Bombay Baby

BOMBAY
Baby

A NOVEL

LOVE
HUDSON-MAGGIO

SWEET AUBURN
PUBLISHING

To my cherished readers,

You breathed life into the characters of Bombay Baby. Your passionate messages, thoughtful questions, and unwavering enthusiasm kept Harlow, Vik, and their world alive in ways I never imagined possible. This book exists because of you.

Writing this sequel was challenging. There were moments when I set it aside, convinced I couldn't do justice to the story you deserved. But like faithful friends, you were there, asking about these characters who had become as real to you as they are to me. Your connection to their stories gave me the courage to return to the keyboard time and time again.

Bombay Baby is a testament to the power of readers who become family, who remind authors why we fell in love with storytelling in the first place. The characters you cherished in *Karma Under Fire* were eager to continue their journey, and your voices helped guide them home.

As you turn these pages, I hope you feel the same magic that sparked your love for the first book. This story belongs as much to you as it does to me.

With deepest gratitude and love,
Love Hudson-Maggio

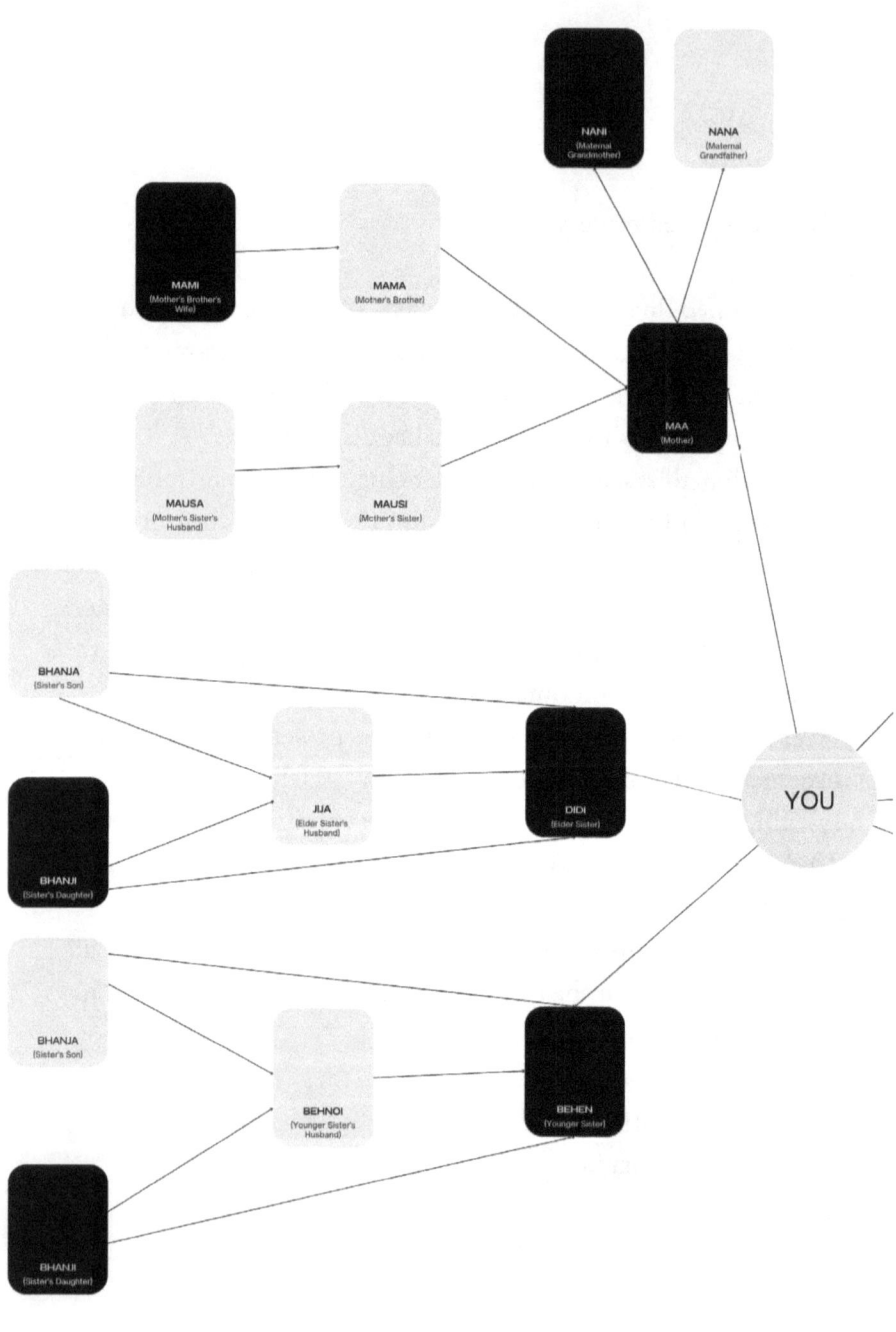

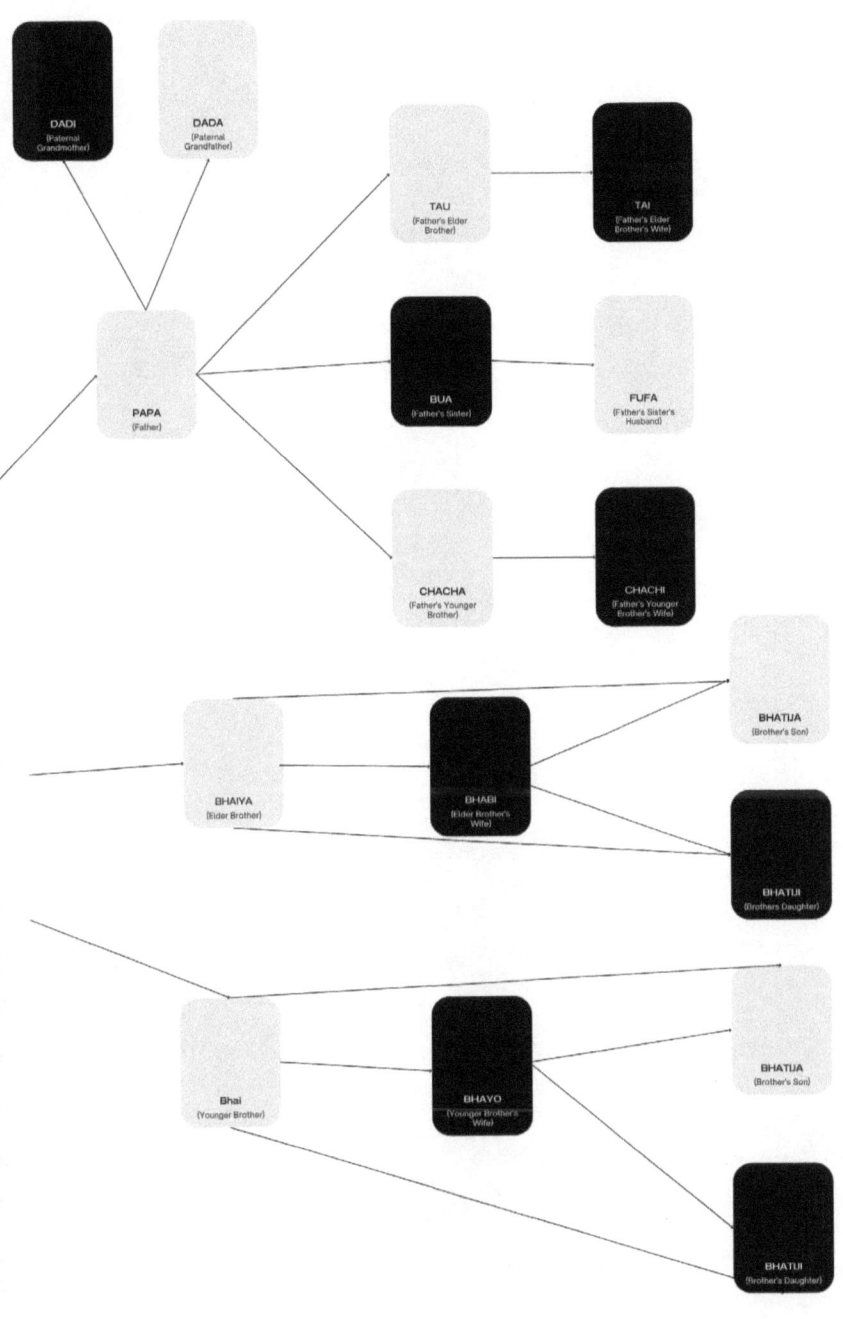

HARLOW

EVEN THOUGH VIK HAD STARTED HIS story with "Once Upon a time," it would be a while before we got to "happily ever after." While my mother almost broke her hip when she stumbled after jumping for joy, the Chatwals were more reserved. It seemed the longer they considered Vik's profession of love the more their enthusiasm waned. Their muted reaction to our pending nuptials stung a little.

Over the next four days, Vik spent hours with his folks on video calls. What started off as easy chats soon deteriorated into an icy standoff. Things finally reached a breaking point.

"You are a man," Mr. Chawal said. I heard every word. I was sitting next to Vik but out of the camera's view. "You can do what you want. But you must know our initial enthusiasm has cooled somewhat after several hours of consideration." Mrs. Chatwal's expression gave no indication of any thought, feeling, or emotion. Mr. Chatwal continued. "We are no longer caught up in a moment of excitement. My son, we have changed our minds regarding Ms. Kennedy's suitability. Next wedding season, you will come home and find an acceptable wife. If you do not comply with our wishes, there may be significant consequences."

Vik did not respond at first. He chewed on his bottom lip so long that I began to fear his response. "*Baapa*," he said, "do not go there. Let's not say anything we will both regret. My devotion to you and *Ma* is unending, but I adore Harlow. And, as you said when I was home, love will find a way. I have finally found the one. And I am at peace in my heart." He took a quick breath. "I hear your implied threat to disinherit me. It is both cruel and trite. I know you are a traditional man, but you have not risen to your position of influence by staying anchored in the past. Times have changed. I want to be happy. I know deep down you want that for me."

Mr. Chatwal began to speak, but Vik held up his hand. "Respectfully, I will finish—then we are done with the discussion. Know this. The family fortune does not factor into my decision. Certainly, I do not want the Chatwal empire to diminish. I want the family to flourish. I would love it—and I am only human. I know your financial backing would enable me to expand my dream—perhaps all over the world. That being said, I am going to succeed with or without your help. So... I am going to marry Harlow—ours is a love match. She is of another country—she is of another race. I love India but the United States is the country of my choosing and I intend to live here with Harlow. For once in my life, I am truly happy, and I plan to stay that way."

He pulled me into the camera's view. There was a slow but unmistakable change in Mrs. Chatwal's expression. And, for the first time in all the conversations I'd witness, she smiled. She whispered into her husband's ear for a long time. I saw the man's face begin to soften, He leaned into her and spoke. We could not hear what he said, but Mrs. Chatwal's reaction was one every husband knows. It said, "You need to rethink that, my dear—and rethink it now. "

Mr. Chatwal stared at the screen for a full three minutes, lost in thought. Then, he nodded.

"Your mothers has always provided an unerring compass to my life. She feels very strongly about this."

I held my breath.

"So, it is settled, Vikram—and this is the last time we will discuss it," Mr. Chatwal said. He smiled broadly. "You will marry Miss—you will marry Harlow, and she will be our daughter. Your *ma* sees the light in Harlow's eyes. It is not a gleam of avarice; she says it is the beam of love. Your ma and I have come to love one another across the years, but she just pointed out how much easier it might have been for us had we started in a different place—a place of affection."

Vik leaned in to kiss me. I close my eyes, then heard his mother gasp. When I opened my eyes, Vik was sitting ramrod straight like a schoolboy who'd been reprimanded, and his mother was looking at him with suspicion. She said nothing, but her gaze said, "Remember your training. Some things are always private."

"Outstanding," Vik said. "We do not want to wait. We plan to be married next weekend—that gives you twelve days. I'll make arrangements for your travel to the US."

His mother leaned in toward Vik's father. More whispering.

"We will not be in attendance," Mr. Chatwal said, "but not for the reasons you might suspect. Your ma, while better, remains too weak to travel. It is, as you know, a very arduous journey."

Vik's eyes reflected a flash of sadness, then the mask of indifference appeared. Vik's eyes went hard until Mr. Chatwal resumed. "We would propose a happy compromise—a resolution," the older man said. "We would love for you to arrange your way for us to attend the nuptials in a virtual manner—like this (he pointed to the screen). Then, at your convenience—when you feel you can leave your Bombay Baby for at least a month—we ask that you return to India and reenact your wedding in a traditional Indian ceremony. Then spend a few weeks with us that we might come to know our new daughter better. You will stay in the guest house where you can enjoy your privacy."

"Vik's Mother lunged toward the screen. "And you will not keep us up all night." She immediately put her hand over her mouth and giggled. We all dissolved in laughter.

Five weeks later.[1]

Not everything had gone as planned. Sure, we were standing in a beautiful space and considering a second location for the restaurant. Everything looked great, business was good, and the possibilities of expansion were promising.

But there was a proverbial fly in the ointment appointment. For reasons we could not understand, three days after our joyous conversation with Vik's parents, they withdrew their blessing and kind tacitly, their approval of our marriage. Communication had fallen to zero. They neither accepted nor initiated any calls.

I returned my attention to Dinesh.

"The lease is signed," he said. "The crew will be here tomorrow to begin working on the kitchen. We will open Thanksgiving weekend, just in time for the holiday crunch."

"That's great," Vik said. "In ten months, we will have our second Bombay Baby."

---

1 Author's note. Fans of *Karma Under Fire* will immediately recognize a change in the time frame and the narrative. I did not anticipate the demand for a sequel would be so strong…hence, a few alterations were made. I beg your indulgence and thank you for your kind response to *Karma.*

I shared a conspiratorial look with Dinesh. "Not so sure about that," I said.

Vik stared at me. "Seriously?" he said. "Do the math."

"Already have," I said. I could feel the corners of my mouth curling into a wicked grin. I took his hand and placed it on my stomach. "Bet this little one gets here first," I said.

And, for the first time in his life, Mr. Vikram Tej Mahur Chatwal was completely speechless.

CHAPTER ONE

VIK

Three weeks later

THE "PARTY IN THE SKY" RAGED, an extravagant affair set against the backdrop of my condo—or, as the gossip mongers online liked to call it, "Vikram Chatwal's breathtaking Atlanta penthouse." The revelers ate, drank, and danced while taking in the sprawling city view below. It was the usual crowd—Atlanta's young, hip socialites. I knew a few of them, but Miguel Calderone, my best friend and wingman, was always in charge of the guest list. Folks mingled around the white marble wet bar and enjoyed whatever libation they requested from my bartender with no regard for vintage or expense. It was a party after all and I had become famous for sparing no expense, for a good time. I watched as the partygoers danced—or attempted to—while I stood against a wall with a "welcome to my home" smile plastered across my face. The scene was the same, but tonight felt different. I was different. In eight weeks, my whole life had changed for the better. I had the woman of my dream, and a little Chatwal was on the way, a secret we kept from everyone—including Sophia.

Harlow and I had decided a trip to the justice of the peace was the only way forward, consequences be damned. I would have to beg for forgiveness from my family for the rushed nature of things. After all, it would be beyond inappropriate in India to host an extravagant wedding with a pregnant bride.

My mind snapped back to the present when Miguel approached and handed me a crystal hosting a double—more likely a triple. The color and smell shouted "bourbon." The taste was unmistakable.

"Picked the most expensive one, didn't you?" I asked.

"Nothing's too good for my best bud," he said.

"Especially when I'm paying for it, right?"

Miguel's thousand-watt grin erupted. "Absolutely."

I listened to the din—music, laughter, shouted conversations, the same old scene. Miguel leaned in.

"What's the problem?"

"I'm over this," I said. "Ever since…"

"I know," he said. "Ever since Harlow. I get it. You're moving into… (he put the back of his hand to his forehead in exaggerated horror) …adulthood!" He clapped me on the shoulder. "And I couldn't be happier for you. You guys are a great couple."

"Thanks," I said. *I wish like hell that Harlow was here.*

Miguel polished off his drink and set the glass on a side table. He pointed to the coaster he'd used. "See, I'm learning." He looked a little wistful.

"You okay?" I asked.

"Fine," he said. "Just realizing I am probably witnessing the last great party thrown by the legendary Tej Mayur."

"Don't use that name anymore," I said. "I'm proud to call myself by the one my parents gave me: Vikram Chatwal."

Miguel shouted, threw a hand into the air, and bolted across the room to speak to someone. I was left with my thoughts.

Long, strange journey. When I'd started my restaurant, Bombay Baby, I decided to go by my middle names. I was concerned someone might recognize the Chatwal surname and put together the fact that I was the heir to one of the largest fortunes in India. Young, stubborn, and more than a little unbridled, I wanted my success to be...well...*mine.* I didn't want anyone sucking up to me, or worse overrating my cuisine, to curry favor with my father.

Unsure of how long I stood musing in the corner, I looked up to see the sun disappear in earnest, casting a kaleidoscope of muted pinks and blues across the skyline. I watched the carousing with a mixer of detachment and self-loathing. For more time than I wanted to remember, this had been my life—over-the-top parties featuring all the "beautiful" people, each gathering an attempt to be more legendary than the last. Now, the entire scene felt empty and hollow, and I was glad I had moved on.

A look around was a reminder that things weren't all doom and gloom. Life had dealt me a great hand. I lived in a spacious penthouse with floor-to-ceiling windows that afforded a breathtaking view of the grandest city in the South. When my realtor showed me the penthouse, I knew I had to have the place if only for the private elevator camouflaged as a butler's pantry. I had routinely used it to afford my female guests the utmost privacy and security for our late-night rendezvous. The lift ran almost non-stop before I met and fell in love with Harlow.

My dear Harlow, my future wife and the love of my life. I would have preferred a quiet night alone with her. We would be watching movies and eating popcorn in bed. But no. I had a role to play, some aspects of my old life were a little harder to shed than I thought.

I moved through the room and offered greetings to the party-goers. I watched some of them ogle the paintings and sculptures that lined the walls of the foyer. The open floor plan was designed for Bollywood-style entertainment like tonight. And almost every single female guest noticed the spiral staircase in the corner of the foyer that led directly to my bedroom. It would soon belong to Harlow and me when she moved in.

I moved outside to the balcony. A row of potted lemon trees pushed their refreshing tangy aroma onto the gentle breeze. The smell relaxed me—and, for some reason made me miss Harlow all the more.

Miguel had detached himself from a gaggle of people he probably didn't know and was making small talk with the bar-tender. She tossed her auburn hair over her tattooed shoulders in time to the music while she mixed a drink and handed it to Miguel with a seductive, dimpled smile. He winked and slid her his business card. Something, either his Goldman Sachs card or his boyish good looks, encouraged her to mouth the words *meet me later* before she returned to crafting cocktails for the other guests. Miguel didn't seem to know and or care why he'd been blessed with such a provocative invitation. He simply winked his acceptance and sipped his drink. Another cool breeze moved through from the balcony. Miguel turned out the suede collar of his tailored corduroy blazer for warmth and wandered to my side.

"Nice work, my friend," I said with a chuckle. "Always with the player moves."

Miguel shrugged and pointed to my drink. "That's not bourbon, is it?" he asked.

"It's not," I said. I unconsciously caressed the Glencairn glass. "This is Macallan 1926. When they took it out of the cask at Speyside in '86, they only produced forty bottles. There are probably fewer than twenty left in the world."

"How come you've never shared it with me, buddy?"

I laughed. "You know me. What's mine is yours—except Harlow and *this* Scotch."

"You share it with your fiancée?" Miguel flinched a little. "Still can't get used to that word."

"I tried," I said. "You know me, the consummate romantic." Miguel mimed a gag. "I told her she was about to have a transformative experience. She sniffed it, then took a nice sip."

"Did she like it?"

"Hell no," I said. "She spit it out. Said it tastes like 'gasoline-infused stump water.'"

"Not even sure what that is," Miguel said, "but it sounds bad."

I swirled the dark liquid in my glass and took an exaggerated inhale. "All I know is she's not getting any more. That sip probably cost about twelve grand." I chuckled.

"Good thing for you I don't like Scotch, or you'd hurt my feelings," Miguel said.

"Sorry," I said. "But I'd rather hurt your feelings than share this."

"Speaking of the soon-to-be ball and chain, where is the delightful Ms. Kennedy tonight?"

"She had a private showing of her jewelry line. Her mother set it up. Some wealthy Buckhead Betties looking to invest in the next big Atlanta talent. Sophia is all too ready to brand Harlow as the next Kendra Scott."

"Why fundraise with Buckhead mavens when she has a rich fiancé?" Miguel said. *I had asked Harlow the same thing.*

"I offered. She wants to do it on her own. I'm trying to give her space. You know I'm itching to do something to help her launch."

"She coming later?"

"That's the plan." *It couldn't be soon enough for me.* I noticed a pair of hungry-eyed redheads standing next to the bar and staring at me with intent. *I'm so tired of that life.* Before Harlow, I would have accepted their clear invitation for a quick tryst—in the past, three was the magic number.

Miguel sipped his drink. "Things sound like they are working for you guys. I couldn't be happier. By the way, everyone loved the *chana aloo* curry. Maybe you should serve it at your restaurant."

"That's the idea," I said. "Try it out on these Guinea pigs before I spring it on my loyal Bombay Baby customers." I looked across the room again and caught a group of women who were staring at me. They made no attempt to look away. "Anyway, thanks for putting this party together." I considered the sea of unfamiliar faces. "Might have been nice to know a few more people here, but I guess that's what I get when I said I wanted an unbiased group. Wait 'til you taste the Jalebi I made for dessert. Our cook in India used to make it for me—and only me. It was our little secret."

"Jalebi?"

"Spiral shaped, crisp, sugar-coated treat made with flour and sugar syrup. You can have it for breakfast or dessert. It's served a lot during Holi and Diwali."

The waitstaff had come out of the kitchen with trays bearing the tantalizing, crystallized sugar delicacies. They placed individual servings of Jalebi on red and white Hermes plates. I waited, then watched the guests move toward the lavish alfresco dining area at the heart of the terrace. Seconds later as expected, faint sounds of satisfaction spread across the table as guests sampled the gooey, comforting confection. Flickering tapers in glittering candelabras cast wavy beams across the table. Silverware sparked. Versace stemware prismed the light around the room in a waterfall of enchanting color.

"Those look delicious," Miguel said. He took a step toward the dining table.

"Let the guests eat," I said. "Plenty more in the kitchen for later."

He looked like a toddler that had been denied ice cream before dinner.

Miguel and I had become fast friends during a Goldman Sachs orientation retreat, two "diversity hires" who bonded right away. Unlike my father, Miguel had been enthusiastic when I decided to leave the world of finance and pursue a career as a chef. In truth I wondered a little at first if his encouragement was only because the sexual playing field at Goldman had been cleared. We were a little notorious and there were always a lot of women all too eager to date *men in finance.* But over the years, Miguel had proved to be a loyal and dedicated friend, even if he was still in the "work hard, play harder" phase of his life.

I felt my phone vibrate and retrieved it from my pocket. I saw an upside-down face emoji from Harlow. *Hope you're having a great time. Won't make it. Wiped out. Sorry.*

Miguel read the text over my shoulder. "Damn," he said. "I know you were looking forward to showing her off—she's something special."

"Yep" was all I could think to say. I tried to hide my disappointment with a quick smile. The sizzle had definitely gone out the night for me.

"You know it's been a while since we've thrown a house party here. Haven't done this since Harlow made you respectable."

"It feels like a lifetime ago, but it hasn't been but a few months," I said.

The last big blowout Miguel put together occurred before I

left for India to check on my ailing mom. At the time, I was long overdue for a visit home. I'd avoided returning after the fiasco of an engagement gone wrong. Two years earlier, I had traveled home for an arranged marriage to a woman named Haiya, a woman of voracious sexual appetites who made no effort to hide her dreams of a life of luxury and indolence.

But when I shared the vision for my life with Haiya, a string of successful restaurants where I would introduce America to the wondrous tapestry of Indian cuisine, she had other ideas. She wasn't wild about leaving her home country. She didn't want to live anywhere other than the Chatwal familial estate while indulging her passion for buying sparkly things and being waited on by a retinue of attentive servants. The Chatwals were the closest thing to Indian royalty on the subcontinent. Haiya aspired to be the lady of the manor, not a hostess at a diner.

Little did she realize how quickly the name "Tej Mayur" would become synonymous with fine dining in Atlanta. Bombay Baby rose into prominence, and unlike so many "it" places in America, the restaurant showed no indication of sinking in popularity. On any given night, one spotted a celebrity. And on *every* night, even the most unknown patron left the place raving about "the best food I have ever eaten *period*."

The night wore on, the genre-spanning party music thumped from the precisely placed Cosmotron 130 speaker. The music summoned the guests back into the penthouse to mingle and dance.

The waiters moved through the party with platters of tapas. While everyone was munching away, Miguel and I shared a moment of camaraderie with a friend from our time at Goldman. We laughed about the "good old days" trading manly back-slapping and guffaws. I was engaged in the conversation, but scanned the room every so often to ensure the guests were happy. Then I saw *her* and felt my smile melt away.

Her pace was slow and seductive. Her eyes never left my face. There was no escape.

It was clear to me she basked in the knowledge of her power as she leaned in on tiptoes and gave me a lingering kiss on the cheek. Her ample bosom pressed against my cashmere sweater; her presence brought an uncomfortable warmth, accompanied by a faint scent of Chanel N°5. I was filled with a mixture of annoyance and irritation.

"Hi, Tej . . . I mean, Vik," she said. "Sorry. Still getting used to using your real name." Her gaze bored into my eyes.

Why was she here? I blocked her number months ago and asked her to not call me again.

"Good evening, Kiara," I said. I backed away. "It's been a minute."

"Longer than that," she said. "I can tell you down to the hour how long it's been since—"

I interrupted her while discretely stepping on Miguel's foot to stop him before he laughed. Kiara had no shame and no problem oversharing. "Where's Jeremy? You're here with Jeremy, right?" I asked and scanned the room.

"I am, unless I get a better offer," she said. She laughed but it sounded hollow. "Don't get me wrong, he's a great guy, knows how to show a girl a good time, but he's not you."

Poor Jeremy. I almost feel sorry for him. Almost.

My purely physical relationship with Kiara had ended when I returned to Atlanta from India with the singular goal of finding a way to solidify my relationship with Harlow. Miguel bobbed his head in my direction. "I'm gonna go talk to Jeremy. He's coming out of the loo. Kiara, always a pleasure."

I put a hand on Miguel's shoulder. To the casual observer, it looked like one buddy chatting up another. But Miguel tensed and resisted the temptation to yelp under my vise-like grip. *This is your fault, old chum. You were in charge of the guest list. No way you are weaseling out of this one.*

"Hang around a sec, *buddy*," I said. "I want to show you something in my office." I looked at Kiara. "Great to see you. You should try the Jalebi. It's a crowd pleaser." I could not bolt fast enough.

Kiara stared at me wide-eyed with disbelief and wounded pride, but I wasn't about to break the momentum of my flight. I guided Miguel to my office. He closed the insulated door behind him, and the sounds of the party shrank to a muffled thump of the bass speakers. Plush rugs and custom-made bookshelves, equipped with a ladder to reach the top row of first-edition hard-cover books, decorated the office.

"What the hell was that?" I asked.

"Just trying to give you room to operate," Miguel said. "You know, in case you wanted a little reminder of old times since you're flying solo tonight."

What the hell! "First of all, I'm engaged, as you well know, and she's with Jeremy now," I said.

Miguel gave a noncommittal grunt and a shrug. "Maybe not for long."

"What?"

"Rumor mill says Daddy's money is running a little low. The old trust fund might not be what it used to me. Didn't diversify his holdings well enough. A little fiscal ED if you catch my drift. She's probably ready to jump ship, or at least pay a visit to another . . . ah, opportunity."

"And this is supposed to matter to me because?" *Why would*

I care about this at all. I felt my hands gathering to strangle him.

Miguel smirked. "Come on, Vik. You tried to keep it on the DL, but everyone knew you and Kiara were—how did Shakespeare put it—making 'the beast with two backs.'"

"Eloquent," I said. *Real classy, but he wasn't wrong.*

"Despite your well-deserved sense of intellectual superiority, there are a few of us who paid attention in school," Miguel said. He finished his drink. "I mean, she's no Rhodes Scholar, but the woman is seriously hot."

I stared out the window. City lights sparkled from below, a testament to the nightlife of the South's most vibrant city. I sighed involuntarily. "I told you it's over," I said."

"Naw," Miguel said. "Party's just cranking up."

"I don't mean the party," I said. "I mean my old life. I have everything anyone could ever want—money, more stuff than ten people need, a fantastic business, and, for better or worse, a high profile. But none of it matters without one thing."

I was sure he knew the answer, but he no doubt knew what I needed to say. "What's that?"

"Harlow." *I've been missing her all night.*

"Understood. For what it's worth, I didn't know Jeremy was going to bring her tonight. He's a bit clueless, as you know." We didn't say anything for a while. I perused a few invoices on my desk. Miguel amused himself by looking over my collectible sports memorabilia. Then he let out a low, long whistle.

"Who is that goddess?"

I followed his stare to the TV mounted on the wall, which played Bollywood movies on repeat. I preferred the ambient sounds of Bollywood music when I needed to concentrate. A little bit of India and a part of my past life helped me relax and focus.

A beautiful actress danced and sang while her hips kept perfect rhythm with the joyful music. She was all smiles, inky black hair, and gorgeous curves.

"I think I need to go to India and get an arranged marriage," Miguel said, "with her."

I stared.

"What's up?" Miguel asked.

"N…nothing. Just reminds me of someone." I forced a smile. "Everyone looks alike in India, you know."

"They most certainly do not all look like that!" Miguel said. "Seriously, you don't know her? You look like you just saw a ghost." He poked at my ribs. When I did not respond to his jab, his voice lost its characteristic joviality. His eyes grew dark and serious. "Something tells me there's a deeper story here, but it can wait. Something's bothering you. How bad is it?"

"Pretty bad."

"Business?"

"Nope. Everything is swimming along."

"So, it's Harlow?" "Okay." He put his hand on the doorknob. "I'm guessing you're going to need another drink."

"Make it a double," I said.

CHAPTER TWO

VIK

WHEN MIGUEL CAME BACK, I HAD turned off the movie, gone to my desk, and brought a series of social media pages up on my computer screen. "Take a look," I said.

Miguel perused the blogs, pictures, and comments. "So what?" he asked. "People are taking shots at you and Harlow. I know it's irritating, and you want to protect Harlow, but you're a public figure. Cheap shots go with the territory."

I read over his shoulder. "'Delhi Playboy Engaged to African American Queen,' really? Oh…how about this one? 'Gold Digging Sister Lands Bombay Boy Toy.' Classy, right?"

"You don't care about this crap," Miguel said. "You've been a target since you got here. Everybody in America who sees this stuff knows it's birdcage liner." He looked at my face and skidded to a conversational stop. "Oh…shit." I waited. "Everybody *in* America…"

"Yeah." I bit my lip for a moment and hoped the momentary pain would help prevent an explosion. "Everyone in America. Except this garbage is everywhere."

"So your parents have seen it."

"No doubt."

Miguel closed his eyes in a moment of revelation. "And all of their relatives, friends, and business associates."

"Uncles, aunts, gardeners, housekeepers, club members, and people they've never met but who now stare at them at the market, opera, theater, wherever."

"They'll shake it off...right?"

I had to take a beat to gather myself. "They sure did...shook and shook and shook until the wedding fell right off."

"What?"

I had to watch what I said. I got angry everytime I thought about my parents going back on their word. Denying me their blessing.

"A little bit ago, we called to arrange their virtual presence at a little ceremony we were going to have here—just a few friends... like you and some others. Harlow's mother, aunts, uncles, and a few cousins."

"I know—and later, you're planning on going over to India for a big Bollywood to-do...traditional wedding...circle the fire...all that really cool symbolic stuff." He stood a little straighter. "I've been reading up on it. Sounds like a very special time."

"It is," I said. "At least, it would have been. But when we Facetimed, something was different. I could almost feel the frost coming from the screen. After a while, *Pa* told me they were not coming—and that they did 'not wish to be part of any nuptial celebrations.'"

"Damn, that's cold." Miguel shut the laptop and the large, desk-mounted monitor went dark—a gaping black representation of how I felt. "How'd Harlow take it?"

"How do you think?" I asked. "She's devastated." I forced

a smile. "But in true Harlow fashion, she's sure this is a speed bump. She is determined we are going to be okay." I was about to continue when my phone rang. I raised my thumb to hit "Ignore." Then I saw the number.

"*Pa,* how are you?"

My father's voice was strained. "You need to come home, Vikram. There has been a break in at Xanadu."

"Is everyone okay?"

"Your mother and I are fine. We were away for a brief respite. We wanted to get out of town because we knew it would be a bit crazy with the Basant Panchami holiday[1] and the long weekend. We gave the staff the weekend off. When we got back, it was obvious someone had ransacked our home. No one was hurt, but the police said they believe this is the work of a gang responsible for over fifty burglaries. The barbarians target posh South Delhi neighborhoods in Jangpura, Hauz Khas, and in the Golf Links Enclave where your home is located. They are stealing fine art, watches, laptops, and jewelry. They struck when they knew they could take advantage of the widespread cell tower and connectivity outages. In fact, I am calling you from our landline now."

"I'm so sorry, *Papa,*" I said. "What can I do to help?"

"As I said, I need you to come home."

Although, the abrasion on my psyche was still raw from his rejection of Harlow and our engagement, I was, first, foremost, and always, a son of India—my parents' only son.

"I'll be on the first flight out tonight," I said.

The line went dead.

---

1 Hindu festival marks the start of spring season marked by worshipping Saraswati, the goddess of knowledge, music, and the arts.

CHAPTER THREE

HARLOW

I WOKE UP LATE THE NEXT morning. Even the finest Egyptian cotton sheets couldn't chase away the grogginess and aches deep in my bones. I ran my hands through my tangled curly mane and sat up in bed. I pushed the remote on the bedside table. The blinds rose. I blinked hard, then lowered them a little to soften the harsh light of mid-morning.

Why do I feel so lousy? Probably coming down with the bug that's been going around.

I reached for my phone. There were several missed calls from Vik. The first registered at close to three in the morning. I played the message.

"Harlow, sweetie, bad news from home. There was a break-in at Xanadu—a string of robberies targeting the wealthy in South Delhi. There were no injuries, but my parents are traumatized, particularly *Ma*. I have to go. They can't handle this by themselves—they need family. And I want to make sure there isn't any possible danger. I'll get this wedding mess sorted out—I promise. But I've got to get home right now to make sure they're okay. I'm all they've got. I spoke to my two uncles—*Pa's* brothers. They are going to hang around until I get there." I could tell he looked at his watch. "I'm booked on the first flight out of Jackson-Hartsfield. Maybe we should have bought that jet." He paused again. "Nothing I can do about it now. I connect through Newark. I'll call before we head across the pond. I hope you are feeling better. I love you."

I had decided to stay at Sophia's while Vik was hosting the party. Well, it was really Vincent's house, her latest fiancé. I didn't want to dampen the spirits at Vik's. He needed one more legendary blowout.

Whatever was wrong with me continued to escalate, but I needed to get up. I dragged my feet to the side of the bed and hoisted myself to my feet. My legs gave way at the knees. "Mom... Mom are you're here?"

No one answered. I crawled across the floor in the direction of the bathroom—or where I thought it should be. It was the last thing I remembered for a while.

When I awakened, I was at the head of the spiral staircase. *Good thing I didn't try to go downstairs,* I thought.

My cell phone was under my thigh. I picked it up to call Sophia. I'd missed another call from Vik. I listened to his silky voice with a mixture of desire and anguish. "You must still be asleep. Good. You need the rest. Taking off in five minutes. I'll call when I land in New Delhi. I love you, Harlow."

Before I type out a text, pain seared through my abdomen, and I passed out.

Even before I opened my eyes, I knew I was in a hospital. Waters Pavilion deserves its reputation as one of Atlanta's best, but at their core, every hospital sounds and smells the same. My senses gradually attuned to the room. Soft, natural light that filtered through expansive windows. This place represented a harmonious blend of modern luxury and medical functionality. The walls, adorned with soothing paintings of Georgia's land-scape. I stretched and settled into the high-tech patient bed that seemed more suited to a five-star resort than a hospital. Pavilion's reputation as an oasis in the bustling heart of Atlanta, where the affluent often retreated for discreet medical treatments, was well deserved.

Mother's beautiful anxious face came from the side. I saw something with which I was not overly familiar—a display of genuine concern across her features. She hadn't been around a lot when I was young. Daddy threw her out of the house for infidel-ity—at least that was his story. When Sophia and I reconciled, I learned the truth…the painful and occasionally ugly truth about my philandering father and the torturous route my mother was forced to take.

"Harlow!" Her voice disclosed more worry than her face. "Harlow, I'm here."

She handed me a cup of ice chips. They seared my raw throat and sent a chill that contrasted sharply with the warmth of the blanket draped over me. The crisp, sterile scent of the hospital mingled with a subtle floral fragrance, likely emanating from an arrangement of fresh lilies perched on a nearby table—an attempt, perhaps, to soften the reality of my situation. My voice emerged as a croak.

"What the hell?"

Information cascaded toward me like hungry mosquitoes on a hot Atlanta evening. Snippets of her sentences painted a chaotic picture…found on the floor… unconscious… bleeding…

ambulance... hospital... and then a word that made my heart sink—"ectopic."

A good-looking doctor, perhaps more fitting for a Hollywood set than a hospital, leaned over me with a calm professionalism. His presence, comforting and kind, somehow reassured me amidst the chaos. "You ruptured. No way you would have known there was a problem this early. You were about seven weeks or so, I would guess. Your mother gave consent to the surgery. It was an emergency procedure. Fortunately, you did not rupture. You're also at the end of a mild case of the flu. Everything combined to make you collapse."

I pointed to my throat.

"Hurts."

"Intubated you to be safe," he explained.

"Vik?" My heart raced. *Where is he?*

"I tried to call him," Sophia said, her tone laced with frustration. "He didn't answer. I tried several times."

My head was beginning to clear from the fog of medication and shock.

"India," I said. The word sounded ominous.

"Yes, dear, I know where he's from," Sophia replied.

"No... he went."

Comprehension replaced confusion on Sophia's face.

"Okay," she said softly, her eyes softening. "You can explain everything later. Right now, you rest. I'll find Vik. I'll tell him."

She gently wiped a tear from my cheek—a tear I hadn't realized had escaped.

"It will be okay," she said. "You're young."

She was out of the room before I remembered I had not even told her I was pregnant.

CHAPTER FOUR

HARLOW

THE PAIN WAS BOTH PHYSICAL AND emotional, a dull ache that radiated from my abdomen and wrapped around my body like a constricting vine. I felt groggy, each blink a laborious chore as my eyelids fought the weight of pharmaceutically induced sleep. My throat felt like it had been scraped with a rasp. Each swallow a reminded me of the physical trauma my body had endured. I was tired—bone weary—heartsick.

The quiet room with its soft lighting, artfully placed flowers, and faint antiseptic smell did nothing to allay my fatigue. I drifted between uncomfortable wakefulness and restless sleep.

When Vik finally called two days later, the digital chime of my phone felt like a lifeline thrown into turbulent seas. His voice, usually a balm seemed distant, disconnected from my angst.

"Sorry, babe," he said. His words cracked through the static of an eleven-hour time difference and poor reception. "Are you okay? I'm so sorry. The baby...all of it. So bloody sorry I can't be there with you right now."

I let out a long, loud breath, my voice a hollow echo in the luxurious room. "Y... yeah...I know, me too. They say I can go home tomorrow. I feel like a truck hit me."

"Your mother filled me in, and I talked to the doctor for a few minutes," he replied. He sounded concerned, but there was something else in his voice—distance...distraction? "Don't worry about anything. You need to rest. I want you—"

There was a pause, the line muted, the silence stretching between us, filled with unspoken fears and frustrations. Thirty seconds... then forty-five. Vik was never good at expressing his emotions even at the best of times. No life can stay charmed forever. So he did what he always did. He changed the subject.

"Things are crazy here," he said. "The cell phone towers were damaged during a series of storms. Connectivity here in Delhi is more a wish than a reality. We have to rely mostly on landlines— and since there was damage to the cables and power plants, I'm just lucky to get a call through. I've been trying for almost two days. My parents' house was ransacked. It's a disaster."

No, I thought, my heart sinking further, *it's a burglary and faulty cell service. I lost the baby, our baby. That is a disaster. You need to be here.*

He was still talking, a litany of troubles back home that seemed inconsequential compared to the void inside me. I didn't care about any of it. I interrupted with a voice firmer than I felt.

"Vik—come home."

"I can't," he said. I wanted to hear regret—I couldn't quite make it out.

"Please."

"It's not because I don't want to," he said. I could hear the mix of resignation and stress. "I'm like that old circus act—you know, the guy spinning the plates on those long sticks. If I lose focus for a second, something else is going to crash. *Ma* is upset.

My *pa* won't come out of his room. I've talked to him maybe five minutes since I got here. He won't look me in the eye. It's like he's broken or something. I'm sorry, babe, the connection here is really lousy I can barely hear you now. I know the timing is terrible. I'm doing my best. I'll try to call tomorrow. I'm hoping things will be fixed soon. I love you."

The line went dead and left me battling a storm in my heart all the whispered luxuries of my surroundings could not soothe.

Sunlight bathed the room in a warm, golden hue. I had been in the hospital for three days. Sitting in even one of the most luxurious beds I'd ever occupied was beginning to get uncomfortable. I was sick of watching reruns of the *Housewives* series and HGTV held little appeal. My life was crumbling—what did I care about a pomegranate farmer and his emu raising partner buying a home they obviously could never afford? The scent of Asian lilies filled the air, their fragrance potent and overwhelming. They were usually my favorite, but today, all they did was remind me of what was missing.

Mother entered my room with another large bouquet wrapped in pink tissue paper and cradled in her arms like a baby ready for baptism.

"They're from Vik," she said. She set the flowers on a small table by the window and began filling an empty vase with water. "Where would you like me to put them?"

"I don't care."

"Harlow, sweetie."

"I can't right now. I just can't," I said. "Take them home, please. Put them anywhere as long as it's not in the bedroom. Right now, I can't stand the sight of them. The smell either.

They remind me of death."

She nodded. Her expression softened. "You know," she said, "the doctor said you can go home today. Your blood work is fine. HCG level is below two."

"So?" My ignorance about medical jargon momentarily distracted me.

"I guess, I'm saying we get you home, rest up a bit, and then maybe you'd be good to travel," she said.

"Did the doctor say I could?" I asked.

"Well," she said, A smile tickled at the edges of her mouth. She was choosing her words carefully. "He didn't say you couldn't. I mean if you rest. You know, they say it's always better to ask for forgiveness than permission."

"Meaning?" My patience was waning.

"Sometimes Mohammed has to go to the mountain," she said. "If Vik can't come home…"

"I need to pack for India."

CHAPTER FIVE

HARLOW

Five hours later, Mom checked me out of the hospital and took me back to Vik's penthouse. She set me up in the bedroom. The California king felt empty without Vik. Mom explained my meds, filled a bedside carafe with water, and brought in a basket of snacks. All afternoon, she seemed really distracted. She mumbled to herself, said something about meeting her fiancé Vincent for cocktails at the Governor's mansion, and then she bolted.

I wasn't upset, really. Sophia was being Sophia. Old habits die hard.

I spent the rest of the afternoon reading, dozing, and watching a really bad movie on television. It was predictable, sappy, and I cried my eyes out. There was a boy and a girl and a situation and another boy—the "bad fiancé" no one watching the movie was supposed to like—the everyone knew was eventually going to lose the girl to the first boy.

I wasn't in any pain, but I was still a little tired, so I went in and out of sleep until...I sat straight up in bed.

"Addison!"

A great many people in Atlanta—hell, in the Great State of Georgia—thought Addison Whitmore was a catch. His parents had, as the saying goes, "enough money to burn a wet elephant on the lawn on Sunday." Generations of Whitmores had risen to positions of political prominence, both statewide and nationally. He was tall, well proportioned, had spectacular hair, had been the president of his fraternity at UGA, and was considered by most of the women he met (regardless of age) as "totes gorg."

Addison and I grew up together. And in an earlier life, we had kinda-sorta been engaged. Yes, I found him off-putting, self-absorbed, and a spectacularly lousy kisser. But Sophia saw him as a great catch. To move things along, she had incentivized the deal by offering five million dollars upon completion of a wedding ceremony. If not for an unannounced Uber ride over to his condo where I caught him playing tonsil hockey on the sidewalk with a blonde wearing a dress so tight I could read the tattoo on her right butt cheek through the fabric, we might have gone through with the plan. Oh yes, and the fact I eventually realized I was in love with Vikram Chatwal.

Addison and I had not spoken since I drove away in the ride share while giving him the one-finger salute of affection and tossing his mammoth "to die for" engagement ring into the nearest storm drain. So, of course, when I called, the first words out of my mouth when he answered the phone were, "Addison, it's Harlow. I need a favor."

I told him what I needed.

He said, "Yes, with one condition."

I said, "Depends on what it is."

He said, "Non-negotiable."

I said, "Is it disgusting and gross?"

He said, "You might think so, but I will enjoy it."

I hesitated all of five seconds. "Okay," I said. "I'm desperate."

Ninety minutes later, the silver metallic Maybach pulled up outside of Vik's circular driveway. I left a message on Soph... *dammit*...Mother's voicemail while a chauffeur ran around to my door and opened it. Addison grinned from inside. "Welcome to my parlor."

I shook my head. "Said the spider to the fly."

CHAPTER SIX

HARLOW

THE RIDE TO PEACHTREE DEKALB AIRPORT took forty-five minutes. The car sliced through the affluent Buckhead neighborhood, the car's smooth purr barely audible over his ceaseless chatter about recent escapades, stock market wins, and the mundane extravagances of Atlanta's elite. I sat ensconced in the creamy leather of the expansive backseat, tension knotting my stomach as I waited for Addison to reveal the catch to the favor he had granted. I'd tried to call Sophia, but she hadn't answered. I'd text her when we were taxiing. She would understand. She was a past master at disappearing acts.

We were nearly at the gate, the sprawling airstrip visible beyond, when I could no longer endure the suspense.

"Okay," I said. "I can't believe you've waited so long. I assumed you were enough of a gentleman not to make whatever I have to do a public display."

"Oh!" Addison's textbook, frat boy smirk made me want to bust him in his perfectly formed lips. "It doesn't have to be public. We can do it right now." He shifted in his seat to face me. I winced and kept one eye closed and the other on alert for creepy eyebrow movement or his hand reaching for his belt.

"What is it?" I asked.

"What do you think it is?"

"Like you said, something gross and disgusting—and probably degrading."

"Only if you let it be," he said. "I think it can be something beautiful."

"Damn it, Addison!" I could feel the veins in my neck expanding. "Get on with it. Spit it out. What do you want?"

"You have to do it, Harlow," he said. "Only you can do it."

Without warning, rationale and reason swept through me like a wave pushing up on the sand. I'd been panicked and hurried. That's why I'd called Addison, but suddenly I realized I didn't need him.

"I only called to use your family's plane because I didn't think I could stand a long, commercial flight," I said. "But, you know what? I am strong as hell. I can do whatever needs to be done."

His signature smile faded. His face was serene and something I wasn't sure I'd ever seen before—from him. He looked sincere.

"Harlow," he said, "I've been messing with you a little. Teasing. Everyone in town knows about your engagement to Vikram Chatwal. Hell, *even I know* you are crazy about him. But still, the favor I want from you in return for using our Gulfstream is something I can only get from you."

"What?" I asked.

"I've always thought you were special," he said. "But I thought I was more special—I thought I was some big shot. I figured you would be lucky to have me when I was really the one who would have been lucky to have you." He reached for my hand. For some reason, I did not resist his touch. "Harlow, what I want from you…"

He swallowed…hard. I'd never seen anything close to genuine emotion from Addison and now he seemed on the verge of tears.

"All I want from you…all I will ever ask of you now or in the future…is that you forgive me. Harlow, I am so very, very sorry for the way I treated you."

I didn't hesitate. I hugged him. He cried. I cried. Then, I said, "I forgive you. I promise. No hard feelings."

He wiped his eyes, kissed me on the cheek, then got out and walked around to open my door.

"The pilot has filed the flight plan. Direct to New Delhi. You'll be there in eighteen hours. Make sure you use the bedroom. From what you told me, your doctor was less than enthusiastic about this idea, so be sure to lie down most of the flight. Okay?"

"Okay," I said. "Thanks, Addison. I owe you."

"No you don't," he said. "We are all square, besides, I always wanted to visit India."

He saw my shoulders clinch. "Harlow," I could tell he was trying not to sound panicked, "this isn't really my family's plane—it belongs to Dad's business. We are required to keep very specific records. If we show too much personal use, there are tax issues. Dad arranged for me to meet a few people in Delhi to discuss business. I won't be in your hair. Hell, you probably won't see me again until we're both back in the States because I assume you're going to come back with Vik. No worries. The bedroom on the plane is yours and yours alone."

"All good," I said. "I get it. And I am grateful. I don't think I'll ever be able to repay you for this."

We started walking toward the plane. "Well, if you *really* want to repay me," he said. I didn't bother to look when he started talking. I knew he had his world-class, shit-eating grin on his face. "It would be very thoughtful if you spend some time in the sewer looking for the ring I gave you."

We were both laughing on the way up the stairs. The second I cleared the cabin door, I quit laughing.

CHAPTER SEVEN

SOPHIA

The second I saw Harlow's face I realized Addison had not told her I was going to be on the plane. I had a lot to explain.

Outside of Harlow's terrible situation, everything in my life had been perfect—right up until the time it all went to hell.

A week before Harlow's trip to the hospital, Vincent and I flitted from one extravagant wedding venue to the next. The more we visited, the more arranging our nuptials felt like a high-stakes social maneuver than a romantic escapade. The Ocala Resort, while dripping with Southern charm and an air of equestrian nobility, seemed almost too pristine as if the grass was too afraid to grow out of line under the strict gaze of the mansion's imposing columns.

At Foxhall, nestled along the Chattahoochee, the promise of leisure activities—clay shooting, fishing, and private pickleball lessons—tempted the notion of a wedding that doubled as an aristocratic summer camp. I couldn't shake the feeling of an orchestrated facade, where every villa and tennis court was just another set piece in our matrimonial exhibition.

Vines Mansion stirred something within us, its gardens twinkling under fairy lights, igniting a spark of romance that prolonged our usual after-dinner tryst. Perhaps it was the wine, or maybe the way the moonlight played on the mansion's facade, but Vincent found an enthusiasm I hadn't remembered for a while.

We considered leveraging Vincent's illustrious connections to secure the Wimbish House in Atlanta, but I wanted something a little out of the ordinary—something out of town. Nothing against the magnificence of the place. It was just a little local.

And there was always The Cloister on Sea Island. It had every amenity with the added attraction of some of the finest golf courses anywhere in the state outside of Augusta. However, the laughter of children and the sight of toddling youngsters made me feel as if I were auditioning for the role of a genteel, aging matriarch rather than a bride.

Returning home, I teased Vincent with the possibility I might announce my preference soon. "Maybe I'll surprise you," I said. My tone was light, but my mind raced with options and the weight of expectations. It was all fun and games—a lighthearted dalliance in decision-making. But I was oblivious to the looming shadow of drama about to engulf me, one destined to transform my carefully curated venue hunt into a tempest of unforeseen chaos.

Harlow's voice snapped me back to the present.

"Mother, what in the world are you doing here."

"Are you upset?" I asked.

Relief flooded her face and she reached for me. Before I knew it, I was experiencing something I had not encountered in a long, long time—holding my daughter while she wept.

"I needed you to be here," she said after a while, "but I couldn't find you anywhere. Are you okay?"

I stroked the back of her hair while her head rested on my shoulder. The position served twin purposes. I could comfort my daughter and I could keep her from reading my face when I lied.

"Everything is fine," I said. "Just a few things to iron out with Vincent."

CHAPTER EIGHT

HARLOW

WE TOOK SEATS ACROSS FROM ONE another and the Gulfstream climbed smoothly into the sky, leaving Atlanta's tumult far below. The initial turbulence gave way to a serene glide. Seated in the expansive cabin, enveloped by the soft hum of the engines, I stared out the window, lost in the sprawling, lazy clouds. The jet's luxury, a sanctuary of high-tech amenities and impeccable design, momentarily distracted me from my turmoil. The leather seat beneath me was as soft as the proverbial baby's bottom. It adjusted with a quiet whir to my slightest movement and provided the illusion of control in a world that felt increasingly beyond my grasp.

The on-board entertainment system, state-of-the-art, offered a selection of films that spanned continents and genres. My eyes settled on *Veer-Zaara*, a classic tale of star-crossed lovers that transcended borders and societal expectations. The poignant strains of its soundtrack filled my headset. The story unfolded on the screen in front of me, drawing ugly tears I hadn't anticipated. The tale of sacrifice and undying love mirrored the dramatic arcs of Bollywood at its best. Every emotion was magnified and every gesture laden with meaning. Lalita and I had spent many a weekend bundled up on the sofa indulging in Bollywood movie marathons and *Veer-Zaara* was one of our favorites.

I switched over to reruns of *Law and Order*. Sam Waterston's dynamism had always captivated me, but I must have been more fatigued than I realized. I sat straight up out of fitful sleep. I felt Mom's hand on my arm.

"Go to the back," she said. "Use the bed. If you keep twitching around like that, you won't be able to walk when we get to India."

I wandered to the aft of the jet, where the ensuite bedroom beckoned. The bed, an adjustable model sheathed in 1000-thread-count sheets, promised a respite from my weighty thoughts. I dialed the mattress to nearly marshmallow softness, a stark contrast to my usual preference for the firm and reliable. The plush duvet enveloped me like a puffy glove and coaxed me into a deep sleep filled with dreams as vivid and exotic as the movie I had just watched.

In my dream, I revisited my first flight to India with Vik, a journey filled with conversation and confessions. Vik, charming as ever, turned the aisle of the jet into an impromptu cricket pitch. He stood in front of the wicket and struck shots that echoed like thunder against the fuselage. The dream twisted bizarrely. He leapt into the air and caught a high-flying ball, transforming it into a plate of steaming tandoori chicken. He placed it in front of me.

When I cut into the tasty dish—even in my sleep, I could feel the spices tickling my nose. The aroma of the wood smoked poultry filled the cabin. I lifted my fork toward my mouth. Vik saluted me with a glass of champagne and flashed his signature smile—only he had no teeth. Without warning, he threw the contents of his flute into my face. It burned like acid; I screamed and clutched at my cheeks.

"Miss Kennedy, Miss Kennedy, are you okay?" Maurice, the ever-attentive steward, peeked through the door, concern etching his youthful face. "Are you decent?"

"I'm fine," I said, my voice raspy. "Just a bad dream. And yes, I am decent."

Maurice, balancing a tray overflowing with a morning feast, entered with a smile. "Oatmeal, toast points, eggs, turkey sausage, and real bacon," he said. "Wasn't sure what you might like."

"All of it," I said, my appetite returning with a vengeance as the aroma of freshly brewed coffee mingled with the savory scent of bacon. Maurice expertly arranged the pillows behind me and transformed my bed into a makeshift dining area.

"Coffee or tea?" he inquired, ready to pour.

"Probably should have tea to get used to the Indian custom," I hesitated, my face betraying my true desire.

"Coffee it is," he said with a wink. "Black with two sugars?"

"How do you know that?"

"Mr. Addison was quite thorough in his explanation of your preferences."

"Thought he might have been responsible for the crustless toast," I said.

"He was adamant about it."

I spread fig preserves on a crustless toast with the focus of an artist at his canvas and asked, "How long was I out?"

"A little over twelve hours," Maurice replied. "We are wheels down in about another two." He paused at the door. "Ma'am I'm not sure if you know but there's a shower through that door. I took the liberty of laying out a fresh set of clothes. You can find whatever you need in the closet."

Refreshed from the shower, with the scent of citrus body wash still clinging to my skin, I settled back into the main cabin. The textures of the plane—soft leather, polished wood trim—soothed me as we neared our destination. With the hospital's sterile smell finally washed away, I prepared to face whatever awaited in India, the last remnants of my dream fading away like smoke in the wind.

CHAPTER NINE

VIK

MY DRIVER MASTERFULLY NAVIGATED THE MERCEDES through the familiar yet somehow foreign streets of Vasant Vihar. The nostalgia of returning home enveloped me.

I stepped into my temporary downtown office. The distant hum of Delhi's bustling activity was a constant reminder of the vibrant life that pulsed just beyond the walls.

A knock on the door snapped me back to the present. "Dinesh! So glad you made it."

"When the master of the castle summons, the vassal reports, even from Atlanta. But I can't remember the last time you sent me an email. How are your parents doing?" Dinesh's voice carried a mixture of concern and levity, a comforting blend of familiarity and professionalism.

"They are doing as well as can be expected. It's been tough for my dad. He misses his estate and wants to go back home. But with the break-in and a freak storm that damaged hundreds of cell towers," I explained, "we've almost been reduced to using carrier pigeons for messages."

"The ever-present danger of abandoning land lines," Dinesh chuckled, sitting across from me. "I've been warning about that."

We shared a laugh, then I leaned forward, my tone sobering. "I wouldn't have asked you here except for something big."

"I figured," Dinesh nodded, his expression turning serious. "Bombay Baby is still booming. As you instructed, we have put the Atlanta expansion on hold while we scout new locations in other cities. I think New York could be a real possibility in time. Our research indicates it may be too soon. The competition there is brutal, and the population is fickle. Today's impossible reservation is next month's boarded-up building. You have asked for my counsel in the past. If you still want it, I suggest we stick to the original plan and move up the coast a little bit at a time. Maybe Charlotte as we have discussed, then Richmond or DC, Baltimore, Philly—you know, crawl our way to success."

"I appreciate your wisdom and advice," I replied, "but we need to put all that on the back burner for now. What we're going to do here in two weeks could change everything."

"Tell me," he urged.

"You are familiar with the National Film Awards."

Dinesh rolled his eyes playfully. "I am older than you and I grew up here. Everyone in this country knows about our nation's Oscar Awards. They give out the Dadasaheb Phalke Award every year. It is the most prestigious prize in the arts community in India. Of course, I know about the Awards. Due respect, but I was not raised by wolves."

"Sorry," I smiled, "I was being rhetorical."

"Are we going?" Dinesh's voice was tinged with excitement, his usual composure slipping just a bit. "Oh... the chance to see Aamir Khan, Mithun Chakraborty, Ranbir Kapoor, Vidya Balan... oh my god! Do you think I might meet Aishwarya Rai

Bachchan? I've always thought she was a goddess. If I could see her... speak to her... shake her hand."

Dinesh was visibly trembling with excitement, a stark contrast to his usual reserved demeanor.

"Calm down," I laughed, half-joking. "You are going to have an aneurysm. Breathe!"

He fell into a chair, his breaths short and quick. After regaining some composure, he looked up with the eager anticipation of a child on the morning of a festival.

"So, we're going?" he asked hopefully.

"Better," I revealed with a grin. "I got a call, which is why I sent for you. The company engaged to provide the food ran into a small problem."

"Staffing?" Dinesh guessed.

"Botulism," I corrected.

Dinesh grimaced. "Nasty stuff."

"But their loss is our gain," I continued, leaning forward. "My friend, I have been asked to cook for the banquet at the National Film Awards Dinner! I will oversee all the food, of course, but I need you to get everything organized with suppliers and the like. You will have to bust it. We are on a tight schedule."

A smile with the wattage of a sunrise spread across Dinesh's face and he bounded to his feet. "Point me in the right direction," he said.

"It's not a race," I said.

Dinesh quickly regained his composure and straightened his tie. "Certainly not," he responded formally, then added quietly, "And I apologize for my outburst."

"It's fine," I said. The old-world formalities between employer and employee sometimes felt burdensome yet necessary. "Everyone is entitled to excitement. But don't let it happen again."

I thought I caught a slight smile as he nodded, a subtle sign of the deep-seated joy he felt at the opportunity before us. On his way out, the energy in his step could have powered the bustling streets of Delhi, all the way from the tranquil green spaces of Hauz Khas to the vibrant markets of Lajpat Nagar.

CHAPTER TEN

VIK

STANDING IN THE SHADOW OF THE vibrant Hauz Khas Village, the backdrop of ancient ruins mingling with the buzzing modern cafes and eclectic boutiques, I balanced my phone precariously to catch just the right spot where the signal ceased its capricious dance. The air was thick with the scents of street food—spicy, tangy, sweet—all colliding in a delightful assault on the senses.

Rishi's voice crackled through the static, bursting with his characteristic enthusiasm. "This is capital," he said, "just capital. It will be epic. You were great with the illegal hotplate we kept in our room during prep school. I can't imagine what you will do with a full kitchen."

"Honored by the chance," I said. "I can't thank you enough, but remember I said my acceptance is conditional."

"This can be huge for you, my friend," Rishi said. "I know you are successful in America, but this will make you a household name in your home country. Why in the name of everything holy would you turn this down."

"It's a little complicated," I said. "Let's leave it at that."

I waited. I knew we were still connected. I could hear Rishi shuffling papers. "Looking for another replacement?"

"There isn't anyone else who can bring this home like I know you can," Rishi said. "I have to have you." He was rapping his middle knuckle on his desk. I recognized his nervous habit. "Let me ask you this. On a one-to-ten scale, how high is your confidence level that you can do this?"

"Ten," I said. "But if you asking me to weigh my confidence of *being free* to do this, let's take it down to an eight."

"When will you know?"

"Can you give me three days?"

"Two."

"Tell you what. If I can't do it, I will pay for the banquet myself."

"Very generous, but unnecessary."

"Least I can do."

Rishi laughed. "And never let it be said that the great Vikram Chatwal didn't do his very least." He insulted me a little more, then got serious. "I really don't want anyone else, you know."

"I know," I said. "To be on the safe side, line it out for me."

We dove into the details of the culinary extravaganza I hoped to helm at the National Film Awards banquet. Rishi's instructions were peppered with his usual flair. "You will have complete autonomy," he said, "but just try to ensure there will be something for everyone. You know, the stars here are as picky as American celebs."

"Got it," I said. I made a mental note to balance the rich traditional flavors with some contemporary twists to appease the eclectic palates.

"While you're here, let's get the gang together for a lunch or something," Rishi said. He sounded more confident with every syllable. I hoped I would not disappoint him.

The rush on nostalgia I felt was accompanied by a lump in my throat. I coughed. "Sounds good," I said. "You know where everyone is? I've lost track a little."

"I can find them." Rishi sounded typically confident.

"Any chance Nitin will show?" I asked. "He's been pretty much of a phantom since we left school."

"I'll get him there," Rishi said. "He and Krish both still live in Mumbai. Krish is an architect as you remember. Nitin plays with computers or something."

"He was always into that stuff," I said. "It would be great to see him again."

Our conversation, rich with the promise of rekindled friendships and new adventures, was intermittently punctuated by the distant sounds of Rishi managing other calls, his voice fading in and out as he attended to the incessant demands of his bustling environment.

"Okay," Rishi eventually said with a hint of regret, "I've got to bolt."

"I will call with my answer in two days," I said. "Hope to see you soon."

"Great." Just as I was about to end the call, his voice came through again. "Hey!"

"I'm still here," I said.

"Forgot to mention something. Since you are doing me such a solid, I wrangled a couple of tickets. Maybe your parents could come."

"I'd rather bring Harlow if she's up to it," I said, hopeful. "She's on her way over here, but with all the communication issues, I haven't had a chance to run this by her. Would it be okay if she brought a friend?"

"Super!" Rishi's excitement was palpable through the phone. "You talk about her in the group emails and texts—and you suck at those, by the way. Try tapping on the keys and hitting send more than once every six months or so."

"Sorry." I chuckled. "I'll work on getting better."

"Anyway, none of us has ever seen the mysterious Harlow Kennedy. We were beginning to believe she is a figment of your imagination."

"Oh, she is very real," I said. A smile spread across my face.

"You guys still engaged? I heard about it through the Delhi grapevine—more reliable than sunrise." Rishi's tone was a mix of curiosity and camaraderie.

"Absolutely," I said firmly. "Working out some things with *Ma* and *Pa*; it's going to happen. You know how it is over here."

"I do," he said. His voice sounded softer. A pause lingered before he spoke again. "Well…you know we're talking about the night of the Film Awards, right?"

"Hence the name of the banquet," I said.

"All the nominees will be there."

"I would assume so."

"Amrita is nominated."

Damn.

CHAPTER ELEVEN

VIK

I KNEW HARLOW WAS ON THE way, but she wouldn't make it any time soon. I needed to lay out plans for the banquet, but family duty interfered. The idea of spending the day with my *chacha* Deepak held all the appeal of enduring a root canal but *Ma* was insistent.

"He is your father's younger brother, and he loves you," she said.

He loves the young women who flock around me when I am in public, I thought. *My chacha's idea of fidelity is keeping the same set of golf clubs for more than two months.*

The morning filtered through the latticed window of our first-class compartment and cast intricate, dancing shadows across the opulent interior of the train speeding from New Delhi toward the storied Royal Calcutta Turf Club. The compartment, a capsule of indulgence amidst the relentless hustle of India, was scented with a blend of furniture polish wood and the faintest hint of jasmine from the fields outside.

Chacha Deepak, ever the caricature of old wealth with his silk handkerchief theatrically pressed to his nose, seemed an anachronism compared to the modern comforts around us.

"Really, *Chacha*, you'll survive the journey," I said. I watched his exaggerated gestures with a mix of amusement and irritation.

"This is a necessary precaution," he said with the drama of a nineteenth century stage actor. "One can never be too careful on these public conveyances." His voice, though muffled through the silk, dripped with the disdain only those born to privilege could muster so effortlessly.

The train ride, normally a quiet time for reflection or catching up on work, was instead filled with *Chacha* Deepak's relentless chatter. After regaling me with tales of his recent escapades in Scotland—each punctuated with a recount of near-misses on the golf course and chance encounters with the fairer sex—I finally raised my hand, signaling enough.

"Deepak," I said, the omission of '*chacha*' deliberate and pointed. "You assume I won't report your shenanigans to *chaachee* Sannvi, but I will not lie for you if she inquires."

He appeared momentarily wounded, then quickly recovered, adjusting his perfectly tailored blazer. "Would you prefer to hear more about the golf then? That might be more to your taste."

"That would be considerably more palatable," I replied, resigned to the fact that the rest of our journey would be spent navigating his less salacious exploits.

While *Chacha* Deepak dove into a meticulous breakdown of his rounds at some of Scotland's most storied courses, my thoughts drifted to the comforting rhythm of the train on the tracks, the subtle vibrations reminding me of the immense distance we were covering, both literally and figuratively, from my life in Atlanta to these fleeting moments of connection with my roots.

He waxed lyrical about a particularly challenging shot at

Royal Dornoch. "They say the hardest shot in golf is the second on the second hole there. It's a par three, you know—"

I almost shouted out loud when I felt the train begin to slow. "We're here." *Finally.* I hoped I hadn't said that out loud.

Deepak, oblivious to my relief, continued, "Anyway, I was about to hit my chip shot—"

"We're here," I said again, firmer this time.

Disappointment flickered across his face. He gathered his things, including an absurdly large valise. "One does not attend the races in the same attire in which one travels." He sniffed as I heaved his bag down. "It simply isn't done."

I considered my own attire, pale blue linen slacks, double breasted navy blazer, crisp white-on-white shirt and club tie. My attired was decidedly more understated yet impeccably chosen for both comfort and style—a nod to my American influences, perhaps, but still respectful of my heritage.

Thirty minutes later, *Chacha* Deepak emerged from the locker room at the Turf Club clad in an ensemble so vibrant I had to squint. The clash of pastels might have been on trend for a garden party in the Hamptons, but here, it bordered on the comical.

"Like a peacock." I laughed—loudly. "You look utterly ludicrous for a man of your... ah... vintage."

"What can I say?" Deepak responded, clearly unbothered. "The ladies find my sartorial splendor quite appealing."

Sockless feet in Gucci loafers completed the ensemble—a desperate grasp at lost youth. I bit back further comment and we made our way to our box to watch the races. The afternoon progressed pleasantly enough, with the thrill of the thundering hooves and my own successful bets providing a welcome distraction from *Chacha* Deepak's earlier conversation.

However, as the day waned, Deepak's words took a darker

turn. "I understand your fiancée is of another race," he said. He had his eyes pressed into a pair of binoculars.

"Pardon?" I asked, not quite believing what I'd heard.

"Your fiancée, the woman you insist on marrying. She's not Indian, correct?"

"Harlow has some Indian background," I replied cautiously. My grip tightened on the rail in front of us.

"But she is predominantly American Black, is she not?" he asked. He was trying without success to sound casual.

"So?" My patience was thinning.

Chacha sighed, his gaze fixed on a losing horse. "Another three hundred down the drain," he muttered, then turned back to his racing form. "What do you think of Delilah's Mischief in the last race?"

I barely registered the names of the horses anymore. "Why do you care about Harlow's race?" I knew I was not masking my frustration.

"I don't." Deepak shrugged and scribbled on a betting slip. "But I believe your father does. Yes, Delilah's Mischief it is." He filled out the slip and handed it to an attendant along with a handful of bills. "Bring me some luck, my good man, and I will share my winnings."

He'll give you a meager tip if you are lucky, I thought. His nonchalant dismissal of my concerns, coupled with his focus on the trivialities of betting, sparked a fierce anger within me. "*Chacha,* talk to me! What about *Papa*?"

"When your father heard rumors about your living with the woman—"

"Harlow," I said in a bark. "Her name is Harlow."

"My apologies," he said not looking up from his form. "When he heard, he felt you were bringing dishonor to the family. Cohabitation may be common in America, but it is not our way. I heard he flew into a rage and commanded your mother to cancel all the plans she was making."

The pieces of the puzzle began to fall into place—the sudden shift in my parents' attitude, the abrupt end to plans. Frustration boiled over as I considered the traditional constraints clashing so violently with my chosen life.

"*Chacha*," I said, but he had suddenly grown very interested in something across the track. He leaned forward, binoculars pressed to his eyes. He focused feverishly. "Magnificent," he said. "She puts all the other fillies to shame. She looks built for speed."

I gritted my teeth. "I don't care about some damn horse," I said.

He handed me the glasses. "Oh no," he said. "Not a horse. The tall one in blue." He pointed and I adjusted the binoculars.

The woman was, indeed, majestic—tall and slender with thick, dark hair piled high atop her head. Her skin-tight saree highlighted her taut, fit figure. Her eyes were deep and penetrating.

"She's lovely," I said.

Chacha laughed. "You are the master of understatement," he said. "By your standards, Sachin Tendulkar[1] was an average batsman." He nodded in appreciation of his own joke, then pointed again. "That is the type of woman your family wants for you—not someone with whom you are living without benefit of marriage—a mate who will produce true Indians and not hal—"

He stopped. He knew he'd gone too far.

I stood. Almost anywhere other than India, I would have told

---

1 Generally considered the most prolific batsman of all time, Tendulkar the all-time highest run-scorer. In addition, he received more "player of the match" awards than anyone else in international cricket.

him of my desire to beat him until he could not walk. But this *was* India, and I was obliged to honor his place in my family. "In the best interests of harmony and only out of respect for tradition, I am going to leave instead of responding more directly to your insult," I said. "Please do not look for me on the train. Enjoy the last race."

CHAPTER TWELVE

VIK

Upon returning to my home in the lush, cosmopolitan enclave of South Delhi, not even the quiet elegance of the evening could quell the simmering frustrations within me. The mansion, a marvel of contemporary design blended with traditional Indian motifs, welcomed me with its imposing teak doors and expansive, sweet-smelling gardens basking under the soft glow of landscape lighting.

The rest of the house slept, the kitchen beckoned—a sanctuary where I could channel my restlessness into the art of cooking. The kitchen was a masterpiece of design, blending sleek modernity with touches of traditional Indian craftsmanship. Stainless appliances, large mixing bowls, and a well-stocked pantry offered the oasis I craved.

Despite the kitchen's usual stock of meticulously organized ingredients, from fresh cilantro to fennel seeds, nothing appealed to my unsettled spirit. Resigned yet determined, I decided to prepare golgappa puri. Perhaps I would find solace in the familiar rituals of my craft.

I began by carefully measuring out the semolina, baking soda, and a pinch of salt and sifting them together into a stainless-steel mixing bowl. With precision, I drizzled in lukewarm water while stirring steadily until the mixture came together in a stiff, pliable dough. The tactile nature of the flour transforming under my hands grounded me amidst the avalanche of my emotions.

Covering the dough with a damp muslin cloth, I allowed it to rest. This pause was crucial—it let the gluten in the semolina to relax, making the dough more workable. I occupied myself with the online *NYTimes* crossword, a futile attempt to divert my thoughts.

After the resting period, I returned to find the dough perfectly pliable. I kneaded it on a cold, marble surface until it became smooth and elastic. Dividing the dough into four equal portions, I rolled each into a ball. With practiced hands, I flattened each ball, then rolled it out to a precise two-millimeter thickness. This was crucial: too thin, and the *puris* would not puff up in the oil; too thick, and they would emerge from the fryer dense and chewy.

Heating oil in a heavy-bottomed pan, I watched until it shimmered, the sign it was ready for frying. One by one, I slid the dough circles into the hot oil. They sizzled on contact, puffing up as they fried to a golden perfection that mimicked the glow of a setting sun. The kitchen filled with the enticing aroma of frying dough, a comforting scent. Simple pleasures are the best.

Once fried, I let the puris drain on a wire rack. I resisted the temptation to bite into them immediately. Instead, I prepared a quick green chutney. I blended fresh cilantro, mint, green chili, ginger, and garlic into a vibrant, spicy condiment, the perfect complement to the subtle earthiness of the puris.

Finally, I spooned a generous amount of chutney onto each crispy puri. The combination of textures and flavors was immediate and gratifying. The crisp shell gave way to the explosive freshness of the chutney. Each bite was a complex symphony of flavors, balancing heat with the coolness of the herbs.

I looked up to find Govind, our elderly cook, standing in the doorway. His white kurta was pristine. Despite decades in the kitchen, his posture was ramrod straight. His voice carried the soft, respectful lilt that had soothed many of my childhood woes.

"You should let me do that," he said. A smile played on his lips at the sight of me in the kitchen at such a late hour.

Laughing despite myself, I replied, "I think I've got it tonight, Govind. But tell me, does it smell right?"

Govind inhaled deeply. "Ah, it smells like your grandmother's kitchen on a festival day." His words conjured up memories of my childhood where my grandmother would tuck sweet treats in her purse to hand to me at Diwali events.

I offered a puri to Govind. He hesitated, ever cognizant of social tradition, then gave into the temptation. We ate and talked for a while. "Food made with passion always tastes better," he said.

When we were finished, Govind insisted on helping me restore the kitchen to its prior, pristine state. I stepped outside to dispose of the trash. I might not have noticed the contents of the waste bin had not the motion detecting light come on the moment I stepped onto the pavement. Just before I dropped the trash bag in the container, I saw a stack of four-by-six cards. I placed the bag on the concrete, reached into the can, and pulled out a card.

It was simple, elegant, and featured flowing calligraphy. *Ma* knew class. She always insisted on it. She would never have sent out any formal invitation that was not engraved and on expensive stock. The simple message in the elegant script tore at my heart. "Mr. and Mrs. Kavyansh Chatwal request the pleasure of your company at the wedding ceremony of their son Vikram to Ms. Harlow Kennedy of Atlanta, Georgia."

The date and time on the invitation indicated my parents had anticipated a ceremony during the next wedding season. They were traditional to the end. *Ma* would have paid a significant premium for such sophistication, and I imagined she bulldozed her way to a prominent date. She had obviously planned on my wedding being the event of the season. On closer investigation, I found box after box of invitations—over 1,500 in all. Apparently, she had ordered them the moment we got off the phone *before Papa* changed his mind.

These were discarded earlier in the week, I thought. *They must have been in some of the boxes the staff brought here after the break-in at Xanadu.*

Now they lay in the trash along with an assortment of other things my parents had determined were not worth keeping.

I went to my room, shut the door, and tossed and turned until I fell asleep.

CHAPTER THIRTEEN

HARLOW

MOM KISSED ME ON THE CHEEK and was already headed across the tarmac toward a waiting limo before I realized she was not staying with me.

"Hey, where are you going?"

She tossed her hair when she turned—ever the ingenue. "Need a little away time from all the fuss and bother," she said. "Eat, pray, love thing you know. I'll holler when I'm done. Tootles."

Tootles? What the hell? The BMW pulled away before I could form a response, much less a protest. *Well,* I thought, *at least that's not one of Vik's cars.*

I watched her go and was lost in thought when a pair of arms locked me in a vise from behind. I struggled for a moment, then leaned over and bit the wrist closest to my mouth.

"Ow!" Lita let go. When I turned, she had sunk to one knee. She was clutching her arm like it had been caught in a bear trap. She tried hard to look wounded.

"You never told me you were a vampire," she said.

"You never told me you were a candy ass," I said.

She scrambled to her feet and wrapped me in one of the best hugs I'd ever had. When we finally let go, she looked at me, then at Addison with a "what gives" expression. I explained the situation.

With everything sorted out, we trooped to her car, a gleaming Escalade. Despite a retinue of porters and a driver, Addison insisted on carrying my shoulder bag.

"What do you have in here, a rocket launcher?"

"Wasn't sure how much defensive capability I would need by myself with you in a plane," I said.

We both laughed. Lita looked a little skeptical. I leaned close to her. "Relax—old friend. Nothing there."

Lita nodded and, in blatant violation of all protocol, climbed into the front seat opposite the driver. Addison tucked a bill onto the porter's shirt pocket. "I've got it," he said—and he opened my door. "Milady," he said.

"Thank you," I said. I stopped halfway in the car. "Seriously, thank you."

"Anything for an old friend," he said. He stiffened a little. "I mean—"

"Don't worry about the *old* comment," I said. "I know what you mean. And, as your *old friend,* I am seriously and eternally appreciative."

With the bags loaded in the trunk and the two of us ensconced in the rear seats, the driver took his position and eased on down the road. We'd been driving about twenty minutes when my phone chirped with a text. It was from someone I knew back in college. She wrote copy for a "news" website.

Call me was all it said.

She answered on the second ring.

"Harlow, where the hell have you been. I've reached out a thousand times in the last half day."

"Nice to hear your voice too, Ophelia. What's up?"

"Sorry," she said. "It's just…well…damn…I don't know how to preface this."

"How about telling me what's going on."

"You follow me online, right?"

I didn't want to admit that I hadn't looked at the gossip rag where she worked for over a year, but I was, technically a follower.

"Yes," I said.

"You haven't read my most recent column I take it."

"Been a little busy. What's it about."

"I'll let you read it. Just know two things. First, I tried to stop it, but my editor threatened to fire me if I didn't write it up."

"Okay," I said. I wasn't worried. Someone on the internet was taking shots at Vik all the time.

"The second thing is…I'm really, really sorry."

Now, I was worried.

CHAPTER FOURTEEN

SOPHIA

THE MOMENT I SAW HARLOW PASSED out on the floor, I understood. I'd seen a lot of women lose babies when I was "studying" with Mama Jasmine. My daughter—it was still an adjustment to think of her that way—we'd been "on the outs" for so long—lay in a fetal position in obvious distress. Though I managed to get her to her feet and downstairs to my car, she had no idea what was happening until she awakened in the hospital after her surgery.

It was a brutal introduction to her about the perils of pregnancy and the fragility of life. Though she had not told me she was expecting, I'd been around more pregnant women than most people. Somehow, I knew. "They" say that a mother always knows. I wasn't sure I was worthy of the title, but I'd been suspicious.

After the wonderful staff members at the hospital wheeled Harlow into a private room and she and I had shared a good cry, I went home. I visited three times every day. Tried to not stay overly long, but I was trying to make up for lost time—if anyone ever can.

After I took her home and got her settled, I promised to give her a call. It didn't happen.

I luxuriated in my favorite robe and sipped my morning espresso in the quietude of my house. It wouldn't be mine much longer. I'd been "shacking up" with Vincent for a while. Harlow loved to use that phrase—I don't know why. But she knew better than to say, "living in sin." Stones and glass houses, you know.

Since her admission to the hospital, I'd stayed at my place because it was closer both to her recovery and to Vik's apartment. I took another sip and looked at the For Sale sign on the front lawn. Pretty soon I would be a permanent resident in Vincent's opulent mausoleum of a house.

There was always a price to pay.

A ping on my phone shattered my serenity...and my future.

An image flickered across the screen—a familiar photograph of myself taken at a gala last season, where I had dazzled and entertained the most select of Atlanta's elite. Below the picture was a headline blazed—the type of salacious intrigue that the upper crust pretends to disdain yet secretly devours with glee.

"Stunning Revelation: Star of Atlanta Party Scene Not Who (or What) She Claims"—article by Ophelia Housel.

"What the hell is this?" The words slipped from my lips, a whisper of silk tearing quietly. The croissant I had been enjoying lay forgotten, its flaky layers suddenly as unappealing as the bile rising in my throat.

The article painted a sordid picture. The prose dripped with the venom only the scorned or jealous could muster:

Sophia Carter Kennedy Ellison Bashelder has long been a fixture on the Atlanta social scene. Although claiming descent from a long line of Southern prominence, the reality is quite different. Sources reveal Mrs. Bashelder (as of this writing engaged to Vincent Allemande of Macon, GA) is the product of a secret, Old South dalliance that until now has been neither revealed nor discussed...

The words blurred and a cocktail of anger and disbelief spiked through my veins. The narrative was a concoction of half-truths taken out of context and outright fabrications:

Sophia Carter Whatever, product of an illicit relationship between her mother, Lizzie Carter, and the son of her White employers... married to a philandering, debt-riddled jewelry maker named Nathaniel Kennedy... thrown out of the house for infidelity (the author of the tripe would not have bothered to learn the extramarital affairs were my former husband's) ...living on the streets for months... taken in by the owner and operator of one of the most notorious (and well-trafficked) brothels in Atlanta.

The insinuation was clear and cunningly crafted to scandalize without slandering. It suggested I had been more than just a cleaner in the unsavory establishment. The last lines were designed not to inform, but to ignite the worst sort of social wildfire. I knew the velvet gloves were off, and the claws of Atlanta's high society were unsheathed and ready to swipe with devastating precision.

Before I could even process the full impact, my phone vibrated with a message from Vincent, each word a cold slap:

S. Forget my name. Lose my number. And return that damn ring.

And then, the coup de grâce, a single word that seared itself into my memory with the heat of a branding iron:

Whore.

My phone rang. I almost threw it against the wall, but when I saw the caller ID, I hesitated, then answered.

"Addison Whitmore, why in the world would you be calling me?" I asked.

"Sophia," he said. "You have always been a friend to me and to my folks. From what I can tell, this may be a good time for you to get the hell out of Dodge. Just talked to your daughter. I think I have just the ticket."

CHAPTER FIFTEEN

HARLOW

I PUT DOWN MY PHONE. NOTHING in the article was news to me, but there was no reason in the world for the rest of Atlanta—and whatever other parts of the world read that crap—needed to dig through my mother's difficult and demeaning past. She'd come clean to me with the entire story.[1]

I tried to call Mom. I finally got connected on the seventh attempt—the towers and such were still screwed up—by the call went straight to voicemail. I wasn't surprised. There was no way, she wanted to talk about this.

Addison looked at me. "Did you know all that before today?"

"No," I said, "I know the truth—and the only thing this column is good for would be to line the bottom of a bird cage."

"Well," he said, "I read it, and it seems to me, this Ophelia person got the stuff *from* the bottom of the cage and just printed it."

I couldn't help myself. I laughed.

"What do we do now?" he asked.

---

1 To catch up, or review, see *Karma Under Fire*, Chapters 65 & 66.

"This isn't your fight," I said. "It's Sophia's."

"I don't abandon friends…well, not anymore at least."

I looked at his blue eyes. *Paul Newman has nothing on you,* I thought. I bit my lip to fight back the tears I could feel rising in my eyes. "She's more than equipped to fight her own battles," I said. "When she's ready to resurface, nothing will stop her. Now, let's go find Vik."

I settled back into my seat while Addison took in the sights. I looked over at him.

He's really changed, I thought. *Wonder what my life would be like if he'd grown up sooner.*

CHAPTER SIXTEEN

HARLOW

WE DROPPED ADDISON OFF AT THE LEELA PALACE, then merged into traffic. The vehicle inched through the dense tide of humanity. The air outside was thick with the smell of diesel and human sweat, a pungent mixture that penetrated into the car's interior despite the air conditioning's best efforts.

Lita, who had moved to the back, reached across the seat to take my hand, her gesture a small island of comfort in the overwhelming flood of sensory input.

"You okay?" she asked, her voice rich with concern.

I sighed and stared out the tinted windows. "Still haven't been able to get in touch with Vik," I said. "I've texted—no response. Every time I call, it goes straight to voicemail."

"Nothing to worry about," Lita said. "Major issues with all forms of communications right now." She watched the intricate ballet of cars, bicycles, and pedestrians weaving an erratic tapestry outside. "A kid on a bike delivered the message to meet you here."

"I asked the pilot to radio," I said. "I guess someone in the tower sent the messenger."

"Very old school India." Lita grimaced in a half-smile. "Almost quaint." Her gaze lingered on a group of children darting between slow-moving vehicles, their laughter rising above the din of traffic. "Don't take this the wrong way. I love you dearly and I'm always excited to see you, especially in Delhi. But why are you here?"

The limo slowed for a group of beggars. Their faces bore the hard lines of daily survival. Their hands reached out, palms upturned in silent petition. They braved injury every time they navigated the narrow spaces between the of air-conditioned cars and the relentless outdoor heat.

"I'm not sure where Vik is," I said. "He left a message about a break-in at his parents' home. I tried calling there before I left Atlanta but couldn't get through."

"They're staying at Vik's enclave at the Golf Links for a while," Lita said. She cracked open the window and slid a ten-rupee note through to a young girl with hopeful eyes. "It is way out—very posh—no bike boys out there."

"Vik has an enclave?" I was genuinely surprised. My knowledge of Vik's assets was apparently not as comprehensive as I'd believed. Lalita's description of the tranquil, green oasis seated in the center of the Delhi Golf Club community was a silent reminder of how little I knew about my fiancée's former life in India.

"Vik owns a lot of things," Lita replied, her tone laced with amusement. "No way he's told you about everything."

"Bet he has," I said, only half-serious.

"You didn't know about the enclave," she said.

"Okay, one thing."

"The polo ponies?"

"Two things?"

"He owns six boats."

"Point made," I said with a rueful laugh. "How do you know about where he's staying?"

"A break-in at Xanadu, are you kidding?" Lita pursed her lips. "It's bigger news in India than Taylor Swift's latest romance. Everyone has been talking about it. There are rumors everywhere. Someone told me the place was ransacked by gamblers who were upset they hadn't been paid."

I grabbed Lita's arm. "Vik's father is not in hock to gamblers," I said with the certainty of a Baptist preacher holding forth on Sunday morning.

"I know that." Lita playfully tossed my hand away. "Everybody knows that. People like to see who can come up with the most outlandish stories when prominent people are involved. But you haven't answered the big question. Why are you here?"

I didn't respond immediately, just stared out the window at the dynamic tableau of New Delhi life. Women cooked at the side of the road, their makeshift stoves sending up curls of smoke mingled with the city's omnipresent dust. Children cavorted in the dirt, their laughter a stark contrast to the seriousness of their surroundings. Buskers played flutes, juggled, or danced, their performances punctuated by the occasional clink of coins in their collection bowls.

"Harlow?" Lita's voice pulled me back from the window.

I blinked back the tears I could feel at the corners of my eyes, turned, and told my dearest friend everything.

"Harlow, I am so sorry." She cocked her head. "Are you sure it was safe for you to travel?"

"The doc wasn't wild about it. I called him before Addison

picked me up, but he said I would be okay if I didn't get too fatigued on the trip. I slept most of the way here. There was a bedroom on the plane."

Lita rolled her eyes. "You always did know how to roll," she said.

Lita's condominium stood in Vikas Puri, a lively quarter of Delhi, amid the colorful chaos of the city. The surrounding neighborhood mixed chaos with purpose. The street buzzed with vendors hawking an array of vivid textiles and handmade crafts, while children laughed and chased one another. The scent of curry, ginger and garlic wafted through the air with the promise of spicy delights.

Lita's personality shone through in every detail inside. The living space blended neutrals, bold colors, and traditional motifs, each element carefully chosen to create a warm, vibrant atmosphere. It was clear to me that every corner was curated with love and attention. In the living room, a bank of windows let in the golden glow of the early evening. It turned the high-rise buildings around us into shimmering pillars against the horizon. I watched residents pass below. They exchanged smiles and nods in a rhythm of everyday familiarity common in any city.

Amar, Lita's husband and Vik's cousin, was absent, still at work, his dedication as unwavering as the city's energy. Instead of accepting Lita's offer of tea, I retreated to the guest room upstairs. The neutral palettes of gray, white, and tan felt provided a soothing balm to my travel-weary nervous system. I removed my black flats and settled into the caress of soft linens. The calming tones and textures lulled me to sleep. Here, tranquility reigned in stark contrast to the lively world outside. The noise of the city faded into a distant hum.

Three hours later, I awakened to the most beautiful sight I had ever seen—Vikram Chatwal's smiling face.

CHAPTER SEVENTEEN

VIK

She looked stunning with dimming light sweeping across her face. The purity of her spirit shown through while she was sleeping. Yes, she was feisty—often fiery—and still had work to do on her self-esteem (way too hard on herself and more than occasionally suspicious of others, understandable given what I knew of her childhood), but she was...well, there was no other word for it...good.

Harlow Kennedy was a good person. Beautiful, talented, loving, excitable, energetic... and good.

My God, I love you and I said so, as quietly as possible.

Harlow shifted slightly, her brow furrowing as if in response to a dream, before settling again. I remembered how our story began, under less than auspicious circumstances, and I still marveled at the journey.

On that fateful flight, when I found myself seated next to the woman I had just fired, I was caught in a whirlwind of emotions, fascinated and somewhat guilt-ridden. Yet, despite the awkward small talk and even more uneasy silences, something within me stirred—the dawning of affection.

"Remember how furious you were?" I chuckled softly, recalling the memory. "And all I wanted was to keep talking to you, keep seeing you."

I scrolled through our adventures in India. A smile tugged at my lips. The pretense of helping her find a marriage arrangement had been absurd, but it led us to a deeper connection, explosive disagreements, and then to a beautiful, fierce reconciliation. The engagement had been as impromptu as it was perfect.

But then, reality intervened. My parents caved in to their reservations and reneged on their endorsement. Now, a shadow hovered over our plans, and cast the gloom of generational bias over our future. Sitting by Harlow now, I could almost laugh at the irony. My parents, while professing modern values, were ensnared by the specter of societal gossip and the crippling fear of scandal. They worried about appearances, about propriety, and Harlow, the embodiment of all that was genuine and true, was unwittingly at the center of their apprehensions.

"Harlow, they don't know you like I do. They don't see your heart," I said. I reached out and gently brushed a stray lock of hair from her forehead. She stirred again. This time her eyes fluttered open. They met mine with a sleepy confusion that quickly warmed to recognition.

"Hey." Her voice was hoarse with sleep.

"Hey," I replied. "How are you feeling?"

"Mmm, better now," she said, Our hands intertwined with a familiarity that sent shivers up my spine. She glanced at the window and the darkening sky. "What are you doing here so late?"

"I finally found out where you were and I couldn't wait any longer to see you," I said. "The folks at the airport were a little reluctant to reveal the name of the plane owner and the passengers, but I worked it out."

"A bribe?"

I squeezed her hand. "I might have led them to believe I was with the counter terrorism division of the army." She scowled. "I said *I might have.*"

"You are such a scoundrel," she said.

"Guilty as charged," I said. "But once I had the intel, it wasn't hard to find Addison. He could not have been nicer. I offered to pay for the jet fuel, but he wouldn't hear of it. When he told me you were here, I think I hung up on him. I'll apologize later."

"It's fine," she said. "He's changed a lot." I hesitated a hair too long. "Vik, I'm not interested in him."

"Wasn't even thinking it," I said. She didn't protest but she could tell it was a lie. "Anyway, we have a lot to sort out, but right now, just being here with you feels like the most important thing."

Her smile was my sunrise. "We'll figure it out, won't we?" she said with a quiet confidence.

"We always do," I said. I leaned in to capture her lips with mine, sealing our silent vow with a kiss that spoke of battles fought and yet to come, but skirmishes always fought together. I pulled back. We stared at each other with the quiet assurance of our mutual commitment to love—our greatest adventure.

CHAPTER EIGHTEEN

VIK

Five days earlier

"Vikram, my son, you must come home," my father's voice cracked over the phone, a rare display of vulnerability that sent a chill down my spine.

"What's wrong? Are you okay? And *Ma*?" I asked, sensing the weight of his words.

"The house was burglarized," he replied. He sounded old. "Your *ma* and I were away for the weekend, a little holiday at the beach in Goa.."

"Where was the staff?" My concern was immediate, the implications of the breach unsettling.

"We'd given everyone time off—and a little money to enjoy themselves. You remember last week was the anniversary of the first day your *ma* and I met."

I winced, having forgotten the date. "Yes, congratulations," I said even as I recognized the inadequacy of my words. "The alarm?"

"Screaming like a hungry two-year-old from what I am told," he said. "But Xanadu is too far out of town for a rapid response. It took the police over thirty minutes to get there."

"Everyone okay?"

"Yes."

"Damage to the house?"

"The foyer windows were smashed, and the backdoors were tampered with a little. Both easy fixes. "

I could tell he was downplaying the damage, but his voice was strained.

"Did the police arrest anyone?"

"No, and they say it's unlikely they will. There have been a great many similar incidents recently. Too many crimes—not enough detectives."

I'd urged him months ago to install security cameras and hire an on-site security team, suggestions he dismissed in his typical fashion. Internally, I kicked myself for not insisting on both precautionary measures.

"Veer is having security cameras installed while your mother and I stay at The Oberoi Hotel in town," he said.

"I'm on my way," I said.

I'd tried to reach Harlow but didn't have any luck. I called from Newark—no answer. I left a message and boarded the plane, my heart heavy with unresolved questions and the unspoken fears of what awaited me at home. When I arrived in Delhi, Hussein, my folks' long-time driver and factotum, met me at the airport.

"My parents still at The Oberoi Hotel?" I asked.

"Yes," he said. "We will be there in a little over half an hour."

"How bad was the break-in?" I asked. He hesitated. "Please, speak freely."

"There was no vandalism. Nothing was smashed or broken.

The thieves took some silverware and the sculpture by Tyeb Mehta."

"*Pa* loves that piece. But it sits over in the corner of his office—not really in any sightline. Those thieves have a very discerning eye."

"I thought the same thing," he said. "Your father has a watch drawer in his closet. There must be close to thirty timepieces—some very valuable. Not a single one was missing."

Very odd, I thought. "Do you think they were after anything in particular? I mean, other than the Mehta?"

"I do not know for sure," Hussein said, "but it seems to me that someone was trying to attract attention."

After checking on my parents and holding the truncated conversation with my father, I had the staff relocate my parents from the hotel to my home in the Golf Links neighborhood. The enclave would give them the quiet and privacy they both needed.

Hussein took me to Xanadu. The once pristine condition of the vast estate was marred by the recent intrusion. The workman polishing the replacement glass on the front window was a stark reminder of the vulnerability that now shadowed our home.

When I was younger, Veer seemed ageless. He was a squat little man with a face dominated by a profound nose of which he was oddly proud. He claimed to be descended from warrior kings—said his proboscis was a sign of virility and courage. I always thought he looked a little like an aardvark.

Strange looks aside, he was a master of organization. I learned a lot from listening to him.

"You do not need to know how everyone is doing their job," he said. "You only need to know they are doing it and doing it well. Show them how, watch them, then let them develop their own style—whether it is mowing the lawn, trimming the hedges, or repairing a leak in a pipe. Give them the tools and the time they need. Pray them up…praise them up…and pay them up and they will repay you with undying loyalty."

Valuable lessons for my later life.

Veer popped up from behind his desk with a spryness that belied his advancing years. "Master Vikram," he said. "It is so good to see you."

He got me up to speed.

"Doesn't sound like a professional robbery," I said. "In fact, with so little missing, it doesn't even sound like a smash and grab."

Veer nodded. "No, it was not," he said. "I think someone was trying to get your parents' attention."

Odd, I thought. *That's the same impression Hussein has.*

I pondered his words and their implications. The estate, a beacon of heritage and comfort, now felt profoundly under protected. The echoes of my footsteps in the hall were a stark reminder of the need for safety, a luxury we had taken for granted.

"Let's step up the security measures, Veer," I said. "I want a full review of all staff and recent visitors and please hire a small security team to be stationed here to provide twenty-four-hour surveillance," I said. On my way to the door, I turned back. "And get the gardens back in order. My mother will want to see her roses in bloom when she returns."

CHAPTER NINETEEN

LITA

When Vik had arrived after dinner, I led him down the narrow hallway to the second bedroom in our two-bedroom condo. His footfalls made no noise on the Persian rugs. I loved the craftsmanship of the intricate patterns, a testament to centuries of skill and dedication. The walls, adorned with silk wallpaper in a subdued shade of ivory, reflected the soft light from the overhead lights and created an atmosphere of warmth and invitation.

We reached the guest room where Harlow lay resting. I opened the door, and waved him in. The four-poster bed with its carved mahogany frame was draped in fine linen sheets and a silk duvet, the soft blues and creams of the bedding complementing the serene palette of the room. The antique furniture—a pair of Louis XVI armchairs upholstered in velvet, a Victorian writing desk meticulously restored, all great finds—came courtesy of my connections at Sotheby's.

I tiptoed into the room to pull apart the heavy damask curtains. The subtle scent of orange blossoms from the potpourri jar on the nightstand wafted through the room.

My whisper sounded like a shout in the quiet room. "She's been out most of the afternoon. She said the doctor told her to rest."

Vik nodded. His eyes scanned the room. He moved closer to the bed, his expression softening as he watched Harlow breathe gently, a peaceful contrast to the storm of worries I knew were swirling in his head.

"Thank you for making her so comfortable," he said.

I gave his shoulder a reassuring squeeze. "She's family now, Vik. We take care of our own."

Amar and I enjoyed living in his small condo. It felt cozy but not cramped. It was all we needed. Whenever my *saas*[1] started talking about how the place was too small for children, I changed the subject. There were a few more important items to address.

To begin, I barely knew my husband. We'd met on a magical evening in New York. In a turn of events reminiscent of a Hallmark holiday movie, he'd managed to get fired and lose my phone number all in a matter of about eight minutes. He was sure he'd lost me. Unaware of his misfortune—and the card with my number he'd run through the washing machine in his pants pocket—I was certain he was nothing more than a smooth-talking cad.

We did not meet again until my engagement party...the one thrown for me in honor of my impending wedding to *Vikram Chatwal*. When I say everything had been arranged, I mean everything. Mrs. Chatwal had employed the preeminent matchmaker in all India, Isha, to find the perfect mate for her only son, who was home. As it was later revealed to me, he had entertained no thoughts of getting married during his visit. But his resolve ran face first into Mrs. Chatwal's iron will. One thing led to another, and we were a matter of days from the Indian equivalent of "I do"

1 Mother-in-law

when Vik discovered my mystery man was his own cousin, Amar.

After a hastily arranged "switcheroo," Amar jumped in as the groom, Isha got paid double, and I became Mrs. *Amar* Chatwal. Everything was wonderful for the first month, which we spent at Ooty, one of the loveliest honeymoon spots in India—in the world. We ate, drank, danced, swam, and everything else we could think of when we decided to take a break from passionate lovemaking sessions.

We were a couple…alone…without outside influences. It was romantic and perfect. And then we came home.

When I'd left my job at Sotheby's, my boss begged me to come back. Even though I did not know who I was going to marry at the time, I was sure I would be expected to remain in Bharat.[2] I'd been assured my mystery husband was a man of considerable influence with business concerns throughout the world but based in New Delhi. As it turned out, had I married Vikram, after the honeymoon, we would have departed for Atlanta. Although I was thrilled with the twists of fate that put me in Amar's life (and bed), I knew the second we were wed that we would live in India.

One afternoon while Amar was snoozing (I wonder why he might have been so fatigued in the middle of the day), I snuck in a phone call to my old boss. When I suggested working remotely from India, he was thrilled. Within a day, he'd emailed a contact, which I signed during another one of Amar's "sudden onset naps."

When I told my *saas* about my remote job, she was confused.

"You are working?" she asked.

"Yes," I said. "Sotheby's wanted me to continue in my former capacity."

"You will be *returning* to Atlanta?"

---

2 Commonly used name for India, which is also often referred to by citizens as Hindustan.

"No, I can work from home."

"Who will cook…and clean?" She ran an accusing finger across the kitchen table and seemed disappointed when it came back without as much as a speck of dust.

"I take care of the house. It isn't very big," I said. I cringed the moment the words came out of my mouth.

"My *beta*[3] offered to buy a much grander place." She looked around with marked disdain. "Apparently, you have simple tastes,"

Best to ignore the jab. "And Amar and I do a lot of take out." She looked blank. "Take away. We eat lot of take away food."

She could have been witnessing an execution in sixteenth century England. Actually, watching bodies torn apart by wild horses running in opposite directions might not had disgusted her as much as the thought of her son eating a meal someone other than his spouse (or mother) had prepared.

"What about his other needs?" she asked.

Seriously, this woman is asking me about having sex with her son?

"Everything will be fine," I said. "I promise." I had moved to the stove. Maybe preparing tea would help shift the conversation.

"When the *bachchon*[4] arrive, will you continue to play on your computer?"

I was "this close" to unloading on her about the complexities of my international job and my *birth control pills* when *Lakshmi* [5] took pity on me from above and Amar came through the door. He greeted his *mummy* with a kiss on either cheek, slumped in a chair, and began complaining about his day.

Sympathy poured forth like water from a broken dam. *Mami-*

---

3 Son.
4 Babies.
5 Wife of Vishnu—goddess of wealth and good fortune.

yar[6] patted his head. When the tea kettle sang its cheery little tune, she nearly bowled me over to grab it and prepare her precious *beta* a cup.

After her darling boy had been soothed sufficiently, she stood. "It is time for me to go."

I protested without much vigor—even invited her to stay for dinner.

"No," she said. "You will have your takeaway," she narrowed her eyes, "after which you should attend to your marital duties."

She left. Amar stared at me with saucer-sized eyes. "Did my *mummy* just tell you we should have sex?"

I began unbuttoning my blouse. "First intelligent thing she has said all afternoon. Bedroom or do you think we should see if we can break the table?"

---

6 What a woman calls her mother-in-law.

CHAPTER TWENTY

VIK

I WATCHED HARLOW SLEEP. THE SLIGHT smile on her perfect lips told me she might have been dreaming of something pleasant. My mind teamed with uncertainty.

Who wants my parents' attention. More importantly—why?

I'd been worrying about them for some time. Both were older and while neither was frail, no one saw them and thought "robust" either.

I still like the idea of moving them to the States, I thought. *There are some nice condos in Atlanta. Finding good staff won't be a problem. We'll get something with enough room for Ma's flowers. Pa can read, meditate, write his memoirs.*

I'd talked with him about golf once long ago. We had finished dinner and the conversation wandered around until it settled on my most recent recreational activities. I said I had taken up golf and was becoming quite accomplished.

"Silly game," *Pa* said. "No challenge. The ball just sits there and waits to be hit."

"Not as easy as it looks," I said.

"Well, it certainly is not as difficult as cricket," he said.

"You never played cricket," I said.

Mummyji giggled. "Oh, you could not be more wrong, my son," she said. "Your father was a magnificent batsman. He dominated every time he stepped onto the oval." There was an interesting twinkle in her eye. I could tell she was seeing a younger version of Kavyansh Chatwal in her memory.

"Tell me about it," I said.

Pa took the sort of breath he always did when he was getting ready to launch into a story, but he never started. *Ma* put down her needlework and stood.

"Later," she said. "It's time for bed."

My father started to interrupt, but he took one look at my mother and said, "Yes, it is indeed."

They walked out of the parlor hand in hand. When they rounded the corner toward the stairs, I could have sworn I heard my mother giggle. I might have been a little grossed out if I hadn't been laughing so hard.

I loved Xanadu and its meticulously groomed surroundings—particularly the gardens. But they had long ago become too much for *Ma*. Not so long ago, she spent hours in the summer heat pruning healthy plants and fussing over struggling ones. But those days were gone and her "gardening" was mostly restricted to supervision. Though she still patrolled them with a keen eye for detail or negligence, the trowel she carried seldom moved any dirt.

There were too many acres to oversee and, frankly, too many staff members to manage. When I considered what might have happened had my parents been at home when the robbery occurred, I shuddered. I would never tell my folks they were too old to live at Xanadu, but in my heart, I knew it was the truth.

Then there were the businesses. The only thing more volatile than the oil market in which Chatwal Enterprises was heavily engaged was the value of the rupee. It took more plunges than the Goliath roller coaster at Six Flags. It rose like a mighty wave only to crash again just before hopes got too high. Watching the daily fluctuations could send even the most experienced financial "sailor" raising to the rail to lose his lunch.

I was bracing myself for the inevitable conversation. I had gone over it hundreds of times in my head. "You've had fun with your little restaurant business, now it's time to come back to India" speech. Someone would deliver it while I was home—probably neither of my parents. I imagined it would be one of my Papa's younger brothers, *chacha* as the elder brother was known all in India. Perhaps, and more likely, the admonition would come from my cousin Sajin. He'd always been a pain in the *arse*. He had picked on me relentlessly when I was a child, at least until I hit my growth spurt after which he knew better. He still loved to tweak my nose whenever he could.

Sajin was the only child from my *chacha's* first marriage. When his mother died, Amar's father had no idea what to do. Like most Indian men of his generation, he'd never imaged being faced with rearing a child on his own. Sajin was sent off to a year-round boarding school at the age of five. Three years later, he came home to discover his father had remarried. Sajin took an instant dislike to *chachee* Bhavita. The animosity multiplied when he learned there would soon be an addition to the family, my *chachera* Amar. The more *chachee* Bhavita doted on her new baby; the more Sajin hated him.

Sajin declined the opportunity to study in America. Although his chances of being admitted to a top school were slim, Sajin remained in India where he'd earned a degree in business. After Amar went off the Boston College, Sajin promoted the idea that he'd bypassed his own "foreign education" out of devotion to his father and because he did not want to be "indoctrinated by Western decadence."

I thought back to a small incident at Amar's wedding. I had asked about Sajin. "Where is he?"

"The cover story is that he is on a vacation with his wife," Amar said.

"*Cover story?*" I asked.

"They haven't lived together for a long time," Amar said. "Best guess is that they are getting or have gotten a divorce and don't want to tell anyone yet."

"Sorry to hear it," I said.

"You'd be the only one," Amar said. "Isha arranged the marriage. Wasn't hard to find parents eager to latch their daughter to a Chatwal but Sajin never thought she met his standards. He always found fault. She was not tall or not slender enough. Her hips were too wide, her eyes too deep set. Her did not cook well; her care of the house was slovenly. I've always thought she was a most attractive and winsome person, but to hear Sajin talk, she is a cross between the Wicked Witch from *Snow White* and a lazy bloodhound basking in the sun. From what I hear, after the first night on their honeymoon, they stayed in separate rooms."

"Ouch," I said. "The joys of married life." I realized what I had said. "Sorry."

"No worries, my friend," Amar said. "Lalita and I are going to be happy. We were meant for one another."

Amar's marriage did nothing to improve Sajin's disposition. He knew Lita would eventually start popping out babies like a Pez dispenser and once Bhavita and Gautam became *daada* and *daadi ma,* Sajin would slip further into irrelevance.

I started to mumble. "No matter who gives me the speech about where I belong, coming back to India full time is not in the playbook. I've worked too hard for too long at learning the art of making Indian food to return to a desk in New Delhi."

Mastery of my craft would never come. Who in the world could claim to know everything about a native land's food? I knew colleagues in the States who were still feverishly trying to create "the world's perfect hotdog."

Indian food, with its multiplicity of spices and the subtle effect even the smallest ingredient change could make, would forever hold some mystery, but I was determined to become as good as possible. And my quest did not involve a home base in Xanadu—or anywhere else in the subcontinent.

It was getting late. Once I was convinced things at Xanadu were okay—and had fulfilled *Ma's* wishes with the execrable day with my uncle—preparations for the awards ceremony in Mumbai demanded my presence. I wanted to tell Harlow about my exciting new assignment, but I was loathe to awaken her given everything she had endured in the past few days. I leaned in to kiss her forehead and remembered the one thing I had yet to do—tell her about my plan to move my parents to America.

And then...Harlow opened her eyes.

CHAPTER TWENTY-ONE

HARLOW

I GRABBED VIK'S NECK AND RAINED kisses on his head, his cheek, his ears, and his gorgeous lips. I yanked back.

"What's wrong?" he asked.

"Morning mouth," I said. "I must taste like there's a marching band in there."

"Tastes just fine to me," he said. He pressed his lips against mine and stayed there for a long, luxurious time.

When he backed away, we both groaned. "I've missed you," I said.

"It's been all of…what…five days? Six? Seven?"

"No idea," I said. "I've lost count. We're in another country with a different time and a different day. Seems like months."

"Indeed, it does," he said. He leaned back in for another kiss.

I moved away. "What's with the radio silence there, Skippy?" I asked.

He looked chastened. "Nothing intentional," he said. "You know there are cell phone issues everywhere. I couldn't get you. You couldn't get me. I was in the air. Then, obviously, you were in the air. *Ma* sent me on a fool's errand with my *chacha*. Glad I got the message you were here at Lita's. And I am most pleased you arranged a private flight. If I had known about your plans ahead of time, I would have set everything up."

"It's okay," I said. "Addison was very kind. He—"

"Addison? As in Addison Whitmore, your erstwhile fiancé?"

Outrage flooded my brain. "What the hell difference does that make? You know that whole deal was a sham from the very beginning. You even helped me look for a husband here before you swooped in with your dark eyes and perfect teeth (my anger was losing traction) ...and... and kissable lips... (it disappeared) ...overall gorgitude."

I'd shone enough indignation. Time for another kiss. A proper kiss. A deep, probing one full of unspoken desire. I was getting revved up—even though I knew I had certain physical limitations—when Vik slowed the pace.

"Something wrong?" I asked.

Damn, he looked at his frickin' watch.

"Well," he said. "I checked with the doctor, and he said you need to take it easy for a few days. On top of that, things are a mess. I've got security people coming to Xanadu in—*his watch again*—less than an hour. I haven't even had the chance to tell you about the awards ceremony."

I was still a little groggy. "You're getting an award?"

"No, long story short, I am cooking the banquet for the annual Film Awards—like the Oscars."

"Don't try to tell *me* about movies, Mister," I said. "I grew up on them—all kinds." I paused a beat to absorb what he'd told me. "Wait a minute. That's held in Mumbai, right?"

"Yes," he said. He sounded like a teenager who'd been caught with a dirty magazine. "Next week...ah...if...ah...if that's alright with you."

"So, what you're telling me is that you are leaving for Mumbai—see ya later?"

"Well, like I said. Only if you approve. But you and Lita can come—I have tickets for you."

My irritation slammed to a halt like a bird flying into a plate glass window. "Do I get to wear a fancy outfit?" I knew the shift in mood made me sound shallow, but this was *the Oscars.*

"No," he said. "You *have to* wear one, several in fact. Very fancy, very expensive, you will have the top designers at your disposal. My treat of course." He smiled because he knew I loved to shop and the idea of getting dolled up by the top Indian designers left me a little breathless.

He stood. "Harlow, I hate it, but I have to run. When you are a little more rested, I'll have Hussein come over and move you to my house in town. You will be more comfortable there. My parents are there but there is plenty of room for all of us I promise. But I am running so, so late. I have to go. I love you."

He kissed me on the cheek and was gone. When the door clicked closed, my excitement evaporated. I could feel hot tears streaming from my eyes.

"Hello," I said. "How are you feeling? Was the hospital terrible? Are you okay? And oh, by the way, I'm *so sorry about the baby!*"

VIK

Hussein had driven about three miles when I slammed my fist into the back of the seat in front of me.

"Damn!"

"What's wrong, sir?" Hussein asked.

"I forgot…"

"I'll turn around, sir."

In my haste, I had thought only about what I had to do—the business, the security system, taking care of my parents, the film awards. Those were big ticket items. But there was nothing more important in the world to me—well, there shouldn't have been—than Harlow's health and well-being.

Sophia had called to tell me about the baby and the surgery. In truth, the conversation felt like it had taken place months ago. When I was at Lita's, I'd spent all my time watching Harlow sleep and thinking about everything on *my* plate.

What an ass.

So much for the new and improved Vikram Chatwal who was no longer self-absorbed—the man more concerned with the love of his life than he was with money, success, parties, his golf handicap, and the next sexual conquest.

Hussein spoke again. "Should I turn around?"

"No," I said. "It's not anything I can retrieve."

I just hope it's something I can repair.

CHAPTER TWENTY-TWO

LITA

HARLOW'S VOICE MADE ME JUMP. "WHAT the hell are you doing?"

I looked up from the mixing bowl and grinned. Harlow leaned against the kitchen doorway wearing flannel pajama bottoms and a sleeveless t-shirt. Her hair braided into two long ponytails.

"I like your hair. You look like a girl that escaped from a boarding school for the criminally insane," I said.

Harlow shook her head. "Ha, ha! Very funny. I was exhausted when I got here. I didn't put it in a braid before I feel asleep. It was all over my head when I woke up. I jumped in your shower and washed it, but I was too tired to blow dry it. So here we are," she said. "It'll take a bit to coax these curls into an updo—if we're going out." She pointed at me. "But I repeat, what the hell are you doing? You can't cook."

"Au contraire," I said. "I *can* cook; I simply choose not to. Wanna help?"

"Well," she said, "Vik has taught me a few things. But I prefer to watch and eat. What are you making? More important—why are you making it."

"Some of the young wives get together once a week to bitch about everything from their in-laws to their husbands' lousy lovemaking techniques."

"Well, I know you are all in on the first topic. Any complaints in the other?"

I could feel the heat rising from the base of my neck. "None at all," I said. "Well, if you don't count the fact that almost every morning Amar's mother calls to 'check' on me. What she means is, 'Are you knocked up yet?'"

Harlow shook her head. "The *Mas* all want to be *dadee mas*." She reached into the bowl and pulled out a pecan. "Whatcha makin'?"

"Sweet and savory nut mix," I said. "A nice little crunch with just the hint of a pop."

Harlow put out her hand for the bowl again. I slapped it with a spatula. "Wait your turn."

"Come on," she said. "One less cashew is not going to ruin the recipe."

"Okay," I said. "But only one. Those things aren't cheap, you know."

Her mouth was full, but I think she said, "Don't I know it."

"So, you stir the nuts into sugar-water over medium-high heat. Once all the sugar is dissolved, you reduce the heat and wait for it to caramelize. Before the nuts cool—"

"No one like cool nuts," she said.

I choked on the water I was sipping. "Girl, you have certainly gotten nasty in your old age."

"That's why the boys like me," she said. "Go ahead with your cool nuts."

"Sprinkle on the seasoning. Separate the nuts that are stuck together." I threatened her with the spatula. "Don't say it."

She giggled.

"Put them in a bowl and let the greedy little whiners talk about how they can't seem to lose any weight while they stuff their faces with deliciousness."

Harlow watched lay the mixture out on a sheet of waxed paper. "Looks good," she said.

"Help yourself once everything cools off," I said. "First thing will be the crunch. Then you'll get a little burst of sweetness. About everything third bite, the cayenne will pop. It's a great concoction."

She pointed to the assemblage of cannisters and bottles on my kitchen island. "Regular assortment of Indian stuff?" she asked.

"Absolutely," I said. "No self-respecting Indian homemaker would be caught dead without all this."

She inspected every item with the eye of someone who knew what she was doing. "Let's see, fresh cilantro and curry leaves, garlic and ginger, fresh green chilies, serrano chilis, black pepper-corns, mustard seeds—brown *and* black—cardamom pods." She looked up at me. "You grind them yourself?"

"Mostly there for show," I said.

She continued the inventory. "Cayenne, chaat masala,[1] ground cinnamon, ground clove, ground coriander, fennel seeds, fenugreek seeks, sweet paprika, whole dried red chilies, whole star anise, and ground turmeric. A little bit of that goes a long way."

"I found that out the hard way. Amar tried to choke it down, but just couldn't."

"He likes your cooking?" she asked, "That is, when you deign to use your own kitchen."

I broke eye contact. "I'd like it a lot more if he didn't compare

---

1 An eclectic blend of black salt, mango, cumin, and black pepper often used when making salads.

everything I make to his mother's version."

Her hands flew to her mouth. "Oh my god, he does not say, "This doesn't taste like *Ma's*.' Please tell me he doesn't."

"He did at first. Once he figured out that meant he slept on the couch, he quit. But I can see him struggling to keep his comments to himself."

"Speaking of the old mother-in-law, how's that going?" she asked.

I ran my tongue around the inside of my mouth—an old trick I'd learned when I felt like I was going to cry.

"That's a whole other topic," I said.

CHAPTER TWENTY-THREE

HARLOW

THE LUNCHEON WENT VERY WELL FOR A WHILE.

The guests struck me as being very much like every other woman of their age, at least the ones with money. They were over dressed—obviously trying to impress. I mean, really, who wears Jimmy Choo pumps to a casual girls' lunch? Two of them looked like they'd applied their foundation with a trowel, and I imagined the Botox budget around the table ran into the thousands per month. Lita, twenty-six, and I, slightly older, were the elder stateswomen of the bunch. A couple of the girls could not have moved their upper facial muscles without a forklift.

I should not have been so quick in my judgments. Inaya and Nyla, though dressed to the nines, were very sweet and judicious in their application of makeup. Lita had agreed with me about keeping my involvement with Vik private.

"This is Harlow, from America," Lita said. "Atlanta, to be precise." The name Vikram Chatwal hung unsaid but palpable in the air.

The chatter around the table was a mix of honeyed words

and thinly veiled barbs. Inaya, with a somber grace, shared her widowhood story, her voice barely above a whisper, hinting at the solitude that cloaked her despite the room full of people. Just prior to the sad tale, Sharvi and Vanya had made quite the entrance, their sarees a swirl of vibrant colors, their conversation less about catching up and more about sizing up. Plates of kale pakora circulated. The crunch of the crisp fritters seemed to punctuate the growing tension. I savored Lita's spiced chickpea soup and tried to focus on the rich, complex flavors instead of the idle chatter. But as soon as Sharvi brought up the burglary at the Chatwal mansion, the atmosphere thickened.

"They say over a million dollars-worth of diamonds were stolen," she said, eyes wide with a mix of excitement and faux concern.

Vanya chimed in, her voice laced with false pity, "But the Chatwals will never miss it—you know how rich they are."

I sensed a casual cruelty of their gossip. The conversation spiraled from there. Sharvi tossed around rumors like confetti, "After Vik passed over Lita—" she started, with a glint in her eye.

"Excuse me?" Lita kept her voice level, but I could tell she was pissed. The room fell silent for a heartbeat.

"I'm sorry." Sharvi backpedaled with a sly smile, "I misspoke. After he wiggled out of the arrangement his parents had paid for by introducing you to your husband..."

I stood, my chair scraping slightly against the tile. "The trip wore me out," I said. My voice calm but cold. "If you will excuse me, I believe I need to lie down."

Someone said something about "jet lag," but Lita knew better. I was exhausted by the relentless drama. When I stepped out, I felt the weight of the afternoon lift slightly. It was replaced by the lighter burden of figuring out how to navigate these shark infested social waters with grace while swimming with a metaphorical rump roast strapped to my leg.

CHAPTER TWENTY-FOUR

HARLOW

Vik's mother was already seated in the parlor when I entered with a slight nervous flutter in my stomach. I'd arrived at the Chatwal home earlier in the day and been welcomed by Mrs. Jain. After she showed me to my room, one I was obviously not expected to share with anyone, Mrs. Jain told me I was expected for tea with "Madam" at four.

Mrs. Chatwal's smile was unexpectedly warm.

"Harlow, my dear, welcome to our home. Have a seat." She gestured to a chair opposite hers. She was wearing an elegantly draped red and gold handwoven saree.

"Mrs. Jain is ready to pour the tea. Milk?" Her tone was polished but not stiff.

"Yes ma'am." I managed to reply without stuttering. My eyes briefly darted to the bourbon decanter across the room, a tempting but forbidden respite.

"How was your trip?" she asked. She took a delicate sip from her cup.

"It went well, Mrs. Chatwal," I said.

My hand shook a little and the delicate floral china cup rattled against the saucer until I steadied it. The tea was aromatic, a blend conveying floral notes—likely Darjeeling. I detected a whisper of cardamom. The brew demanded appreciation. I sipped and savored its warmth and complexity.

"Would you care for something sweet?" Rachana asked.

Mrs. Jain presented a plate of diamond-shaped treats gleaming with hints of cardamom and rosewater. "Barfi," Rachana said after my gaze lingered a tad too long. "Are you familiar?"

My small laugh was pitiful and defensive. "I thought I knew a lot about Indian food, but I've never seen these before."

Her expression remained unchanged, though I caught a micro-twitch of silent judgment from Mrs. Jain's eyebrow.

"The sweets are infused with cardamom, rosewater, sometimes fruit. There is a wide variety. Some have cashews, pistachios, or peanuts. You're not allergic, are you, my dear?"

"No," I said, "though it might be safer if I were. The food here makes it too easy to indulge."

My attempt at a joke landed in silence, the cultural gap wider than the table between us.

"Well, enjoy," Rachana said. Her courtesy remained impeccable.

I selected a pistachio barfi, the sweet dense yet meltingly soft flavors of milk and nut mingling with the subtler undertones of spice. I almost quipped about needing a cigarette after such a delight but settled for a contented murmur of approval.

Rachana was the epitome of an Old-World hostess; my teacup was never empty, her inquiries about my health and career thoughtful. She complimented my lapel pin, a delicate design from my budding jewelry line, yet skillfully steered clear of any mention of Vik.

The conversation drifted to lighter topics—art, music, and some of Rachana's favorite recipes, which she promised to teach me. "I hope you find our traditions to be as enriching as we find your presence refreshing," she said. I thought her gaze looked more inquisitive than imposing.

I smiled and fought for courage. "I'm eager to learn, and hopefully, bring some joy into the family as well."

Rachana nodded. A hint of approval flickered across her features. "Vikram speaks very highly of you, Harlow. He believes you have the heart to embrace our ways."

"That's very kind of him," I said, my voice a mix of gratitude and nervousness. "I know there's a lot to understand, and I appreciate your patience."

"We are family, after all," she said, pausing as if to choose her next words carefully. "And family is about more than just sharing a name or blood. It is about building a life with all its complexities and joys."

As our time together drew to a close, signaled by Mrs. Jain clearing the tea service, Rachana stood. "Thank you for a lovely afternoon," I said, rising. "I am deeply honored to be a guest in your house."

"Think nothing of it, my dear, it's Vik's house actually" she responded with a smile that reached her eyes for the first time.

Stepping out from the parlor, a flutter of optimism took hold of me. Rachana's welcoming demeanor over tea ignited a hope that, perhaps, acceptance within the Chatwal family was within reach. On the way back to my room, the mansion no longer felt as imposing; the weight of tradition seemed less daunting. A soft smile spread across my face. There was work to be done, relationships to forge, and understandings to deepen, but for the first time since my arrival, I felt the promise of belonging.

I could not have been more wrong.

Later, I dressed and walked downstairs to dinner. The table, which could accommodate three dozen guests, was set for two.

I'd learned Mrs. Ch…*umm*…Rachana was "otherwise engaged" with one of her many charitable activities. Vik's father was still "indispose." I had yet to lay eyes on him. My dinner companion was Sajin, Amar's younger half-brother and Vik's first cousin. I'd heard him described as "insufferable," but I'd been unjustly labeled before, so I wanted to make my own determination.

The conversation was non-stop. And one-sided. I was reminded of something my father loved to say. "If bullshit was music, he'd have a brass band."

Dinner proved to be an exercise in restraint. The korma was divine, its aroma a comforting embrace. The ghee rice was a perfect symphony of cashews and raisins, each spoonful better than the last. Every dish from the kitchen was as loaded with flavor as Sajin was with self-importance.

"You know, I thought about turning pro after my prep school cricket days," he said. He nearly choked on a cashew from the ghee rice in his rush toward self-adulate.

"Mm," I said. I focused on the creamy korma in hopes my interest in the food would hasten the end of his interminable monologue.

"Suffered an Achilles tear in the last game of my senior year," he said. After a dramatic pause meant to heighten the tragedy of his misfortune, he continued. "Totally rehabbed, but it put off the scouts."

"Mm."

He shifted gears. "The award banquet is a big deal for Vik.

He's a cook in America—very different here in India," he said. When I looked up, I caught the fading remnants of a smirk.

"He's a well-known chef," I said. I sliced through a piece of naan.

"Works in a restaurant."

"Owns it," I said. Even though I had vowed to remain non-committal, I heard the pride in my voice.

"Well, I hope it goes well. So many businesses crash in the first year." His words dripped with feigned concern. He waited for a reaction that never came. "Did he ever tell you about the woman I've been dating since my divorce?"

"Ah," I said.

"She would make Deepika Padukone jealous."

"Mm," I acknowledged, my mind racing to Vikram and the secrets he might have kept.

"I'm considering ending my marriage. Dastardly woman—unfaithful and conniving."

"I met Fariha last night. She seemed charming…quiet but charming."

"All part of the act," he said. "She is quite devious. Has most of the family fooled."

Vik told me she was quiet, demure, loyal, and obedient. My mind drifted to Rachana. *Does she really like me or was she just being polite?* Sajin was still talking. He'd moved to his career.

"…in the Finance Department. They have me in a very high-profile position…" Sajin's voice faded into the background, but I caught snippets. "…grooming me for better things. Since Vik has abandoned the work, I imagine I'll take over pretty soon. Then people will see how a real business should be run."

"Indeed."

"Oh," he leaned in closer, lowering his voice as if about to share state secrets, "Very interesting that Vik is cooking for the Film Awards. It's probably good you'll be going. Everyone will be there. Do you know Amrita Rai?"

"Mm." Of course I knew who she was—everyone did.

"She's stunning—almost as beautiful as my girlfriend. Which reminds me, Ms. Rai used to be Vik's girlfriend. They were inseparable in prep school. His first love, his first everything as you can imagine."

I knew there had been a myriad of women before me, but the revelation of a former involvement with an international star was something altogether different. Now Sajin had my attention.

CHAPTER TWENTY-FIVE

VIK

IT HAD BEEN A LONG TIME since I'd eaten a meal from anyone's kitchen other than my own. It had been even longer since I'd broken bread with my family. The table, elegantly appointed, had been shortened to only fourteen places. *Ma* occupied one end. I was to her right, the place of honor.

Pa would have normally presided at the other end, but he was noticeably absent. Uncle Kanak took his place after *Ma* made apologies. I saw Deepak roll his eyes, but no one had the temerity to make a derogatory comment. To *Ma's* left were Harlow, Aunt Bhavita, Fariha (Sajin's wife), Lita, *Chachee* Sannvi, and a young woman I did not know. Even though we were in my Delhi's home, it was my mother's place to sit at the head of the table. I sat to *Ma's* immediate right in the place of honor as befitted my status as the eldest (and only) son. Down the line next to me were an empty chair, Sajin, Amar, *Chacha* Deepak, and, another empty chair.

Odd, I thought. *The space across from Aunt Bhavita I understand. Her husband is fill-in as the host. The vacant place honors his marriage. Everyone else is seated across from their significant other except for the pretty young woman next to my uncle. Someone must be late because I know Ma did not make a mistake with the chairs.*

Mrs. Jain appeared at *Ma's* shoulder and whispered something into her ear. *Ma* nodded gave a look, and the table fell silent. "I understand our last guest is approaching the house," she said. "It seems he was unavoidably detained by the vagaries of Delhi traffic." Everyone laughed—we'd all been there. "We will begin when he arrives."

Her eyes grew wide. "I am so embarrassed. I have been remiss in not introducing our other guest. Seated next to Uncle Kanak is Ezhil Balakrishnan. To use an American term, she is our absent guest's 'date' for the evening." She looked up. "Ah, here he is now."

With an entire garden of roses in one hand and a bottle of what I suspected was very expensive wine in the other, Addison Whitmore walked into the room. I recognized him from the internet. To be honest, the pictures did not do him justice. He was handsome in an all-American boy way and very at ease—a man who'd worked more cocktail parties than a politician.

He strode to *Ma* all the while begging everyone to "Keep your seats, please. I am so embarrassed." *Ma* offered her hand. He took it, then leaned in for whispered apologies. I'd never seen *Ma* blush before—after which she did something else completely out of character. She giggled.

Addison waved to every person around the table in turn after he shook my hand. He walked to his place in a circuitous fashion by way of each woman on the other side. He paid special attention to Harlow, which I assumed was only natural since she was the only one he knew. Still, I did not fail to notice the sparkle in his eyes when he took her hand.

When *Ma* introduced him to Ezhil, Addison greeted her with most gallantry than Lancelot could have mustered. He complimented her gown, commented on her stunning looks, and expressed the "honor" she was doing him by allowing him to be in her company during the evening—all without sounding either obsequious or creepy.

For her part, Ezhil played her role perfectly. She passed the evening with a pleasant smile on her lips and even made appropriate small talk throughout dinner. She was exactly what she was supposed, a prop intended to balance the table.

After Mr. Movie Idol put his ridiculously toned glutes in his place, *Ma* picked up a small silver bell at her left and gave it a twitch. Immediately, servers bearing plates of kachumber salad appeared—one server per guest. They posed behind each guest until one of them gave a signal even I couldn't spot before slipping the plates onto gold chargers (from the left, of course).

The chatter had been lively before the food arrived. Once it came, conversation ceased for a while.

CHAPTER TWENTY-SIX

VIK

THE ELEGANT GOLD ANTIQUE FLATWARE GLITTERED next to bone china. The table was laden with *thalis.*[1]

Dessert was one of my favorites: falooda. Made of vermicelli, jelly, rose syrup, sabja seeds, milk, and ice cream, it has best been described as the subcontinent's answer to an ice cream float. Tempted as I was to ask for seconds, I demurred for the sake of propriety and my growing awareness of how long it had been between serious workouts.

Ma looked at me. "I believe Vikram has some news to share," she said.

All eyes turned my way. I was suddenly and inexplicably self-conscious. Because of my station—and my parents—I had lived in the spotlight from the moment of my birth. Center stage seldom bothered me. But in that instant, I would have rather been anywhere else. I wanted to stall for time to collect my thoughts. I stood and cleared my throat.

---

1 Indian style meal made up of a selection of various dishes served on a platter.

"Before I address *Ma's* announcement, I would like to thank Addison once again for his generosity in bringing Harlow from the United States on his parents' jet."

I wondered if anyone made note that I had said 'parents,' but the only face I could read was Ezhil's. She was, as her name suggested, a "beauty" with flawless skin, a perfect figure, and the most seductive eyes I had ever seen. At the mention of the word 'jet,' I swore I could see dollar signs flash in them.

Is she here for Addison, or is Ma trying to replace Harlow?

I shook off the thought and continued. "One more detour, *Ma,* if I might be so bold. Would you ask Govind to come out for a moment?"

My mother looked a little puzzled, but after the briefest of hesitations, she nodded to one of the servers who dutifully trundled off to the kitchen. Moments later, Govind stood next to my mother.

"Madame," he said. "You wish to see me."

Ma looked at me. "Govind," I said. "Food is a very important part of my life. I am very blessed to have the gift of cooking. My restaurant in Atlanta is one of the most sought after eating establishments anywhere in the city. But I must say, tonight I have enjoyed the best meal...*of my life!*"

Enthusiastic applause broke out around the table, Govind was so startled by my comment that he momentarily lost his balance. He steadied himself, then put both hands over his heart and bowed his head. When the clapping stopped, he wiped a tear from his eyes.

"Thank you, Master Vikram," he said. "You have given me a great blessing."

"I learned most everything I know from *Ma* and from you," I said. "Thank you."

I walked to him and wrapped him in a fierce bearhug—protocol be damned.

HARLOW

I watched the scene unfold in quiet amazement and more than a dash of hope. From what I knew of Indian culture, members of the working class, while appreciated and generally treated well, were seldom singled out for approbation and *never,* like never in a gazillion years, embraced by their employers. Vik's gesture was impromptu and absolutely genuine.

His action did not surprise me. I'd seen how he treated his employees. He was unfailingly gracious, polite, and complimentary. When someone needed to be corrected, Vik did not pass the assignment to someone else. He shouldered the responsibility of leadership and had the difficult conversation. But he did it in a way designed to lift up the person he was addressing—to make them better at what they did—to teach them the value of pride in an outstanding effort.

I saw the uncles' reactions. Deepak smirked. From what little I knew about him, he loved to tweet society's nose. On the other hand, Kanak recoiled as if someone had made a rude noise. He whispered something to his wife, who made a great show of nodding gravely.

What shocked me was how Mrs. Chatwal reacted when my dear fiancé hugged Govind. There was not so much as a single raised eyebrow. In fact, Mrs. Chatwal started the applause.

The times, they are a changin', I thought. *Maybe…just maybe Vik and I have a real chance.*

CHAPTER TWENTY-SEVEN

VIK

THE MOMENT THE GOVIND RETURNED TO the kitchen, *Ma* resumed her assault on my privacy. "So, Vikram, you have news, do you not?"

"Well," I said, "what *Ma* is referencing is that I have been offered a chance to produce a meal of a certain notoriety."

Ma clucked. "Don't keep everyone in suspense, Tell them, son."

Mumbled assent flitted back and forth across the table.

"Okay, okay," I said. I have been invited to prepare all the food for the banquet the night of the National Film Awards."

More applause. I noticed, however, that Sajin did not take his hands from his lap. For reasons I never understood, he never liked me. True, I was closer in age to his half-brother Amar, but blood is blood.

"Very exciting news, Vikram," Deepak said. "What do you suggest by way of attire for the evening."

I was not expecting his question. Deepak's assumption of an invitation was presumptuous at best. Some would label it arrogant. But he was my uncle. I had to be careful not to insult him.

"*Chacha*, in this instance, I am providing a service. I am not an invited guest. As you can imagine, with all the directors, producers, investors, and innumerable stars, space is limited. While I would dearly love to offer you a place, alas I have only been given two tickets. One was to be given to my *fiancée* Harlow (I intentionally leaned on '*fiancée*'). Since it would be inappropriate for her to attend without an escort of some kind, I had intended on giving the other to Lita."

Ma scowled. "What do you mean 'intended?'" Her eyes lasered Amar. "Surely her husband has no objection."

Amar raised his hands in surrender and was about to offer a defense when I came to his rescue.

"I am sure he does not," I said, "but it does not matter. I have decided to decline to offer."

🔥

HARLOW

For a moment, consternation swept across the room. No one raised a voice, but the objections to Vik's announcement were swift and plentiful.

"What do you mean?"

"You must be joking."

"This is the greatest opportunity of your career."

"The film community will view this as an unforgivable insult."

"Isn't your old friend Rishi involved? He will be crushed."

I lip read Sajin's comment more than I heard it, but I could tell exactly what he said. "Afraid you'll choke, cousin?"

If anyone heard Sajin's comment, they ignored it, but I was ready to throw myself across the table and stab him with a fork. Despite my anger, I felt a wave of relief wash over me. We had been reunited for less than two days. Only hours before dinner did I finish moving everything from Lita's home to his. I wasn't happy about being in a separate bedroom, but I knew we were trying very hard not to splash any more water into the boat of parental disapproval.

"Unbearable" hardly described the weight of my emotional angst and physical exhaustion. When Vik talked to me about the opportunity in Mumbai, my external reaction had been as supportive and enthusiastic as I could muster. But I did not want him to leave and was thrilled the moment he said he wasn't going to do it.

Mrs. Chatwal ended the bruhaha by raising a palm. "Please," she said, "such an uproar is unseemly and disrespectful. I would remind you that Mr. Chatwal is abed upstairs. He is still quite spent from the upheaval of recent events." She waited a moment before reaching out her hand and taking Vik's.

"My son," she said, "can you explain your reasoning? As *someone* said—I honestly cannot tell you who it was because it sounded like the train station in here—anyway, this *is* quite an opportunity. I just think we are all a little confused. Please give us your justification."

"*Ma,*" he said, "you and *Pa* have been through a very traumatic event—"

She cut him off—not something she did very often. "We survived a minor inconvenience. You have already met with people who are experts in the protection field, and I am considerably comforted in knowing the security measures around Xanadu will be updated. Your father and I may be old, but we are neither doddering nor afraid. There must be something else."

"Well," he said, "Harlow just got here—"

Once again, an interruption. "The two of you were separated

for less than a week. You said yourself that she is invited to the gala. She can join you in Mumbai in a few days. That is not an eternity. Try again."

"Ah…there is another matter."

"Which is?"

"Harlow is recovering from…from an illness."

Mrs. Chatwal looked at me. Her eyes carried a message of concern along with a hint of suspicion. "Should we take measures to quarantine?"

Vik was trapped. Now he had to go to Mumbai—and I was crushed.

CHAPTER TWENTY-EIGHT

VIK

As much as I loved the city, I had mixed feeling about being here. My time with Harlow at Xanadu had been severely limited. When I learned we were assigned to separate rooms, I intended to protest to *Ma,* but after her declaration that I *would* go to Mumbai, initiating a fight before my departure did not seem appropriate.

The note I slipped under Harlow's door was brief.

Darling, this was not how I envisioned our reunion. I am sorry to be gone. I hope you understand… family duty and all that. Leaving so soon after you got here makes me feel worse than I look—and I look like an insensitive heel. Please forgive me. I promise to make it up to you with a magical time at the Awards.

Don't let Ma push you around. Let there be no doubt in your mind as to my intentions…or my love. You are everything to me.

VIK

Even though I was a reluctant visitor, I didn't realize how much I had missed Mumbai until the city overwhelmed my mind and senses with a flood of memories.

Bandra, the vibrant jewel in Mumbai's bustling crown, aptly known as the "Queen of Suburbs," was home to celebrities, models, and designers. It buzzed with an eclectic charm, a perfect combination of old and new. The bustling energy of the neighborhood enveloped me like a warm embrace and reminded me of my school days. Nestled along the Arabian Sea, the neighborhood featured pastel-colored colonial bungalows standing proudly beside sleek modern cafes and urban *chaiwalas*.[1] A soundtrack of children at play mixed with the strums of a street musician's guitar and the chatter of vendors hawking their wares.

My car passed Theobroma, my favorite bakery from my boarding school days. Freshly baked *pav* beckoned with invisible yet seductive sensory fingers; nearby street food stalls did their best to lure me into a gluttonous frenzy.

Minutes later, I stepped out of the bustling streets into a large industrial kitchen. I was immediately engulfed in a world of stainless steel and bustling activity. The air was filled with a blend of aromas—freshly baked bread, simmering sauces, and the sharp tang of citrus. Overhead, bright lights shone on expansive countertops cluttered with an array of culinary tools while busy hands meticulously prepping ingredients. The rhythmic clanging of pots and pans mixed with the sizzle of frying pans and the steady chop-chop-chop of knives. This always felt like home.

"What do you think?" Rishi's voice always made me envi-

---

1 Tea seller.

sion a chipmunk on speed, high-pitched, a little squeaky, and fast as a buttered slide. (I'd heard the expression once in Atlanta—I liked it. Southerners do have a way with words. Another of my favorites was "Lower than a snake's belly in a wagon rut," but I didn't use it very often. I taught Harlow how to cook Indian food; she gave me Southern speech lessons.)

"What's going on?" I asked.

"Local banquet tonight," Rishi said. The place will be pristine tomorrow, but I thought you'd like to 'see the field,' so to speak."

"Good idea. You can tell a lot from a kitchen when prep is underway," I said. "It's nice."

"Nice?" Your mother is nice. A warm evening in June is nice. Helen Mirren is nice. Vikram, my old friend, this is *the big time.*"

"Rishi, perhaps you forget I am running one of the most successful restaurants in Atlanta."

"You have celebrities in there every night?"

"Pretty much. Players from the Braves, the Hawks, the Falcons, the Dream. We get actors, actresses, politicians—the whole enchilada."

"Enchilada? Tell me you are *not* serving Mexican food."

"Lighten up," I said. "Just an expression. To get back to your question, my place has someone high profile in there all the time. We try our best to give them private tables where they won't be bothered—unless, of course, they are there specifically to get people to look at them."

"But is there ever one night when everybody in your restaurant is somebody—and don't hand me the old line about how all of your customers are special. You know exactly what I mean."

"Well, one night, the Rotary Club of Atlanta rented the entire space." Try as I might, I could not keep my face straight. I was giggling within about ten seconds once I looked at Rishi's confused expression. "To answer your question, my dear old chum, no… we have never had a 100% celebrity evening."

Rishi tried to look superior—hard since he was seven inches shorter than me, even in his Santonia shoes, in which I knew he had put lifts. "Well, *old chum,* six nights from now, every star in the Bollywood firmament will have their arses in the seats in that dining hall. Every agent in the country will be in attendance. There will be football players, cricket stars, badminton studs, you name it. I know for a fact that Suraj Narredu[2] will be in attendance. It will be virtually impossible for you to go in there without dropping your jaw. The men will be dressed by the most prominent designers—and the women…oh my god …the women will look ravishing."

The door to the banquet hall entered and a tall stick of a man entered. His pewter hair had enough pomade to lubricate a race car but matched his Armani suit to perfection. He walked with the air of someone in charge. His presence was so powerful, I barely noticed the limp.

"Rishi," he said, "this must be our savior." He extended his hand. "Kabir Prabakar. You must be Chef Vikram Chatwal."

Interesting name his parents gave him. More likely he chose it when he started his career.

I accepted his outstretched hand. "I appreciate the honorific," I said, "but please call me Vik."

"Vik it is," he said. "You may call me Kabir."

"Have we met before?" I asked. "You remind we of some-one—I think."

"I am deeply honored to make you think of someone, per-haps an old friend, but we have never met." He raked a hand through his thick hair, an odd gesture reminiscent of someone in

2 One of India's premiere contemporary jockeys.

my past—I might have placed it, but he kept prattling. "Thank you for coming to our rescue at such short notice. From what I hear of your reputation, I anticipate an evening of wonderful entertainment bolstered by spectacular food."

"I will do my best not to let you down," I said.

"Can you perhaps share the menu for the evening?"

I had no reservations about disclosing the plans for the meal to the man who was obviously paying for the evening. I reached inside my jacket for the list.

The door behind me opened. I didn't bother to look. I assumed it was a delivery. There would be plenty of those in the next one hundred and forty-four hours and I could not be distracted every time the door hinges growled.

"I thought we'd open with—"

I jumped when a hand clapped down on my shoulder. I turned and saw three, stern-faced members of the Greater Mumbai Police. The one in the center, higher ranking than the others, looked at me with an expression that was anything but pleasant.

"Vikram Chatwal?"

"I am," I said. I looked at the three stars on his shoulder. "What does a chief inspector from the Special Branch want with me?" I forced a smile even though there was a knot in my stomach the size of a cantaloupe. "You're a little early for lunch but I am sure we can find something for you and your men."

"You are correct. I am Chief Inspector Hasha Bakshi of the Special Branch. We are not here for sustenance, Mr. Chatwal, and you would do well to take this seriously."

"How can I assist," I said. *This division deals with State security. I need to quit fooling around.*

C.I. Bakshi nodded to the constables with him. They approached with handcuffs.

"Hands behind your back, please, Mr. Chatwal," he said. "You are under arrest."

CHAPTER TWENTY-NINE

VIK

I was too stunned to say anything. But not Prabakar. He limped closer, furious and shaking his fist...at me.

"This is an outrage, Chatwal. You come here, ostensibly to help with the biggest awards ceremony in India and disgrace us by being arrested by the Special Branch. What sort of vile misdeed have you brought to our door. It's a good thing this happened before the ceremony—otherwise it would have been catastrophic. You would have forever sullied the reputation of the National Film Awards. You, sir, are a scallywag of the first order. I should have known better than to agree to engage someone with your checkered reputation. No wonder you fled to America."

I knew it was coming. I waited.

Prabakar took a deep breath. "You'll never work in this country again."

There it was.

We were already outside before I found my voice about ten feet from the patrol car—a four-door, Mahindra Bolero, white with three horizontal stripes: red on the bottom, dark blue in the middle, and yellowish orange on top. There was a loudspeaker mounted in the roof just to the left of an orange "bubble gum machine" style light.

"There's been some mistake," I said. "I haven't done anything. I've been in the country less than a fortnight. Didn't bring anything with me except for some clothes."

The officers on either side had control of my arms. They never stopped moving. The stubby one opened the rear door. The other one put a hand atop my head.

"Mind your head, sir," he said.

With one foot in the car, something came to me. I locked my legs and shook off the hand. "Stop! Wait a minute! I am a United States citizen. I demand to be taken to my country's embassy."

Prabakar smiled and looked at his watch. "Four minutes and twenty-two seconds. Who had that in the pool?"

I heard an odd noise—not really odd—simply out of place. This was not a situation where anyone would expect hysterical laughter. I looked. Rishi, Prabakar, and one of the constables were guffawing and falling all over each other. Only "Prabakar" now had dark hair. He'd pulled off a thick wig and was scratching away at a prosthetic nose. The constable was peeling off a phony, thick-as-bear-skin beard with his right hand, digging padding out of his cheeks with his left index finger, and trying to flip off his sunglasses by tossing his head like a spirited stallion.

Rishi held up a hand. "I had the four-to-five-minute square. You each owe me nine thousand rupees. Oh, and I get an extra forty-five hundred apiece because I picked the phrase correctly." He lowered his voice the best he could—I assume to attempt to sound like me. "I demand to be taken to my country's embassy." He threw both hands over his head, a sprinter breasting the tape at the Olympics. "I won it all, babeee!"

The constable, now revealed as my old school chum Nitin, stomped his feet in mock fury. "I was so damn sure we were going to get, 'Do you know who my daddy is?' He used to say it all the time back in school."

Prabhakar—now recognizable as Krish—stuffed his wig into his pocket, ran over as best he could, and embraced me.

"I *knew* there was something fishy about you," I said. "You still scrape your hand through your hair—that's your old poker tell. And who came up with that name? *Kabir Prabhakar*—'great, powerful leader—cause of luster'—wow, think much of yourself?"

"I thought the limp might give it away. Hasn't gotten much better over the years," he said.

"Damn cheap shot you took in the football match, but at least we won," I said. "Mostly because you scored three goals before they decided to take you out."

"Don't try to change the subject by reminding me how *lustrous and powerful* my football skills were." He laughed. "See there was a reason for the name. Still, you should have seen your face when they arrested you."

"Not nearly as good as the expression he had when you said, 'You'll never work in this country again.'"

The hair on the back of my neck stood up. I knew the voice coming from behind me and as soon as I turned and saw the other constable who'd peeled off the "fat suit" she was wearing and was just now shaking out the luxurious mane of hair for which she was best known the world around, I knew the face as well.

"Hello, Chatwal," she said.

"Hello, Varma."

CHAPTER THIRTY

VIK

THE ONLY ONE LEFT WAS THE chief inspector. I squinted when he took away the phony handlebar moustache.

"Mr. Oommen," I said. "It's been a long time. How did these degenerates talk you into such a vicious prank."

He looped his arm around Rishi. "When my son told me about it, I wanted in," he said. "You are a fine young man now, Vikram, but when you were in prep school with these boys, you were often proper little wanker."

"Father!" Rishi looked horrified. "Vik was never anything but gracious to me."

"I know," Mr. Oommen said, "but you must admit, he masterminded most of the shenanigans your boys engaged in but usually managed to sidestep the punishment."

"Good point," Rishi said. He looked at Varma. "And, he got the hot chick."

Varma brushed by him. "I'll ignore the sexist remark," she said, "because you were and always will be a pig." She was smiling when she hugged me. "How are you, Chatwal?"

All of a sudden, I was a teenager again holding my heart in my hands.

Varma (we always called one another by our last names) was the prettiest girl I'd ever seen. We met at a party—a dance organized by our respective schools. From the moment I saw her on the other side of the room, I was smitten. There was a force about her, a magnetism. I walked across the dance floor as if drawn by an irresistible, invisible beam.

"I'm Vikram Chatwal," I said, "your new boyfriend."

For reasons I never understood, she did not slap me. Instead, she looped her hand around my arm and guided me to the middle of the room.

"Nice to meet you, Chatwal," she said. "We'll dance first. Consider it your audition."

I must have passed because we became inseparable—well, except when I was playing sports with the fellows, in school, or imprisoned at study hall. My prep school was prestigious… and expensive. Her all-girls' school, while just down the road, was miles away on the socio-economic scale.

We met when we were fifteen and stayed together for three of the most glorious years of my life. Then one day, she was gone. No one seemed to know where she was. I could have asked *Papa* to hire someone to find her, but I would have had to explain an awful lot and the extent of our relationship—especially the physical part—would have come to light. Perhaps my father would have understood in the way Old World fathers accepted such behavior as part of the natural order of things. In his mind, men needed to know certain things.

But *Ma* would have been horrified about a lot of things.

Varma's lower class status would definitely have been a point of contention. So, like a coward, I let her slip away. Didn't see her again for a long time until one day...

CHAPTER THIRTY-ONE

VIK

I WAS ROUNDING THE CORNER A year after university when I spotted the poster, I'd heard about the new film; there was considerable buzz. When I saw the notice, I realized why. The movie was introducing a new starlet to the Bollywood firmament—a woman with a dazzling smile. Her captivating eyes, and sensational hair dominated the advertisement. It took me a moment to realize she had changed her name, well, at least her last one—and she had reverted to her full first name. India was about to be introduced to Ahmi Varma—now, Amrita Rai.

I was brought back to the present when Krish chucked me on the shoulder. "Really had you going there, old boy, didn't we?"

I pursed my lips in defeat. "Yes, you did. By the way—fabulous makeup. How did you clowns manage?" I looked at Mr. Oommen. "No offense—I meant them."

"None taken," he said. "I think they're clowns as well."

Rishi took the lead. He usually did when I wasn't around.

"You forget where you are," he said. "You are about to cater the Film Awards ceremony. All the great actors are here as well as every technician in the industry."

I got it. "Along with makeup and costume experts. I get it. Who did you bribe?"

Rishi tried to look hurt—he didn't pull it off. "You wound me," he said. "Don't you think my sparkling personality is enough to charm folks into helping me."

"No."

"You're right." He laughed. "But those good and talented folks are always up for a prank. Once we explained what we were doing, they were all in."

"Well, they did a marvelous job," I said. "You really had me going. I was already trying to remember the name of my father's *pratinidhi.*[1] Now, let's celebrate our reunion."

Rishi raised his hands in victory. "We have defeated the master prankster, Vikram Chatwal," he said. "Drinks are on him."

We locked arms and stumbled onto the sidewalk, a lively group in search of the nearest pub, laughter trailing behind us like a merry echo. We settled into the pub's dingy ambiance. Even in dim light, Varma's striking features shouted for attention. She possessed a kind of timeless beauty, reminiscent of classic film stars with lush, wavy hair cascading down her shoulders and framing her beautiful face perfectly. Her eyes, large and expressive, looked like polished chestnuts. They revealed a soul seasoned and wise beyond her years. Her skin glowed even in the shadows, a flawless, radiant canvas without the need for embellishment by heavy makeup. Her smile drew in everyone close with a gentle allure. She'd always been more than just another pretty face, but her beauty had matured with a grace and warmth as comforting

---

1 Attorney.

as it was stunning.

We chatted with the same ease as people who saw one another every day. I purposefully avoided sitting next to Varma. No reason to increase temptation with proximity.

We prodded her for tales of Bollywood intrigue and while she talked freely about film making and acting, she steadfastly refused to engage in gossip. Even though we lauded her with accolades, she remained humble, almost shy when we talked about her considerable abilities. Though she routinely brushed shoulders with the likes of Shah Rukh Khan, she spoke with an earnestness that echoed her modest beginnings. This was no starlet held captive by glitz and glitter. This was a powerhouse of talent, a woman dedicated to her craft and destined for greatness.

She was, in a word, ethereal.

CHAPTER THIRTY-TWO

HARLOW

"MY FRIEND, HOW DID YOU COME to be in charge of the awards ceremony?" I asked.

The evening was waning into night. The reunion hadn't lasted as long as I would have liked. Nitin claimed to have a dinner appointment with a client. He seemed nervous about it. He'd only taken three sips of his beer before he was out of the door. Varma begged off after a series of vague excuses none of which sounded the least bit true. I didn't worry. I could tell she was as uncomfortable as I was.

The rest of us ate dinner. Krish had polished off his third Kingfisher[1] and bid us goodbye. I looked at Rishi.

"Sorry about being so bad about keeping in touch," I said.

"No worries," he said. "We're all busy building our empires."

"You know," I said, "I have no idea how you ended up in the hospitality business."

"Started right out of university," he said. "Took a position with a nice firm in Delhi. Worked my way up. It didn't hurt that

---

1 Largest selling beer brand in India.

a lot of the C-suite people were standing with one foot over the grave and another on a banana peel when I began. They started dropping like flies. The industry was changing rapidly. They needed people with computer skills, social media savvy. I was in the right place at the right time."

"Good for you," I said. "And I am honored you thought to call me when the ox went in the ditch."

"Pardon?"

"An Americanism," I said. "Sorry. Thank you for reaching out in your time of distress."

"Five minutes after I got the call about the botulism, I heard you were in India. Couldn't pass up a chance to rub elbows with America's celebrity chef."

"Shut up," I said. "Just grinding away like everyone else." Rishi was too good a friend to mention the massive financial head start I had. "How did you know I was back?"

"Are you serious?" he asked. "There was a break-in at your parents' house. Everybody knows about it. And I knew you would come home. Which reminds me, I've been a jerk not to ask about your ma and papa—they okay?"

"They're fine," I said. "No one was home. There were no confrontations or sword fights or anything."

"No doubt your pa would have grabbed that old cavalry saber from above the mantle and gone all Erroll Flynn on someone's ass."

"No doubt," I said. We both laughed at the image of my fearless, swashbuckling father. I did not bother to mention I had barely laid eyes on him since my arrival. He refused to leave his room. When I inquired about visiting in the mornings and evenings, I had been politely rebuffed.

I took a sip of beer. "Good to see Nitin," I said. "He's been

MIA for a long time. Missed our last two reunions—and if I remember correctly, didn't stay very long at the first one."

"Always claims he's busy," Rishi said. "You know how it is when you run your own business. The customers set the calendar."

"Yep."

"Besides, he's always been pretty jealous of you. You know that."

I did not. "That's ridiculous," I said. "He was faster, taller, and stronger. Sure, I was a better cricket player and student, but the last one if only because I bothered to open a book every so often. I absolutely could not keep up with him on the football pitch, badminton court, or playing basketball. He's a gifted athlete and pretty much of a computer genius."

"All true," Rishi said. "But you had something he didn't."

"Nothing I can do about who my parents are. I never flashed papa's money around and you know it."

"That's not it and you know it," Rishi said. "You had Ahmi. That's her name, you know."

CHAPTER THIRTY-THREE

VIK

WE WERE BOTH SILENT FOR A moment. I coughed to cover my discomfort and took a sip of my drink. I was desperate to change the subject. So was Rishi. "What are you planning for the banquet," Rishi asked.

I paused as if in deep thought, but I already knew the answer. "I have something very special in mind," I said. "It's a little un-traditional, but I think it will work. Come by tomorrow after lunch and I will show you."

It was after 2:00 pm when Rishi arrived outside the kitchen. I had posted security at the door to keep anyone from barging in. When preparing a feast for several thousand people, one cannot take too many precautions.

Nitin was his usual bubbly self. No wonder he'd crushed the hospitality world. He knew everyone on the event center staff by name. He remembered things.

"Rohan, how are you, old boy? Is your daughter still scaring all the boys on the pitch? Strong leg on that one—she's going to be a star."

"Kashvi, I was so very sorry to hear about your mother's surgery. How is she progressing? Good…good…keep me informed. I will continue to pray."

It took us almost half an hour to get into the kitchen, but Rishi left a wake of smiling faces behind him. I paused at the door.

No wonder he's crushing it, I thought.

"Okay, open mind," I said. "This is a different approach. We always tout the *Indian* way, our life, our culture, our people. What better way to celebrate our heritage than with authentic Indian food?"

"That's why you are here, old chum," Rishi said. "You are the hot new master of Indian cuisine."

I shrugged. "Perhaps in the States. But here, in this ancient land we call home, the real food of India comes from the people… it rises from the Earth like a plant…it has breath…it has…" I stopped. "It is impossible to explain. Let me show you."

We entered the kitchen. I kept walking and talking, but two feet inside, Rishi stopped like he'd run into a brick wall. Seated on the floor and bunched around not-yet-lit fire pits, about eight dozen women looked at us. Traditional cookware littered the floor. Here a khal dastal ural,[1] there a karahi.[2] Stone pots and wooden spoons were everywhere.

Rishi stared at me. "What the hell?"

I spread my arms like Vanna White revealing a puzzle. "Behold—a traditional Indian feast unlike any other. Instead of taking the banquet to the streets, we will bring the streets to the banquet."

---

1 Mortar and pestle set.
2 Cast iron pot similar to a wok.

"Where did you get these people?" he asked.

"Here and there," I said. "They cook all day on the highways and byways of this fair city. They sell their wares to passersby. I am paying them to cook for the banquet. They will make more over the next few days than they will in a year. This is a great service you are allowing me to provide. Imagine how it will smell in here when all the fires are burning, and the food is cooking. The aromas will fill the place. They will filter into the grand hall where the patrons will salivate in anticipation."

"Or gag while the smoke assaults their designer outfits." Rishi's face was nearly purple. The fumes will ruin everything. The smoke will cause massive damage. Hell, the sprinklers will be triggered. The guests will be soaked—hair will tumble—makeup will run."

I was still grinning. "It will be a wonderful occasion. The tastes…the smells…the ambiance."

Rishi hopped, a giant, angry bunny. "The only ambiance will be the charred remnants of my career." His shouts bounced of the copper pots hanging on the walls and reverberated against the gleaming floor. "You *bastard!* You have ruined me. This will cost me everything. I will be a laughing st—"

He stopped mid-rant and pointed an accusing finger. "You snake," he said. "This is all an elaborate joke, isn't it?"

I tried to keep my game face, but quickly dissolved in laughter. "Had you going, didn't I, *puraane dost?*"[3]

Rishi could not quit sputtering. "How could…why…you sorry…"

"You mess with the bulls, you get the horns," I said. "Certainly, you knew I would retaliate for your stunt with the cops."

I looked at Dinesh who was snickering in the corner. "Thank

---

3 Old friend.

these wonderful women for helping in the charade. Pay them double what we agreed."

"Yes sir," Dinesh said. He began handing out money. The women clapped and smiled.

Rishi began to relax. "A whoopee cushion would have sufficed."

I draped an arm across his shoulder while he sagged in relief. "Not my style, buddy," I said. "Not my style."

CHAPTER THIRTY-FOUR

HARLOW

WHEN MRS. CHATWAL SUGGESTED A TRIP to the National Gallery of Modern Art, I accepted with more eagerness than I felt. I was hurting. Physically I was coming along fine, but my heart might well have been stabbed by a thousand thorns. I'd awakened to Vik's note, which was fine. I understood the social propriety of Old India that prohibited us from sleeping in the same bed, but I felt a little abandoned.

Even though I knew the Awards dinner was great for his career, I didn't want Vik in Mumbai. Worse, I didn't like it because I suspected his mother had pushed him to go as a way of keeping us apart—the old divide and conquer gambit.

"Wonderful," she said. "Hussein will be out front in an hour. Does that give you time to prepare?"

I wanted to ask what was wrong with my look. But I knew almost immediately where I'd made the mistake. I should have selected one of the designer saris Vik had purchased and placed in my room. I thought it would make sense to wear a simple sari, something more subdued. But my new reality here in India was clear. I was soon to be a Chatwal and every time I left the house, I could and would be photographed and tabloids would be sold detailing my appearance from head to toe.

"Mrs. Jain had one of the upstairs staff lay out something for you," she said. "I think you'll like it, but it takes a while to get it right."

On the way to my room I considered the jaunt. I grew more excited with every step. Initially proposed by Barada and Sarada Ukil, artist brothers and students of Abanindranath Tagora, the museum was registered in 1929 as the Delhi Fine Arts Society. As if often the case in any enterprise involving "artistes," there were wranglings and squabbles along the way. The year 1946 saw the First International Contemporary Art Exhibition at the fledgling institution.

I could not wait to see *The Arnolfini Portrait* by Van Eyck. The painting of a fifteenth century, Bruges merchant couple had been a focal point of study in an Art Appreciation class I took in college. It is considered one of the masterpieces of the Northern Renaissance. Some labeled it a wedding "photo." Others saw the rendering as a double portrait. I always considered it a memorial and said so in my final paper. I got an A!

When I opened the door to my room, I realized why Mrs. Chatwal gave me an hour. Nine yards of silk presented a considerable challenge. Forty-eight minutes later, I came down the stairs in an emerald-green saree embroidered with gold thread and wearing matching green sandals with two-inch heels. My hair was up. After the young woman assisting me with my mummification left the room, I had looked in the mirror.

"Wow!"

Mrs. Chatwal wished me a pleasant day and I stepped into the mid-morning sun. The car, gleaming from a recent detailing, stood in the driveway. Hussein walked up the front steps and offered his hand.

"If I may," he said.

"Thank you, Hussein," I said. "It would look bad for me to fall on my face."

I heard him suppress a chuckle. He opened the door and gasped.

Addison sat on the other side of the Audi's expansive back seat. "What! Why are you here?"

He switched on his thousand watt smile. "Harlow, this is a great idea. Gives us both something to do today."

CHAPTER THIRTY-FIVE

HARLOW

I DIDN'T WANT TO MAKE A scene, so I decided not to throw Mrs. Chatwal and her little scheme under the bus. I settled into my seat and buckled the belt.

"Well, I've got some time before I head to Mumbai—"

"And make all the beautiful people jealous."

I looked for some indication he was being his usual creepy self, but he seemed oddly genuine.

"Sure," I said. "That's my plan."

"And it will succeed," he said. "Especially if you wear something like that." He pointed to my saree. "Got to tell you, Harlow, green is definitely your color. You look amazing."

Again, not even the slightest hint of creepy.

"Thank you, Addison," I said. "Mrs Chatwal picked it out."

"Very nice woman," he said. "She was very gracious to invite me to dinner last night."

You have no idea what she has in mind, I thought. *Neither do I, but I suspect she's dangling me like bait and hoping some other man will snatch me away from her precious Vikram.*

"Know much about the museum?" I asked.

"A little," he said. "The building used to be the residential palace of the Maharaja of Jaipur. A new wing was added in 2009. If I remember, the museum has an impressive collection of Indian bronzes, terracotta, and wood sculptures, but I may be confusing it with some other place."

I checked to make sure my mouth wasn't agape. "How do you know all this?" I asked.

"Harlow, I know you think I am just a pretty boy from a rich family. And I am." He paused, then winked. We burst into spontaneous, genuine laughter, and the tension was broken. "But although I did some serious partying at UGA, I was a pretty good student. I majored in business, but my parents insisted I get a well-rounded education. I took classes in everything from music appreciation to photography. They had a good idea. I found out that I really like art. When I graduated, I was one course short of a minor in Art Appreciation."

"Impressive," I said. "I didn't know."

"There's a lot you don't know about me," he said, "but that's on me. Whenever we were together, I focused too much on trying to impress you with the stuff my family owns. I was a jerk."

I held up a hand. "You don't need to do this again, Addison. You apologized; I forgave you; we're starting over. Deal?" I offered my hand.

He shook it. "Deal."

We spent six hours at the museum. I had a marvelous time. I almost forgot how heartbroken I was that Vik was in Mumbai. *Almost.*

CHAPTER THIRTY-SIX

VIK

RISHI LOOKED A LITTLE WORRIED AFTER my practical joke. "Seriously," he said, "you've got to fill me in. What's the plan?"

I patted him on the head. "Relax, old friend. I would never do anything to hurt your sterling reputation—at least, what's left of it."

His laugh was nervous. He looked like he might throw up.

"I've got this," I said. I led him into the main hall. "Here it is. Imagine at train against the rear wall. I've already been talking to some set design people. They could see it before I finished describing it. There will be a mock-up of an old steam engine followed by a string of cars to scale. The engine will be complete. The cars will be cut in half, longways as it were. In each car I will feature food from a different region of India."

"Tell me more," he said. "You know I'm still a little suspicious."

I laughed. "Based on our history, you have good reason," I said, "but I am taking this very seriously."

"Go on."

"Appetizers in the first car. I'm seeing chicken tikkam, momos—oh, I made some the other night…delicious—paneer tikka, sev puri, maybe even chili paneer."

"So far, so good," he said.

"Next car, we introduce the delicacies of the North: Delhi, Jaipur, Agra, and the surrounding towns. We have malai kofta, chole bhature, tandoori chicken—"

"Of course," he said.

"Don't interrupt a genius at work," I said. When he quit laughing, I continued. "Aloo paratha, biyani, chicken tikka masala."

"Sounds like a greatest hits album," he said.

"Now you're getting it," I said. "Central area foods in the next car will be tikka masala (they make it a little differently in that part of our country), butter chicken, korma, malai kofta, vindaloo—"

"Ah, the world's hottest curry," he said. "I must say, I love it more than it loves me."

"Definitely not for the faint of heart," I said, "or of stomach."

"Keep going," he said. "But, I warn you, we will probably have to go eat when you are done. This discussion is making me ravenous. Will there be rogan josh?"

"What kind of a chef would I be without lamb curry?" I asked. "I would be run out of the country. May I continue?"

He bobbed his head—a child answering, "Would you like to go to the toy store?"

"As you know, Southern India cooking revolves around rice, lentils, and stews. There will be dosa, idli, saaru/rasam, and huli. Everything will be delicious."

"Sounds like a feast, my friend," he said.

"Not quite done yet," I said. "The last car—I've talked the geniuses in the set department into building an old fashioned caboose—will feature a full-service bar and desserts. We will prepare sandesh—"

Natin couldn't help himself. "With or without pistachios?"

"Both, my friend…both. There will be galub jamun—after all, who doesn't love donuts dunked in rose sugar coating?—rasmalai, jalebi, falloda, kalakand—before you ask, I will have two varieties, one flavored with cardamon, the other with mango—nankhatai for those who want something a little lighter. I might have to cover my shortbread biscuits with a pan to keep them from floating away."

Rishi wiped the corner of his mouth. "You are killing me," he said.

"I know," I said. "But wait until you are there. Do not take a plate—just wander up and down the line while stuffing your face. For custard fans, we will have kulfi. There will be rasgulla for anyone who wants a bite-sized dessert."

"Those little cheese balls dipped in floral sugar syrup?" he asked.

"Yes," I said. "There are one or two more like soan papdi, but you are beginning to drool, so I will conclude by telling you there will be a huge bowl of mango lassi at the end. You can drink it to your heart's content." I paused. "What do you think?"

Rishi's eyes were wide. "It's brilliant, Vikram," he said. "Positively brilliant."

CHAPTER THIRTY-SEVEN

HARLOW

I opened the carved wooden door of Kavyansh Chatwal
office door. My heart pounded. The grandeur of the room with
its colorful handwoven rugs, golden miniatures and handblown
glass lamps, filled me with anticipation. This was my first official meeting with Vik's father, and I said a little prayer that our
conversation would at least be non-combative. Light from the
outside struggled to penetrate the partially drawn shades. Even
in semi-darkness and propped up on a mountain of pillows at the
end of a leather couch, Mr. Chatwal was a formidable figure.

"Good morning," I said, voice shaky. "You sent for me."

I was not prepared for the scrutiny of his squinted gaze. "Yes,
Miss Kennedy. I would tell you to come in, but you have already
managed."

I flushed and stepped into the imposing room. "Sorry, didn't
mean to disturb."

"No bother." He waved it off with a regal hand. The room
smelled of cologne and old books. "I did, indeed, send for you."

"How can I help you, Mr. Chatwal?"

The air felt heavy with tension. "Miss Kennedy, why are you here?"

I tightened my grip on my purse and tried to sound casual. "You summoned me."

His frown deepened. "Please, spare me the witty repartee. You know what I mean. Why are you in India?"

"I came to see Vikram," I replied. "We are engaged, after all."

Maybe he thought the ticking of the antique clock would cover his sigh. It did not. "I understand you have been ill," he said without a hint of sympathy.

"It was nothing contagious," I said, but I knew his concern was more for form than genuine worry.

"That gives me some small comfort," he said. His voice was stiff as the collar of his purple morning coat. "I am an old man in failing health. I cannot afford exposure to anything."

The undercurrent of his words hinted at something more, and I pressed. "Mr. Chatwal, you did not ask me here to discuss either my health or your age."

"You are direct." His voice was clipped and not without a hint of malice. "Rude, but direct. I will respond in kind." He continued and my heart sank. "I can die a happy man if you would assemble your belongings, leave India, and never see my son again."

I wanted to flee the room, but my legs locked and smelled the aroma of his morning tea lingering like a forgotten promise.

LITA

I could not remember the last time Harlow had been this mad. She wasn't "rage against the machine, throw stuff, cursing" mad. She was *scary* mad.

"If that old fart is dying, I'm frickin' Beyonce," she said.

"Well, you're pretty 'Heated,'" I said, "even for a 'Brown Skin Girl' who's 'Crazy In Love.'"

She glared at me. I couldn't help myself. I was on a roll. "You're a 'Grown Woman,' girl. 'Just Stand Up,' go back in there and tell him, 'I'm Somebody.'"

She'd been sitting on the bed. She stood with slow deliberation. Her eyes never left mine. "One more Queen Bey song," she said, "and I will 'Move Your Body' right out that window."

She stood over me for a good three or four seconds before she burst into laughter.

"You always know how to get me to unwind," she said.

"Well," I said, "'What's It Gonna Be?'"

She doubled over and clutched her stomach like someone had kicked her. "Enough," she said. "I give up. You are incorrigible. And please don't tell me it's time to 'Start Over.'"

"I see what you did there," I said. "You're getting better. That's the S—"

"Do *not* say 'spirit,'" she said. "I've had all the Sasha Fierce references I can take."

"Okay," I said. "So, what's the plan."

"I don't know," she said. "But I am going to get that old man up and out of bed if it's the last thing I do. I am in love with his son. He needs to understand that. If I can't marry Vikram Chatwal, I'd…"

We said it together. "Rather Die Young!"

Once we quit giggling, I took Harlow's hand. "It's going to be okay," I said. "You guys will find a way."

"Well," she said, "there is a silver lining in all this. I've text Vik five times today and gotten one, entire heart emoji as a response. This being in love with a chef business can get old. It's a 24/7 deal, but right now, I'm not overly psyched about playing the understanding partner, you know.

Lita shrugged. "Look at it this way," she said, "He's going to be too busy in Mumbai to get into any trouble."

CHAPTER THIRTY-EIGHT

VIK

THE KITCHEN BUZZED WITH THE ELECTRIC energy of the bassline of a Bollywood soundtrack. Each station contributed its unique rhythm to the ensemble. The scent of cardamom and saffron filled the air and intertwined with the smoky notes of tandoori cooking. I stepped into this orchestrated chaos and caught the sharp tang of freshly chopped coriander mingled with the sweetness of simmering mango chutney—a vivid olfactory portrait of tonight's feast.

"Keep it together," I said quietly, a calming mantra I'd repeated all night. "Everything will be fine. My crew knows the recipes inside and out. They are as committed as I am. The committee will be ecstatic."

Although the kitchen was noisy, the prevalent attitude was joyous. The world of high-stakes catering was often a hotbed of fiery tempers and sharp tongues, but I had molded my approach to be one of nurture over force. Encouragement, I had found, was the spice that best enhanced performance.

Navigating through the stations, I reached the masala hub

where busy hands were grinding spices. The air was thick with the earthy fragrance of cumin and turmeric. I took a pinch of the spice mix, rubbed it between my fingers, and inhaled deeply. "Just a touch more garam masala," I said—a soft suggestion, one the chef accepted with nodding appreciation.

At the next station, a chef was adjusting the heat under a large pot of dal makhani. I dipped the spoon in to taste the creamy lentils. They needed a hint more kick. "Add a bit of *asafoetida*," I said. I was careful not to shout despite the clatter of utensils.

Moving towards the dessert station, the sweet aroma of frying jalebis almost made me shout for joy. I sampled one, its crispy sweetness precisely balanced with the floral notes of rose water. "This is perfect," I said. The pastry chef's face broke into a wide, satisfied grin.

After making my rounds, I splashed cool water on my face at the sink, the droplets a brief respite from the pervasive heat of the kitchen. Catching the eye of my assistant, a young man whose potential had been spotted in a famous local eatery, I signaled my need for a short break.

"Headed out back for a moment," I said, patting him on the shoulder. "I need a quick breather."

"We've got this, Chef," he said.

I pushed on the door while the title "Chef" echoed in my ears, a badge of my passion and commitment to this craft. Bolstered by his confidence, I stepped into the balm of the cool night air. I intended the momentary respite to provide a snippet of solitude and calm.

Fate had other ideas.

All I caught was a glimpse of her at the head of the alley, but I would have recognized the saunter anywhere—I'd memorized her every movement in my youth.

"Varma!" The nickname slipped out again, just like it did on the day of the gag, a relic from a past life but I'd never shouted it in such a brazen, public manner. In the halcyon days of our elite prep school. "Ahmi" to our circle of perfectly groomed acquaintances. I began calling her by her last name in retaliation for her steadfast refusal to refer to me as anything other than "Chatwal." Our relationship seemed simultaneously a lifetime ago and just yesterday.

For a split second, I doubted my senses, but before I could reach for door handle to retreat back into the kitchen, a second look toward the street solidified my reality. She was headed down the alley. A lump formed in my throat, stubborn and unyielding. Then, suddenly there she was, her hands a gentle weight on my shoulders, her lips pressing a chaste kiss on my cheek.

"Hullo, Chatwal," she said. Her voice was a melody I hadn't realized I'd missed. "Chatwal." While I called her "Ahmi" in our private moments, she had used my given name exactly—never.

The guys claimed she was somehow mocking me, but I knew better. It was a defense mechanism—her way of keeping some distance from a guy whose parents would never approve of our relationship—under any circumstance.

"What are you doing out here?" she asked with a tilt of her head. "Shouldn't you be in there, burning the naan?"

"I never burn the naan," I said. The corners of my lips twitched into a reluctant smile.

Her laughter erupted, unapologetically boisterous and utterly unfeminine, filling the space between us. She embraced me with such ferocity that breathing became a luxury. We held each other until the silence frayed, nicked and cut by a thousand unspoken words. I pulled back. The air cooled the spot where she had been.

"You are a little early," I said. "The event is a few days off."

"Some publicity thing—photos—I don't know," she said. "My manager says, 'Show up,' and I show up."

"You're nominated this year, I believe," she said. She smiled and bowed her head while smoothing a non-existent wrinkle on her dress.

"I am," she said with pride evident in her voice.

"When you win, it'll be your second, right?" I asked.

"Third, actually. But who's counting?" she said.

"You are, as I knew you would—and rightly so," I said.

"Thank you," she said. She pointed to the kitchen door. "I look forward to tasting your brilliance once more."

I had no idea what to do, so I stood…and stared. I don't know how long it was, but in those moments, my head and heart were flooded with memories both poignant and painful.

She did not insult me by feigning to look at the diamond Piaget on her wrist. "I have to go, Chatwal," she said. "We should catch up."

"Sure," I said. "Maybe tomorrow. Coffee or something."

She'd always been able to tell when I was lying. "I mean it," she said. I could see her mind working behind those stunning eyes. "We really need to talk. There's something you should know."

Before I could respond, she kissed me on the cheek again, but not hard enough to spoil her perfectly applied lip gloss. "I'm serious," she said. "Tomorrow morning. Ten sharp. *Wankhede.*"

I watched until she turned the corner, the echo of her steps mingling with the pulsating rhythm of my racing heart. When I touched the knob, I breathed deeply.

Same perfume, I thought. *Did she wear it today on purpose?*

CHAPTER THIRTY-NINE

HARLOW

ADDISON SOUNDED LIKE AN EXCITED CHILD. "I've never seen such an amazing animal! I had no idea they were so huge."

He was right, of course. A male Royal Bengal Tiger grows to close to 450 pounds, stands four-and-a-half feet at the shoulder, is almost seven feet long with a three-foot tail, and displays canine teeth close to four inches long when it issues its earth shaking roar. When encountered in the wild, the *Felis tigris*, while still stunning, presents a terrifying sight. Still, Addison's awe seemed a little over the top.

"You've never seen one?"

"Pictures and the like," he said. "One of my favorite movies as a kid was *The Jungle Book*. Shere Khan scared me to death."

I cocked my head. "There's a Sumatran tiger in Zoo Atlanta, Bob. He had a companion named Chelsea, but she died last year. Surely you saw them."

Addison's eyes focused on something far away—something in the past. "I've never been to the Atlanta zoo." I couldn't think of anything to say. I'd never seen Addison's face register such profound emotion. He looked...forlorn. "Mother always said it was 'common.' She claimed the only thing worse was going to a Braves game."

"You never saw a game at Turner Field or Truist Park?"

"Hard to believe, huh? Pretty gaping hole in the resume of a guy who's supposed to run for governor one day."

I'd forgotten all about the Whitmore Master Plan for World Domination, but there was a more important matter at the moment. I stomped my foot in mock fury. "Well, it's settled then. When we get back to the States, Vik and I are taking you to a game. Vik has a box. Maybe we'll sneak down and sit in the regular stands and have something disgusting like a chili dog."

Addison smiled. "You'd do that with me?"

"Sure," I said. "That's what *friends* do."

"I'd like that," he said.

And we went back to staring at the tiger whose name was certainly not Bob.

CHAPTER FORTY

VIK

VARMA TOOK OFF HER SUNGLASSES WHEN she sat in the booth, but she kept her baseball cap low across her forehead.

"Running from the law?" I asked, even though I knew what was happening.

"I'd rather not be hounded while we're having coffee," she said. "Don't get me wrong. I love my fans—they are wonderful. But every so often I like to have a normal day."

I saw two teenaged girls pointing in our direction. They were trying to decide whether to approach.

"I've got this," I said. I pushed back from the table and stood. "Excuse me, everyone," I said in Hindi. "Ms. Rai is here enjoying a cup of tea. She would very much appreciate if you would allow her some time. When she is done, she promises to sign an autograph for everyone who is here." I noticed the girls picking up their phones. "But, if you text your friends and tell them to come, the deal it off."

The phones went down.

"You didn't have to do that," she said. "I can handle myself."

"As well I know," I said. "That was selfishness, pure and simple. I would like to have a moment or two to catch up."

"Thanks," she said. She sipped her chai. "But that's about all I have, especially now since you have sentenced me to a half-hour of signing things."

At first, I thought she was angry, but I saw the corners of her mouth twitch.

"You're not mad, I can tell," I said. "You may be a great actress, but I know you too well."

"How do you know I'm a great actress?"

"I've seen everything you've ever made…more than once. I've even introduced your work to Harlow, my fian…"

Someone sucked all the air out of the small café. If Varma was waiting for me to speak, she was going to be disappointed. For reasons I could not explain, I could not even look her in the eye, much less say anything.

After what seemed like an hour, I heard her smooth, alto voice. "Chatwal, look at me you candy ass." I looked up. She was smiling like someone who knew the truth but didn't necessarily like it. "Harlow Kennedy," she said. "Atlanta, Georgia, tall, beautiful, has her own jewelry line."

"You knew."

"You think there's anyone in Delhi—check that—anyone in India who doesn't know every move you make? You are bigger here than Jagger is in the UK. Relax…and don't flatter yourself."

"Excuse me?"

"Despite what your elephantine ego leads you to believe, not every woman in the world is pining away for you—least of all me."

Her tone was flat and without malice. She could have been reciting the morning weather forecast.

"That's a little harsh," I said. It sounded defensive and a little wounded.

"Don't get your knickers in a bunch," she said. She laughed and broke the tension. "We go back a long way." She took a long pull on her tea. "Let me ask you something if I may."

"You can ask anything you like."

"Does she make you happy?"

"Indeed she does."

"Then, I am thrilled for you, though a little surprised. I never thought anyone would lasso the great Vikram Chatwal."

It was my turn to laugh.

"What's so funny?" she asked.

"I think that's the only time you have ever uttered my first name," I said.

"And it will probably be the last," she said. "Now, let's finish our tea. I can tell the natives are getting restless and I have to be somewhere in a bit. But I can't leave immediately because *someone* made a promise on my behalf."

The moment we stood, every person in the place rushed our table. Ahmi already had a pen in her hand and began signing everything shoved in front of her. She looked at me.

"Tomorrow," she said.

"Where and when?"

She mouthed the location and the time. I nodded and left.

CHAPTER FORTY-ONE

HARLOW

I DIDN'T DO ANYTHING TO MAKE it happen, and I was horrified after the fact. But it happened and I have to live with it.

The evening outside the Purana Quila was wonderful. Night didn't fall; it slid in as if on skates—smooth, gentle, gliding. The air carried all the wonderful aromas of Delhi I had come to adore on my last trip—jasmine, lavender, gardenias, and all the spices of the land. The temperature remained mild; humidity was low. My full-length, rose-colored saree felt wonderful against my skin and though I was sleeveless, it was just warm enough to be without a chill and cool enough to avoid stickiness.

The Ishq-e-Dilli unfolded like a sub-continental version of the light show at Cinderella's castle in Disneyworld. The scale was enormous, the story fascinating. It told the story of ancient Dilli—how it had been destroyed and rebuilt seven times, then rebuilt. Audience members stood spellbound by the tale of Prithvi Raj Chauhan, who ascended to the throne in 1177 CE at the tender age of eleven. His mother served as regent until he reached the age of majority. Under his reign, the nation flourished. A statue of him firing a bow from astride a horse in battle stands at Ajmer as a reminder of his heroism and unifying rule.

Pictures projected against the "Old Fort" built in 1538 combined with colorful lasers, bombastic music, riveting sound effects, and marvelous narration (fortunately in English) to make a most memorable experience. Amazement painted the faces of every tourist—pride was reflected on the face of every native of India.

The show ended in a blaze of pyrotechnics...and then the sky and everything around the venerable old building went black. The darkness only lasted for a few seconds, but it was enough time for me to turn to Addison and say, "Wasn't that amazing?"

"Not as amazing as you," he said.

He kissed me.

And I did not push him away.

CHAPTER FORTY-TWO

HARLOW

I STARED AT HIM. HE STARED back at me.

"That was nice," he said.

All I could come up with was a grunt. He let go of me. We both stared at the Purana Quila. Now it was illuminated with blazing spotlights. The crowd was dispersing. I imagined every person there was staring at me.

"It was nice," he said again.

"The laser show or the tonsil hockey?" I asked. I gritted my teeth at the sound of my tacky comment.

"Damn," he said, "that sounds like something I might have said not too long ago."

"Addison—"

He broke in. "Shouldn't have happened. Won't ever happen again."

"Damn right," I said. I wanted to be angry, but I realized I wasn't. "And you shouldn't apologize. I get it. We've been spending a lot of time together. Maybe I've given you the wrong impression. I'm sorry. It's probably selfish of me to spend this much time with you when I'm engaged to be married."

"Have you been having fun? Hanging out with me?" he said.

"Huh?"

"Eloquent as always," he said. And there it was—the thousand kilowatt Addison Whitmore smile—the toothy grin destined to reside in the Governor's mansion in the Peach State.

"What are you doing here Addison. I know it's not about your father's plane and your desire to see India. Why are you here? Please explain?" I asked.

"I want to…and, …I need to. But you've got to promise me a few things."

I was suspicious. "No more kisses, please you have to stop with that," I said.

"No…no more," he said. "But you have to hear me out."

"Okay."

"No hitting me."

"Check."

"And, most important—absolutely no laughing."

He could read the confusion on my face. "Fine, Addison. Go ahead."

"A few years ago, we had an evening together at my apartment." I didn't like where this was going. I squared my shoulders. "Remember, no hitting."

"Then you better get on with it."

"I fell asleep. When I woke up, you were on your way out."

"I know," I said. I could feel the humiliation of my first sexual encounter welling up inside.

"I stumbled to the steps and asked if you had to go, but—"

"But you didn't ask me to stay," I said. Tears rolled down my cheeks. I made no effort to hide them. "All you had to do was ask. I would have stayed—I wanted to stay. It was my first time. I *needed* to stay. Why couldn't…why didn't you?"

He reached out with both arms and took me by the shoulders. I buried my head into his chest and sobbed. "Why didn't you… why didn't you."

The embrace was tender and unthreatening. He stroked my hair and waited until my breathing returned to normal.

"Harlow?" he asked. "You okay?"

"Getting there," I said.

"When you are ready, I need you to look at me. I have to say this to your face, or things will never be right."

It took a moment for me to feel a little more composed, but after a while, I stepped away, wiped my cheeks with my hands, and locked onto his eyes. "Okay," I said. "Go."

"I didn't ask you to stay because I was embarrassed," he said. "Our time together was a caricature—wham, bam, thank you ma'am…thirty seconds of making noise and then falling asleep like a sated buffalo."

I would have gotten mad, but I saw his face. "Well," I said, "I wasn't exactly experienced."

He shook his head so violently, I thought he might hurt himself. "No, no, no, no, no. You were wonderful. You were tender. You were loving. You were every bit as beautiful as you are today. You were what every man wants—what every man needs. I was the problem. I was lousy, and crude, and unpolished, and uninspiring. I ruined it for both of us by trying to act like I was some kind of a stud." He swallowed hard. "Harlow, it was my first time."

CHAPTER FORTY-THREE

VIK

NESTLED AMIDST THE STREETS OF SOUTH Mumbai near the iconic
Marine Drive, Wankhede Stadium represents the city's enduring
love affair with cricket. The stadium overlooks the Arabian Sea. I
knew this place. Wankhede Stadium speaks to a detente of sorts
between the Cricket Club of India and the old Bombay Cricket
Association. The organizations had been in a long argument
about ticket allocations. The decision was made to build a new
stadium in what was now South Mumbai. It was named after
S.K. Wankhede, the politician who had proposed the solution.
Expedited construction took only thirteen months. The stadium
opened for play in 1975, just in time for a Test between India and
the West Indies.

Inside the stadium, stands were usually packed with passionate fans, their voices rising in unison with each boundary scored
and wicket taken. Today, the crowd was nowhere near capacity,
but the lush green outfield was still beautiful, a pristine canvas
upon which the drama of cricket unfolds.

I'd played here on numerous occasions. Always loved the

"batsmen friendly" park.

The gate was open. There were cars in the lot. Someone was playing. I muttered to myself on the way in.

"Why in the hell does Ahmi want to meet me at a cricket match?"

AMRITA

I'd been watching the match for an hour when Chatwal arrived at ten. He hadn't protested my request to meet, but he couldn't stay long. He needed to be in the kitchen to oversee the evening's banquet. But I knew he would have everything planned. It was Vik's way. He could spare thirty minutes or so. I saw him at the top of the breezeway and waved. We greeted one another in an overtly socially appropriate manner, then sat. Vik's gaze locked onto the field.

"Never figured you for a junior cricket fan," he said. "I always thought you had a weakness for dashing prep schoolers."

I suppressed a smile. "You still think an awful lot of yourself, don't you, Chatwal?"

"Not really," he said. "Life can have a very humbling effect." He waited. "I figured it up on the way over here. It's been twelve years."

"Twelve years and four months," I said, "but who's counting."

Our mutual laughter sounded forced—nothing like it had been twelve years and four months in the past.

After a while, Vik pointed to the field. "That young batsman has talent. They can't get him out."

"He's quite accomplished."

"Might not have much of a future in the sport, though," he said. "Seems a bit smallish. This looks to be a Boy's Sixteen team."

"It is," I said. "And he is…small, I mean."

"Wicked gifted with the bat. Can he field."

"He's a black hole. Sucks in everything he can reach—and he gets to a lot of balls. Quick hands, strong arm, fast, and a wonderful kid. He's too accomplished for his own age bracket, so the league moved him up two classifications. The reason he looks small is because he's barely twelve."

"Oh, you know the boy?" Vik looked at me with interest.

"I should," I said. "His name is Pratham. He's, my son."

CHAPTER FORTY-FOUR

HARLOW

STANDING IN THE HEART OF COUTURE designer Tarun Tahiliani's celebrity-filled boutique, surrounded by a sea of glittering fabrics and gleaming accessories, I was sure I had stepped out of the nightmare of my own creation and into a dream. The gown I had slipped into was nothing short of breathtaking, a masterful cascade of sheer sapphire layers intertwined with subtle silver threads. Every movement caught the light in a different way. Lita, always the vibrant commentator, wrapped her arm around my neck.

She released me. "Twirl, honey, twirl!" I spun and clapped her hands in delight. "Girl, you look astounding!"

The fabric swirled around me. Adopting my best influencer pose, I sucked in my cheeks and pouted my lips. Lita's laughter rang clear and true.

"Amazing," she said. Her eyes scanned the mirrored walls reflecting our glamorous outfits.

"Not too shabby," I said, "for a country girl from Atlanta."

"Country girl, my ass," Lita said. "You're going to outshine the biggest stars there. Trust me, that's saying something."

Though I smiled, a tight knot of anxiety twisted in my stomach. The ride back to the Enclave with Addison had been more than quiet—it was peaceful. The war we'd been fighting for the last few years was over. The kiss had sealed the armistice. And it had made us realize we would never be more than friends. It was a sweet gesture, but instead of being an invitation to passion, it was a beautiful way to say goodbye.

Still, I had a hard conversation with my fiancé coming up… no way around it. I swallowed my anxiety, at least on the surface. "I guess Vik will be surprised. I've transformed from the caterpillar to the butterfly just in time."

Lita's eyes twinkled with mischief. "And just in time to flutter right past that famous Bollywood ex of his, right?"

I felt my smile falter, but I quickly masked it with a grin. "Well, if I'm going to be scrutinized, might as well be in a dress that screams, 'Look at me!'"

"Exactly!" Lita grabbed another gown off a nearby rack—a daring ruby red creation. "And I'll be right beside you in this little number. If we're going down, we're going down in style."

I helped her with the zipper. "What did your boss say when you told him you were jetting off to the Indian Oscars?"

"He was thrilled," she said. "I work at Sotheby's for crying out loud. He said it was a perfect opportunity to network. Probably hopes I'll charm a prince or two to put their crowned jewels up for auction."

"And Amar?" I asked gently, knowing Lita's relationship was always a tender subject.

She rolled her eyes. "He's under his mom's thumb but said he'd cover for me. Auntie Bhavika thinks I should be a dutiful housewife. She would not approve of gallivanting around in designer gowns."

"Every mother's dream," I said, adjusting the fit of my own dress.

"No kidding." Lita sighed and met my gaze in the mirror. "But enough about my soap opera. The next few days are about us, glamour, and not letting anyone dull our sparkle, especially not with Vik cooking and all eyes on us."

I nodded, the nerves (good and bad) alive and tingling in anticipation. "Let's dazzle them so fiercely, they need sunglasses just to look our way."

"Cheers to that!" Lita raised an imaginary glass. "Now, let's go make some unforgettable memories and maybe even stir up a little envy."

We shared a laugh and brushed aside our worries for the thrill of the upcoming event—at least for a while. We changed into our clothes, paid for the outfits (with matching Ferragamo heels), and walked out of the store.

Mumbai awaited. Lita was readying for an event. I was headed into a moment that would define my entire future.

CHAPTER FORTY-FIVE

VIK

"He's my son," she had said.

Blood whooshed in my ears. My heart thumped. The world narrowed to the arithmetic churning in my head. "Who's the father?" I heard myself ask, a part of me wishing for a swift retreat into the Earth's embrace.

Maybe Varma didn't wait an hour before answering, but the pause surely seemed long. When her lips parted, releasing the words I had anticipated, they did not fall hard. Instead, they floated, light and irrefutable. "I believe you already know." Her gaze never left me. The space between us seemed to shrink.

The years rolled back; our history replayed in silent vignettes— shared glances, peals of laughter, stolen moments. I looked out at Pratham, the way he commanded the field, and the last piece of an ever-present puzzle clicked into place.

I sat in my car for thirty minutes or so until I felt calm enough to drive. Varma had said nothing more about Pratham's paternity. In fact, after, "I believe you already know," she hadn't said much at all except in one instance. Most of her responses had been grunts or silence. But she did react when I said, "I have every intention of supporting the boy."

She'd said, "I know. That's all been taken care of."

Her demeanor at my departure could best be described as "distant." I saw none of the effusive nature she'd exhibited when we'd chatted behind the pavilion the night before.

I took my time on the drive home. I was in no great hurry. I needed time to calm down before I stepped into the kitchen. Once I arrived, my every focus *had* to be on the evening's meal.

Harlow! She would be there tonight. *I'll deal with it when it's time.*

I drove. I thought. And I remembered.

The last time I'd been intimate with Varma was two days before prep school graduation. As was always the case, our time was rushed. We were both terrified of being caught—her more so than me. She was painfully aware of what a sullied reputation meant to a young Indian woman.

Still, she'd promised to come by my room the next evening. Said she had something "special." *Papa* visited me and stayed longer than expected. Varma never showed.

Perhaps that was why I'd struck such a terrible bargain.

CHAPTER FORTY-SIX

HARLOW

THE BLANKET OF EXOTIC PERFUMES COMBINED with sharp pangs of near panic almost overwhelmed me when we stepped into the cavernous venue of the Bollywood Film Awards. Every corner of the room featured exquisitely attired, and famous, attendees. Dressed in our resplendent Tarun Tahiliani creations, we navigated a path through the throng, our senses assaulted by the clamor of chatter, laughter, and the incessant clicks of cameras capturing the evening glitz.

"I think these alleged VIP passes are the basic model," I said. I thumbed the glittering lanyard around my neck. Looks like everybody's got one. We're the regular fish is a very large ocean."

"What do they have that we don't?" Lita asked. She couldn't quit staring. I didn't blame her. Stars and their glamorous "others" were as numerous as shells on the Jekyll Island beach after a storm.

I sort of liked our underdog status. "I think we're on double secret probation."

Lita was blank. She'd never seen the movie *Animal House*.

"Never mind," I said. "We are surrounded by the crème de la

crème. They've got money, fame, and—"

She gave me a playful shove "Don't you dare say 'looks' because, honey, we are fiiiiine."

In a moment of cheeky defiance, we stopped, traced our fingers from lips to hips and made a sizzling sound. The little performance was lost in the larger spectacle, thankfully unnoticed amid the surrounding fanfare.

The closer we drew to the dinner line, the more magnificent were the smells. I feared sensory overload. Each inhalation drew in a banquet. We finally arrived at the food station, marked by a velvet rope that divided the guests. To the left, the elite dined in a setup resembling a series of opulent railroad cars, while we were guided right to a less extravagant but still elegantly appointed buffet.

When Lita popped a momo into her mouth, her expression transformed into one of pure bliss. "Sweet Mother Mary, this is good!" she said.

"Interesting choice of words for a good Hindu girl," I said. I took one for myself. The taste was an explosion of flavors—tangy, spicy, and utterly delicious.

"Would you rather I slip into the vernacular and say, '*Hey Bhagwaan*?" she asked, clearly enjoying the culinary delights.

"Whatever floats your boat." I laughed. The playful back and forth was helping me relax.

Suddenly, the crowd parted slightly, and there she was— Amrita Rai. Her stunning saree shimmered like liquid platinum under the lights. The fabric, basically a second skin, accentuated every graceful movement as she laughed and bantered with an entourage of admirers. My heart tightened a little. She was breathtaking—without even trying.

Lita, sensing my sudden quiet, squeezed my hand. "She's

gorgeous, but so are you. Remember that."

I nodded and took a deep breath. I forgot all about the momos and everything else. I was nearly blinded by her radiance.

"It's like a culinary symphony in here." Lita pulled me back to the present and I listened to the people around us who were moaning with every bite.

"Basically a dining orgy," I said, I tried to shake off the nerves and focus on the excitement of the night. "And my man is the maestro of this madness."

As the evening unfolded, each star we recognized, each snippet of overheard conversation, added layers to our experience. This wasn't any ordinary night out; it was a plunge into a world where every gesture was magnified, and every smile held a story. Here, amidst the stars and the spectacle, I realized this was my moment to sparkle, too.

I had other issues to address—but I decided to push them aside until later.

CHAPTER FORTY-SEVEN

HARLOW

I WAS AS FULL AS A tick at summer camp by the time the show started. Since it was being broadcast live nationwide, the preliminaries began about thirty minutes before eight. As the giant clock in the grand hall inched closer to "go time," a palpable buzz swept through the audience awaiting the live broadcast that would display Indian cinema to the nation.

Before the main event, a couple of dignitaries took to the stage, their speeches meandering through pleasant but forgettable territories. The crowd shifted restlessly in their seats, their attention waning until the unexpected happened.

To everyone's delight, Shah Rukh Khan, the undisputed *Baadshah of Bollywood* and tonight's Master of Ceremonies, made an early entrance. Known affectionately as SRK, his fame spanned over a hundred films and countless accolades. As he strode confidently onto the stage, the room erupted into a roar of applause that reverberated for a solid two minutes before simmering down to a hushed awe.

Grasping the microphone with charismatic ease, he flashed

his signature boyish grin, the kind that made every one of the 2000 attendees feel personally acknowledged. "Thank you so very much," he said, his voice smooth as silk, his presence magnetic. "I realize I am not due out here for another few minutes, but there is something I feel compelled to do before my official appearance. Tonight, we will celebrate the best of Indian film. I am thrilled to be a part of it, and I do not wish to change the focus of the evening. But I think it is important to recognize the gentleman responsible for getting tonight's festivities off to a rousing start with the most outstanding assortment of indigenous cuisine ever assembled. Please, someone back there in the kitchen, ask him to come out." He waited twenty seconds during which everyone could hear shouting from the back. When the door opened, Shah Rukh Khan began to clap. "Friends, I give you Chef Vikram Chatwal!"

Clad in his pristine white chef's jacket, Vikram Chatwal emerged bashfully, a contrast to his bold culinary creations. He leaned into the mike someone held in front of his face. His smooth baritone wrapped around the audience like an embrace.

"This honor is not mine alone," he said. "It belongs to the soil that grows our produce, the hands that prepared our meals, and to each and every one of you that gives meaning to your creations by sharing them with your loved ones."

Sometimes standing ovations feel a little forced. You know, the lone, overly enthusiastic fan leaps up and cajoles a neighbor to stand. The crowd, eager to depart, rumbles to its feet and claps, hoping against hope they can head off an encore.

Such was not the case here. It was as if someone had simultaneously electrified all the seats in the house. Every patron stood. Decorum evaporated. Men cheered. Women screamed. The chant echoed off the walls: "Vik-ram…Vik-ram…Vik-ram."

And I was yelling the loudest of them all.

The last guest stumbled out into the night. I sat at the table with Lita. She looked at me.

"Go," she said.

When I pushed open the kitchen door, there were only three people inside—a guy with a mop who was finishing up, a vendor loading the last of the unused dishes into a crate, and Vik sitting on short stool—arms on knees, head bent, exhausted. I walked over, careful not to clack in my heels.

"Hi, sailor," I said. "New in town?"

When he looked at me, nothing else mattered—nothing from our recent past—nothing in Vik's distant history...or in mine. He stood and kissed me with the perfect combination of tenderness and passion. It lasted a while. I stood back.

We spoke the same words at the same time. "We need to talk."

"You go first," he said.

I chickened out. "Still furious with you," I said.

"I know," he said. "And you have every right. I have been a self-absorbed, single-focused ass. I should have stayed with you. Coming here was nothing but ego."

I hit him on the arm. "That's not fair," I said. "How am I supposed to stay angry when you are being chivalrous?" I kissed him again. "Okay, your turn."

"Later," he said. "We have some catching up to do." His eyes grew wide. "I mean...ah...if everything is okay...you know."

"I know," I said. "My doctor said I am good to go, but just remember we're not trying to set any kind of records. Okay, cowboy?"

"Yea hah," he said.

CHAPTER FORTY-EIGHT

HARLOW

ONCE WE GOT TO THE HOTEL, Vik quit telling me how sorry he was and began showing me how happy he was to see me. We had a glorious night of laughter and love. We were still mostly awake when Lord Surya[1] flicked his whip and seven horses began to pull his chariot over the eastern horizon.

Vik stepped out of bed and reached to pull on a pair of silk pajama bottoms. "Don't you dare ruin my view with those pants," I said.

"As you command, your highness," he said.

I shook my head at the magnificence of his toned glutes. "My, my, Mr. Chatwal. You have a mighty fine ass."

He looked over his shoulder while he was making coffee. "Mr. Chatwal is my father," he said. "And I hope you never say that to him."

I screamed in mock horror. "I may never get that image out of my head," I said.

---

1 The Indian god of the sun, Lord Surya is traditionally depicted in a chariot pulled by seven horses that represent both the days of the and the colors of visible light.

"Well, maybe this will help." He handed me a steaming cup of coffee on a plate with four pieces of *besan ladoo*.

"Where'd you get the pastry?" I asked.

"Left over from last night," he said. "I thought we might need some sustenance this morning."

"Awfully sure of yourself, weren't you buddy?"

"You've always been a sucker for an apology," he said.

The atmosphere was unincumbered by the past, at least for the moment. We were back. And it was wonderful.

VIK

Once Harlow told me to quit telling her how sorry I was, the evening was wonderful. We greeted the dawn, had coffee and pastry, and prepared for the trip back home to Delhi.

"What time do you want to head out?" she asked. "I figure you can drive me back in your car. Lita has her own car. Hussein won't mind the trip by himself."

Typical Harlow. Thinking about someone else's feelings—even those of a person who was going to have to drive when he was paid to drive.

"I have to go back to the pavilion and ensure everything is squared away. There are some vendors to pay and a few other things to get settled. Will probably take several hours. You'll be bored sick. Hussein will drive you home. Did Lita have a good time?"

She assured me Lita had been "over the moon," whatever that meant. "But I would have thought sleeping with the master chef would have gotten me a better seat," she said, "something maybe next to a star—maybe someone like Amrita Rai."

My heart sank. *Does she know?* I opened my mouth to tell

her—or to try to tell her, I hadn't rehearsed anything—but she kept going.

"Just kidding," she said. "We had a great time."

"Good, I will be back to the enclave in time for dinner. I promise."

"Okay," she said. "But I'm happy to stay."

"Don't be silly," I said. "Besides, I'll get done faster if I'm not worrying about you."

She looked at me with her best *I'm serious* gaze. "I better not see you zooming past us in your Lambo," she said. "You have to be careful."

"Always," I said.

"When you are by yourself, you drive quicker than a hiccup."

"You say the weirdest things I've ever heard," I said. "But I think I understand. I will stay way under hiccup speed."

"Good," she said. "Can't have anything happening to my man."

An hour later, she waved from the rear window of the Mercedes. I waited until she was out of sight, then dug my phone from my pocket.

CHAPTER FORTY-NINE

VIK

THE BUTTER CHICKEN AT *MA'S* DINNER tasted superb. Govind seemed most pleased when I complimented him on the tenderness of the meat and the perfect blend of ginger and garlic in the chile paste. The texture of the basmati rice indicated he had cooked it with great care. I knew a great many chefs who took the quality of rice for granted. Govind was not one of them. He fussed over every aspect of every meal. The naan and a chilled brown ale offered a wonderful balance to the meal's inherent heat.

Neither *Ma* nor Harlow said very much. Once again, Papa was absent from dinner. My encounter with Amrita had robbed me of any zeal for a lot of conversation. Sajin was more than happy to fill the void. He'd been a blowhard his entire life, the hero of every story, the outstanding player in every contest.

He took a bite of chicken, and I made a mistake.

"How are things at work?" I asked.

He responded without benefit of swallowing. "Smashing," he said. "Everything is just capital."

"Really, even with the recent devaluation of the rupee?" I

asked.

"Tempest in a teapot," he said. "Everything is ship shape. The devaluation made some people panic, but I've been doing this long enough to be able to read the fiscal tea leaves as it were. Nothing about which to be worried." He shoved a piece of chicken about the size of an egg into his mouth and smacked away. "Seriously, everything is under control."

While he launched into a soliloquy about his triumphs on behalf of Chatwal Enterprises, my thoughts were 1400 kilometers away. When Harlow departed Mumbai, I'd called Ahmi. The conversation didn't last long, but I learned a lot.

"Hey, I have a question," I said.

"I would think you had a lot of them, Chatwal," she said, "but go ahead."

"When I said I would take financial responsibility for Pratham, you said, 'I know.'"

"Yep."

"What made you say that?"

She told me.

Sajin was still talking. He took a breath and I stood. "Well," I said, "I very much appreciate your keeping a tight watch on things. I'm sure everything is as you report. But I owe it to my parents to take a look. I would have been there sooner, but I could not pass the opportunity to cook for the Film Awards Ceremony. *Papa* said he understood, but I have taken care of the situation at Xanadu and now need to earn my keep as part owner of Chatwal Enterprises. I have put off my obligation to him and to this family long enough."

Sajin began to stand. I place a restraining hand on his shoulder. "I know you are about to offer to accompany and assist me, but I work better alone sometimes. Thank you do very much." I looked at *Ma.* "Please excuse me."

I kissed Harlow on the head, a show of affection of which, perhaps, my *ma* disapproved, but I hardly cared.

The Mercedes was waiting outside. Hussein stood by the back door.

"The office, sir?" he asked.

"Yes, please," I said. "Thank you."

CHAPTER FIFTY

LITA

Flatware clicked against dishes. An occasional *Pass this…* or *pass that* broke the silence. But, all in all, I'd been in louder libraries. Amar finally spoke.

"How were the awards?" he asked.

Jangling nerves made me answer a little too fast. I knew I sounded rattled. "Wonderful, just wonderful. I saw everybody—every big movie star. They were all so elegant. And the food. Vik outdid himself. I've never eaten so much in my entire life. There were foods from all the regions, amazing appetizers, and fabulous deser—"

A chainsaw grinding against concrete would have sounded musical compared to Bhavika's voice. "So, you went alone?"

I stepped right into her trap. "Oh no," I said. "I went with Harlow. Vik got us tickets."

"Two unaccompanied women—one an American with no appreciation of our norms and customs—wandered amongst a collection of *entertainers* without benefit of an escort? You bring shame upon this family."

"*Mummyji,* stop," Amar said—but if he intended his words to serve as a rebuke, they missed the mark. She turned on him and hissed like an angry cat.

"Do not speak to me with such disrespect," she said. "You are supposed to be the man of his house, but you cannot control your wife. I have heard about the way actors conduct themselves—drinking, drugs, jumping from one bed to the next."

"There was no bed hopping," I said. Weak, but it was all I could come up with on short notice.

"Who can verify your story?" she said. She knew she had the upper hand and was determined to press her advantage. "Were you with your *American* friend all evening?"

"Well, until she and Vik went to their rooms," I said.

Horror etched her face. "Where did you stay?"

"I was in my own room," I said. I abandoned all pretense of respect and responded as I would have to someone when I lived in the States. "I'm a big girl, you know. Can dress myself and everything."

Someone at the other end of the table dropped a fork—perhaps an attempt to break the death stares my mother-in-law and I were throwing at one another. Amar audibly gasped.

His voice quavered. "Lalita," he said. "Perhaps you and I could have a word in private."

I lost it. Even though I knew I was breaking every rule in the *How to be a Proper Female in India* book, I spewed out the venom that had been building since we'd returned from our honeymoon. I put my knuckles on the table and leaned across toward my mother-in-law.

"What business is it of yours?" I asked. "I am a grown woman. I make my own money. I support well over half of this household. I cook, I clean, I take damn good care of my husband. Maybe I don't dote on him like you did…maybe I expect him to carry his fair share…but we have a good life. But I guess that's not enough for you. Well, here's an idea—why don't we see how well things go when I'm not around!"

It was the wrong thing to do. My tirade shattered every social norm. Younger people were expected to be deferential and respectful at all times. But I'd lived in America too long—tasted the sweet fruit of freedom from the doddering traditions of yesteryear. I loved Amar. I had never been happier in all my life. But his mother and her constant whining… continual presence… nagging expectations…and endless comparisons suddenly became more than I could take.

When I finally quit screaming, Bhavika was the color of old newsprint. She made to open her mouth, but I was not going to listen to anything from her anymore. I looked across the table at the quivering mass of helplessness that was my husband.

"I'll let you know where to send my things," I said.

I was out of the house and driving down the street before I had a thought. *What now?*

CHAPTER FIFTY-ONE

HARLOW

Dinner had passed. Rachana and I were sitting in the parlor.

"Is everything all right with you and my son?"

I hoped I didn't flinch. Her question just seemed so out of character.

"Everything's fine," I said. "The Awards dinner was a triumph, and we had a nice time in Mumbai."

Something a little devilish brushed across her face. "Good," she said. "Still, he seemed a little troubled this evening at dinner. Quieter than usual."

"I believe he's tired," I said. "And who in the world can slip a word in edgewise with Sajin at the table."

I stopped, horrified by the insult I had just uttered. Rachana bailed me out by choking on her wine. "He does prattle on," she said.

"I meant no disrespect," I said.

"Never fear, my dear. Everyone in the family thinks him a frightful bore sometimes."

She put down her glass, picked up her knitting, and soon

established the easy rhythm of an expert.

"What are you making?" I asked.

A sly grin creased her lips. "A baby blanket," she said. She saw my eyes widen. "Never fear, my child. There is no expiration date."

I couldn't think of a response.

"Have you ever wondered why children are so important to Indian families?" she asked.

"I guess it's like every other culture in the world," I said. "Everybody wants grandbabies."

Her chuckle was soft. "In some ways, you are correct. Parents want to see the continuation of a line. In this country, having a grandson is particularly prized."

Ain't that just the way, I thought. But I didn't say anything.

"A male heir has three very important functions. First, he continues the lineage. Second, he provides for his parents in their dotage."

"Both very important," I said.

"Yes," she said, "but the third responsibility is the most critical. It is the son's duty to perform the last rites at his parents' funerals to ensure their souls will make the journey home to their ancestors without difficulty."

"What about girls?" I asked.

"Our culture values its women," she said, "but not in the same way as sons because when a woman marries, her loyalty shifts to her husband's kin. Consequently, we are very careful about selecting spouses for our sons. We must be sure the girl is suitable."

I nodded like I understood, but I didn't—not really. Now Rachana was lost in memory. She continued.

"My husband and I were not blessed with daughters. I had four miscarriages before Vikram was born. The first was a son; the other three were females. I mourned each of them for months. We were certain we would never experience the joys of parenthood. Then, miracle of miracles, we were blessed with Vik. I fear we might have spoiled him a bit."

"Ya think?" I said. I immediately regretted my outburst. "I am so sorry, Mrs. Chatwal. Sometimes I forget I'm not in America."

"It is fine," she said. Her smile radiated understanding. "You are not one of us." Now it was her turn. She dropped her handiwork; her hands flew to her mouth. "That was a terrible thing to say. I only meant—"

I interrupted. I'd already stepped in a social cow pie, so what was another faux pas?

"I understand," I said. "While I have some distant blood connection to this country, I am not of the Indian culture, but I *am* from the American South. We can be just as brutal with anyone we see as an outsider. You are welcome to be a part of the tribe, as it were, as long as you do things *our* way."

"So, you forgive me?" she asked.

"There's nothing to forgive," I said. "This is just two ladies talking."

"Correction," she said. "This is a *ma* talking with her *betee*.[1] And so it is only right for you to call me Rashana."

We talked long into the night. I was unaware she'd attended Ethriraj College for Women, perhaps the finest in the country. She earned a degree in business.

"Kavyansh has always stressed the importance of education," she said. "Even when he knew my parents did not approve, he insisted I should go—and graduate. Neither of my parents attended the commencement ceremonies, but my husband was there, and he made enough noise for two dozen."

---

1 Daughter.

I had a hard time picturing the reserved, quiet man I knew as Mr. Chatwal standing on a folding chair and whistling while his spouse walked across a stage.

Probably didn't happen exactly like that, I thought. "You're from Mumbai, aren't you?"

"How do you know that?" she asked.

"Vik…Vikram's restaurant is named Bombay Baby. It's a tribute to you," I said.

She leaned forward. "Is it any good?" she asked. "And do not lie. I want the truth."

I sat on the edge of my chair and took her hands in mine. Her fingers were thin like drinking straws, but surprisingly strong. Her eyes were deep and all-knowing.

"It is easily one of the finest restaurants in Atlanta," I said. "As you know, not everyone cares for Indian food."

"One must feel pity for them," she said.

"Absolutely," I said. "But among those blessed enough to appreciate the cuisine, the word is that Bombay Baby is the best of its kind anywhere outside of the country in which we are currently residing."

Joy flooded her face.

"I believe it is a sign, my child," she said. "I am thrilled to hear of my son's success. Now, we must figure out how to convince my husband of the blessing your marriage to our son will provide for this family. You know I love Kavyansh, but sometimes, he can act like a cantankerous old goat."

CHAPTER FIFTY-TWO

VIK

EVERYTHING SEEMED IN ORDER AT THE office. I spent several hours scrutinizing P&L statements and reviewing the audits for the past several years. Our holdings, while diminished in value in a few places, appeared solid. Our former comptroller, Vanesh Shakar, had been with Chatwal Enterprises for decades. He was a man of unlimited integrity. I remembered his retirement ceremony from just a while before I left for America.

Pa stood before the assembled with Vanesh at his right. "In recognition of your devoted and stellar service, we have a token of appreciation." He handed over an envelope. Vanesh started to put it in his pocket. Staring at a dollar amount would be gauche. *Pa touched* his arm. "Open it, please."

When Vanesh took out the paper, he saw a certificate announcing him as a five percent owner of Chatwal Enterprises. He wept without shame.

Since then, we had divided responsibilities amongst a retinue of junior accountants, each with his (and they were all men) area of responsibility. I'd noticed a slippage in excellence after Vanesh's retirement. No fraud, but things were not quite as buttoned up and tidy as they had been during his watch.

For one thing, there were the desks. When Vanesh had been in charge, he required every desk in the Finance and Accounting Department to be kept in "a neat and orderly fashion." A bit of a stickler, he'd been known to straighten pens and pencils in desk-top holders. He insisted on conservative business attire—dark suits and subtle ties. When the mavens of international fashion determined it was chic to accessorize a navy or black suit with brown shoes, Vanesh was nearly catatonic.

But the biggest issue of which he would not have approved was personal discretionary accounts. After his retirement, and probably as a kneejerk reaction to his tightfisted control, every-one in the department above a certain level received a monthly allocation for "business related expenses." While these funds were subject to audit, since they represented a fraction of the company's net worth, any review usually consisted of, "Show me a receipt for this dinner and tell who was there." But as anyone knows, lax oversight eventually lapses into no oversight at all.

My father trusted all the people who worked for him. Before anyone was hired, he always insisted on meeting every single employee from the top executives to the hourly guy who worked on the offshore oil rigs. When face to face meetings were impos-sible—because of the global nature of the enterprise –*Papa* used Zoom. Anyone who got a check from Chatwal Enterprises had access to a phone number through which they could contact the *mukhiya aadamee*[1] with any issue—large or small.

Captains of industry all over the world had admonished Papa. There needed to be space… distance…some even said "a sense of awe" …between top management and the worker bees. But

1 "Chief man."

every year, two things happened. Employee surveys rated Chatwal Enterprises the absolute highest in employee satisfaction and increasing numbers of executives from other companies asked to parlay with my father for advice on how to create and maintain happy workers.

Still, my father was not naïve. He understood the need for checks and balances. Hence, he maintained a list of the key codes for every office, file cabinet, and desk. I checked my phone and unlocked random drawers. I looked for anything untoward. I flipped through folders and checkbooks. Nothing seemed amiss.

I was just about to replace a checkbook in a drawer when a name on an entry caught my eye: "East India Talent, Inc."

Wait a minute. I saw the same payee a moment ago.

I reopened the large ledger and flipped through the stubs. There it was again: "East India Talent, Inc." I kept looking. Again…one month later. I looked at the amount—a sum equal to fifteen thousand U.S. dollars. I went back to the previous item. Same amount. An expanded search uncovered two more ledgers covering a total of six years. Every month there was a duplicate payment.

I googled East India Talent. The website on my phone screen trumpeted: "The #1 agency for Indian artists."

I'd been so busy I had no idea whose desks I was scrutinizing. I took pictures of all the check stubs, replaced the ledger, made sure the drawer was locked, then reached for the name plate at the front of the desk. I turned it around.

Sajin Chatwal.

CHAPTER FIFTY-THREE

VIK

Sajin reminded me of some of the kids I'd seen in my restaurant—the ones who didn't want to be there. They were used to eateries with ball pits, video games, and loud animated figures that danced and sang silly songs. They liked their chicken fried and in bite-sized nuggets along with fried potatoes (curly or sticks or waffled, they seldom cared) and lemonade or sodas. Sitting in a dark booth while sitar music played closely approximated their idea of eternal torment, so they fidgeted and squirmed.

Sajin looked uncomfortable. He'd put two and two together. Since I'd been to the office, he assumed he was in trouble. I couldn't prove anything yet, but I suspected he was right.

Ma sat in her chair with her knitting. She appeared focused on her craft, but I knew she was absorbing every word and movement with the intensity of a hawk spying on a field mouse.

"So, I went to the office," I said. "Looked around a bit."

"Good," Sajin said. "Place looks amazing, doesn't it. Been a little expansion since the last time you were there. You probably noticed. Upgraded the lighting too—fabulous ambience."

"Yes," I said. "Looks nice."

"P&L's are pretty solid. We're still riding on the crest. Other places are sinking. Some have crashed, but CE keeps rocking along."

"Financial statements look good," I said. "And I had the occasion to look over the last few audits as well."

"Everything's copacetic, right?" he said. "Clean bill of health all around."

"Took a look at a few of the check ledgers too," I said.

"Boss's son's prerogative to snoop, I guess," he said. "Seems a little petty to me…a little micro-managing, a little invasive, but like I said, can't stop you."

"I hold a twenty percent share," I said. I clenched my teeth to keep from saying anything else. *He never quits goading me.*

"Well aware," he said. "Pretty good chunk of the pie for a guy who's never there and spends all his time in America wearing a paper hat and asking customers if they want fries with their order."

Fifteen years ago, I would have flown into a rage. But, unlike Sajin, I'd matured. He was still the older cousin intent on making my life miserable. I refused to rise to the bait.

"Sajin," I said, "you need new material for your act. You know every well I am an accomplished chef not a fry cook. You know I only present authentic dishes from our mother country. You know because I offered you a position at Bombay Baby several years ago."

"Only so you could lord it over my head," he said. His voice got brittle. "You knew damn well I would never go to work for my baby cousin."

From the corner, *Ma* cleared her throat. A signal—a warning. "Sorry, *chachee*," he said. "But Vikram's arrogance angers me."

She never took her eyes off her knitting. "What you perceive as arrogance may well stem from your own insecurity, *priy bhateeje*,"[1] she said.

There was nothing else for him to say.

"So," I said, "I reviewed your discretionary account." He couldn't help it—his jaw tightened. "There are checks to East India Talent every month equivalent to fifteen grand, American. Care to explain?"

He feigned searching his brain. "Oh yes," he said. "Several years ago, I determined it would better serve the business to spend *your papa's* hard-earned money in an investment in the future rather than on entertainment. Yes, I enjoy the occasional dinner or round of golf with customers and suppliers, but I decided to help sponsor some rising talent in the Bollywood arena. The money I send to East India Talent is intended to assist struggling young artists early in their careers. Documentation is all there—letters and the like."

"I saw them," I said. "They lacked…ah…specificity."

"Well, perhaps you consider yourself an expert, but who am I to suggest to a trained professional which rising star is more than just a pretty face? I anticipate when the young people we have supported hit it big, we will reap the rewards."

"How is an actor or actress supposed to help a corporation predominantly engaged in energy, transportation, and tech?"

"See," he said, "this is what I mean—you lack vision. You are so transactional. It's about relationships. One of those new stars might speak a good word about Chatwal—you know how the public eats that stuff up."

I nodded as if impressed by his sagacity. "Good thinking," I said. "I might not have considered that."

---

1 Dear nephew.

Sajin looked a little smug, then tapped his temple with a finger. "It's called vision," he said.

"Any results?" I asked.

"Promising," he said. "In fact, one of the people we have assisted has become quite successful. I am anticipating great things."

"Oh," I said, "anyone I would recognize?"

"I am sure you would," he said. I could feel the blow in my gut before it landed. "Amrita Rai. Any chance you know her?"

CHAPTER FIFTY-FOUR

HARLOW

IT WAS MORNING. I ASSUMED VIK had come home, it was his house after all. Since he was on the other wing of the house, I was not certain. Right now, however, I had a more pressing issue on my mind—something I had decided to do after my conversation with Rachana.

I paced in front of the window while I practiced.

"Listen, old man," I said. "No, that's not right. More respect. I can't speak to him like I used to talk to Mother. Custom, Harlow, remember the custom. Utmost deference to elders. Okay, try again."

I stopped for a second and checked the mirror. I had chosen a peacock saree by Lashkaara. Elegant with its rainbow of colors, it fit perfectly. To appear demure, I was wearing a matching silk blouse under it. I did not think an exposed shoulder would be appropriate. I started over.

"Mr. Chatwal, there are a lot of things you don't know about me. But there is one thing of which I am sure you are aware."

Good…use formal language. He'll like that.

"You know I love your son. I firmly believe Vikram and I are destined to be together—it's karma. We have endured a lot to get to where we are now."

I could feel my temperature rising. "All he wants to do it please you. He has busted his ass…nononono, Harlow…no ass. Okay… he has worked like a dog to make his restaurant a success. It's the biggest thing in Atlanta. His frozen food line is blowing up."

Is he going to understand "blowing up"?

"Ah…his frozen food products are flying off the shelves in markets all over the States. People everywhere are learning to appreciate fine Indian food—all because of Vikram…no—your son. Yes, that's better—all because of your son."

The more I lectured, the angrier I grew. *What's wrong with this man? Can't he see how much Vik wants to please him?*

"Can't you see how much Vik loves you and wants to make you happy? He's done everything you asked. He suffered with an investment firm for years at your command. He was miserable. He had to think about money and interest rates and all sorts of other…crap—yes, I said it—crap. The whole time he wanted to be in the kitchen with his spices and mallets and mixing bowls. He needed to be perfecting his recipes, not in search of fame, but to make people happy."

I had a rhythm. *This is good.*

"Yes, Mr. Chatwal—he makes people happy. You should see their faces when they take a bite of his galouti kebab. They look like they've seen the face of God. Do you know how hard it is to make that dish?"

My breath had shortened. I could feel the pulse in my neck. "Of course, you don't because someone else has always made it for you. He's painstaking in its preparations because, as he always reminds me, it is one of your favorites. Has he ever made it for you? Have you ever asked him to? I doubt it. All you want him to do is put on a suit and tie and sit at a desk while he sifts through reams of paper and wonders how to increase your holdings."

I'd been doing so well—and then I absolutely lost it.

"That's bullshit, Mr. Chatwal…absolute bullshit. You son is an artist—a genius—a man who can change moods, maybe even lives with his skill in the kitchen. You should have seen the crowd at the Film Awards. At dinner—the dinner *he* created in very little time I might add—everyone in attendance was transported to a different level of life—to a plain they'd never experienced. But you wouldn't know that, would you? You wouldn't know anything about his brilliance…"

I was beginning to gasp. Angry tears were not far away. "You don't know how much he loves me…you don't know I am the best damn thing that ever happened to him because I adore him…you don't know any of it b-b-because…be…because… well because you are a *selfish… cantankerous…old…goat of a man!*"

My hands were clenched. My jaw was set. I felt like I was breathing fire.

I basked in the heat of my impassioned, practice speech. I was ready. And then I heard the sickening sound of someone applauding from the bedroom door behind me followed by the soft sound of Mr. Chatwal's voice.

"That was a very moving presentation, my dear."

CHAPTER FIFTY-FIVE

HARLOW

I COULD NOT HAVE BEEN MORE paralyzed by terror if there had been a king cobra coiled just inside my room.

"M…Mister Ch…Cha…Chatwal," I said. "I…I…I…"

Nothing came out. For one of the few times in her life, Harlow Kennedy could not think of anything to say.

Vik's father bowed a little. "May I enter?"

I nodded like a bobblehead doll in the rear window of a Chevy with bad shocks. I was afraid to speak. No doubt he'd already suspected I was a whacko. Now he knew it.

He sat in a corner chair, perched on the very front with the ramrod posture of a member of the Gorkha Regiment.[1] If he was waiting on me to speak, he was going to wait a long time.

Finally. "Miss Harlow," he said. "The last time we spoke, I was rude and abusive. You are a lovely young woman deserving of nothing but respect. That you have great affection for

---

1 Highly esteemed regiment in the Indian Army dating back to the 19th Century of whom it was said, "If a man says he is not afraid to die, he is either lying or a Gorkha."

my son, I have no doubt."

I noticed he did not use "the L word."

"But there are numerous reasons why the two of you should not be wed. My family descends from Indian royalty. We can trace our line all the way back to the Mughal Dynasty, the last emperor of which was deposed by the British in 1858. While I have brothers, tradition dictates the line of succession flows through me. I realize what I am about to say will sound horribly prejudiced to your American ears, but everyone in India will understand when I tell you about the great burden, I feel to keep our familial bloodline as pure as possible. There can be no questions about inheritance and leadership."

He saw me take a deep breath and headed off my outrage with a simple wave of his hand. "I do not think less of you as a human being—as a child of God. Frankly, I imagine my sentiments would be profoundly different were I not the eldest son of my father. My stance is not about fears of what some might call 'mongrelization.' You are in no way 'less than.' I am simply an old man held captive by tradition even if I imagine I am fighting a losing battle about which future generations will not care one whit. But that is not the primary reason for my opposition to a marriage between yourself and my son."

I bit the inside of my lip, whether to keep from crying or to stop an explosion I was not sure. "There's another reason?" I asked.

"Yes, Miss Harlow," he said. "Only recently I have come into some very disturbing information, something I have yet to discuss with Vikram."

"Yes?"

"It seems he already has a son."

The air left the room. Suddenly, I could not find either words or breath. My head started to pound; my vision blurred. Alarm bells sounded in my ears like so many screeching crows.

"Huh?" was all I could manage.

"Reports have come to me that a youthful dalliance he had while in prep school produced a child—a young man. The mother is apparently someone of considerable prominence in the theatrical world." He stood to end the audience. "So, you see my problem. I cannot allow confusion about who will one day head this family. Despite the shocking nature of this development, I hope it has illumined the situation somewhat."

He moved as if to leave, then stopped and looked at me with penetrating earnestness. "And I trust you will not discuss this with Vikram until I have had a chance to speak with him about it."

I was halfway out the door when I spoke over my shoulder.

"Screw that!"

CHAPTER FIFTY-SIX

VIK

KALI, THE GODDESS OF VENGEANCE, HAD nothing on Harlow when she burst into my room.

"What the hell?"

I had been changing my clothes—one leg into my pants, the other halfway into my trousers. I hopped on my right foot for a moment, lost my balance, and crashed to the floor. Harlow stood over me like Apollo Creed over a fallen Rocky Balboa. She'd made me watch the movie three times.

"I repeat—what the hell?"

Once I got my leg into my pants and zipped up, I struggled to my feet. "I have no idea what you are talking about," I said.

"The hell you don't." I'd never seen her this mad, not even when she "caught" me in a lascivious embrace engineered by Haiya on our last trip to India.[1] The air suddenly went out of Harlow's balloon of wrath. She sagged onto a bench and let her head fall into her hands.

"Harlow, talk to me. What's wrong?"

---

1 Chapter 56, *Karma Under Fire*.

Her voice was muffled but I understood every terrifying word she said. "Were you going to tell me about your son or just let it be a surprise when he showed up for Christmas sometime?"

🔥

HARLOW

"I just found out about it when we were in Mumbai," he said. "I was going to tell you, but there's so much other crap going on, I could barely think. You're right, it's possible I have a son.

The words were not news—I'd heard them from Mr. Chatwal—but the weight of reality crashed on me like a boulder smashing Wile E. Coyote. It took a moment for the words to register and when they did, my anger went *poof.*

I guess I realized what sort of guy Vik had been in his younger days. I'd read all about him on social media for a couple of years when he was cutting a wide swath through the Atlanta social scene. His presence was impossible to miss. This was the hottest new face in the Peach State—one of the hottest in the country. And in every photo of him, his was escorting a different woman—always young, always smokin' hot.

His restaurant rocketed to the top of the "I've got to get in there" list. He went by the name Tej Majur—was still using it when we first met—when he had me fired.[2] Facebook, Twitter, (now X), Snapchat, it didn't matter. In every picture he was flashing his devastating smile and always—as sure as the sun rises in the East—accompanied by some stunning woman.

I think I might have a son. Well, duh.

We talked until the wee hours of the morning. There were tears, but they were mostly tears of regret. When Vik and I had a child—if that were still a possibility given my recent medical

2 See Chapter 12, *Karma Under Fire.*

issues—it wouldn't be his first. Despite telling Vik I was okay; I was still quietly grieving about the ectopic. The body heals a lot faster than the spirit…or the heart.

"Okay," I said, "we need to get some sleep. This evening, I'll have to tell *Ma.*"

"You don't think your father has told her."

"Not something like this," he said, "not in India. This is *man stuff.* I don't think he'd want to upset her. But at least now I know why he hasn't been doing anything or coming out of his room. He's disappointed and worried—too worried to do anything else."

Vik was standing by the window, searching for something in the pre-morning haze. When he looked at me, I gasped. "Damn, you're almost transparent. You, okay?"

"Terrified," he said.

I hugged him. "Relax," I said, "we all have a past."

The color returned to his face in a rush, and he cackled. "*You* don't," he said. "Not unless you count your scandalous trips to the public library."

I shoved him, gently. "Shut up. Seriously, your folks will be upset, but they will understand."

"That's not what scares me the most," he said. "Without knowing it, I've put the entire future of Chatwal Enterprises in jeopardy."

"I don't understand."

"When my father took over the business, it was struggling. He didn't want it. He'd trained as a surgeon in London.[3] But he was the eldest of three sons; it was his duty. He offered the top spot to each of his brothers. Neither wanted it. In fact, they asked him to buy them out. He paid them faithfully every month for three years until the terms were fulfilled."

---

3 Chapter 20, *Karma Under Fire.*

"Then they should be happy, right?" I asked.

"Not particularly," he said. "A few years after they were out of the business, things took off. No one suspected *Pa* had a mind for business. He was the egghead who was going to be a doctor. But he surprised everyone by being shrewd and savvy. He hired experts in every field of the company's holdings—and he listened to them. Within a decade, Chatwal Enterprises because the largest conglomerate on the subcontinent. Now, it is one of the most influential in the world."

"And your uncles feel left out, right?"

"They won't say anything, but the only reason Sajin has anything to do with the business is to placate Uncle Kanak."

"And a baby complicates that exactly how?"

"Everyone knows I have no interest in the business. Naturally, my uncles assume when my father retires or passes, control will fall to them. Every—"

"Everything changes if there is a little Vikram."

"Well, his name is Pratham, but you get the idea."

It was the first time I'd heard the name. For some reason, it made me weak in the knees. "Any more surprises?" I asked.

"No," he said. "Anything else you want to say?"

"Yes," I said. "Addison kissed me."

CHAPTER FIFTY-SEVEN

HARLOW

IT WAS THE FIRST TIME I'D seen Vik's father dressed and out of bed since my previous whirlwind adventure in India—the one where I'd fallen for Vik. Kavyansh looked drawn. His face, a handsome one for a man of his considerable years, had developed crags and crevasses. I could tell he had not been in the sun for a while. His skin looked pallid—unhealthy.

"You insisted I come down," he said. "This must be important."

"Crucial," Vik said.

"To whom?" his father asked.

"To me, to you, to *Ma,* and to the future of the company."

Kavyansh played along. "What is it then?" he asked. He was going to make Vik say it.

"*Papa,* you already know. Harlow and I have talked," he said. He looked at his mother. "But you need to be informed as well, even though this is embarrassing and potentially disastrous."

"You can tell me anything, *beta,*" she said.

What a sweet, unsuspecting woman, I thought.

To his credit, Vikram did not launch into a long prologue full of excuses. "I think I have a son," he said.

I braced myself for an onslaught of maternal protests and tears. It never came. Rachana took her son by the hand.

"I know," she said. "Your father told me some time ago. I am already handling it."

CHAPTER FIFTY-EIGHT

LITA

My ENTIRE LIFE I HAVE HEARD the expression, "Look before you leap." Well, I had leapt and was pretty sure the landing was not going to be pleasant. I had no clothes except the ones I was wearing. Money wasn't an issue. Amar and I kept separate accounts. I was pretty sure my balance was healthier than his. Little comfort to someone driving along a country road in the middle of an Indian evening.

Whether I consciously steered toward Vikram's home, I don't know, but after an hour of two of aimless driving, I found myself in his driveway. I stopped the car and stared at the house in all of its spotlight-bathed magnificence. It never ceased to amaze me how people with so very much could remain humble and kind.

I thought about it for a moment. I knew Vik's mother regularly spent time in hospitals. She assisted the nurses; she rocked babies in the pediatric ward. Every Thursday afternoon she distributed boxes of food to the impoverished citizens of Delhi from a pantry built and stocked largely from donations not from Chatwal Enterprises, but from the family itself. She churned out knitted baby blankets like an assembly line, spent time teaching children how to read, and even served in a local soup kitchen where she cooked then took time ladling her rich concoctions into bowls held out to her in trembling hands by men, women, and children with emaciated faces.

Not once in all my twenty something years had I seen a single photo of Mrs. Chatwal at any of those events. I realized that while the Chatwal's charitable contributions often came from their expansive wealth, the family's true generosity sprang from their hearts.

I looked at the dashboard clock—9:45 PM. *What the hell*, I thought.

Mrs. Jain answered the door.

"Please wait a moment," she said. She came back and indicated I should enter by sweeping her palm through the doorway. "They are in the parlor."

I walked in on what looked like a family preparing for a funeral. Every eye was red-rimmed, every expression tense.

"Bad time?" I asked.

HARLOW

Lita and I went up to my room. I explained everything. She was her usual matter-of-fact self.

"Oh shit," she said, and she went in to brush her teeth. When she came out, her voice was shaky. "Y…You okay, hon?"

"Been better," I said, "but whatever happens, Vik and I are going to see this through together."

Her expression communicated pity more than anything else.

"I don't think you understand," she said. "If Pratham is Vik's son, you and Vik have no future."

"Hmm," was all I said. "You take the side nearer the window."

I turned out the light. At least tonight I was not sleeping alone—small consolation.

CHAPTER FIFTY-NINE

RACHANA ("MA")

Two days earlier

I ALWAYS LOVED VISITING BOMBAY. I seldom called it Mumbai. I lived in Delhi, but in my heart, I always felt more comfortable here.

Memories flooded my head, especially recollections of a dashing young prep schooler named Kavyansh who'd swept me off my feet long before I learned who (and what) he was. Once I discovered the truth about his legacy, his ancestors, and his wealth, it was too late. I was already in love.

But today was not about the past. Today was about the future. I stood on the stoop of the modest, one-story home and admired the fastidiously maintained lawn—and the flowers. Running alongside the house was a...well, I didn't know what else to call it...water garden. It curved around the corner, a moat-like arrangement in which grew a vast assortment of lilies: yellow pond, large blue water, lemon mist water, tropical water, pink water, white water, and the magnificent Meghalaya red water. On the other side were Carolina fanworts, nilofars, golden irises, leopard flowers, and harlequins. While my gardens at Xanadu were larger, this explosion of color put my meager efforts to shame.

I knelt down to examine one of the plants. "Someone spends an awful lot of time on you," I said.

A voice from behind me made me jump. "It's kind of you to notice."

I stood and turned. The beautiful young woman extended her hand. "Mrs. Chatwal, it is an honor to meet you after all these years. I'm Amrita Rai."

She made tea and we sat for a while without speaking. I finally realized she was waiting on me.

"How did you know who I was?" I asked.

Her laugh surprised me—a little too hearty, borderline unladylike—but it worked with her for reasons I could not explain. "Would anyone in England not recognize Kate Middleton or Meagan Markle?" she asked. "In India, you are every bit as famous."

"I'm not a big fan of publicity," I said. She almost said something. It would have been something about Vikram's love of the limelight, but she stopped before she spoke. She seemed a little stuck—or a little trapped. It was difficult to tell. "I believe you know my son."

"We were acquainted in our prep school days," she said. "He attended the boys' school down the road."

"I suspect you were a little more than acquainted," I said.

When she put her teacup down, her hand trembled a little. "Meaning?"

"Ms. Rai," I said, "my husband and I are not the only reluctant public figures in India. You are notorious for three things: your beauty, which may I say is not exaggerated in the least."

"Thank you."

"Your considerable acting talent. I have seen all your films and liked most of them. But even in the ones I did not care for, your ability shone though."

"Any in particular?" she asked.

I would not be deterred by her attempt to veer the conversation off course. "And your nearly fanatical pursuit of privacy."

It had taken a moment, but she'd regained her cool. "Thank you so very much for the compliments. I'm not surprised by what you said about my films. I didn't like some of them myself."

"Like our gardens, not everything we plant turns out the way we planned."

"True," she said, "but you did not come here today to discuss either movies or horticulture."

"Quite right," I said. "My husband is very security conscious. He regularly employs a Mr. Waman to conduct background checks and the like."

"And you had me investigated?"

I nodded.

What, may I ask, triggered your interest?"

"A family discussion about checks. My nephew is not as clever as he thinks he is, and I am not as clueless as the men in my family would like to believe."

"Men have been underestimating women from the beginning of time," she said.

Nod.

"So, you sent Mr. Waman out to dig and he learned about my son."

"You've never tried to hide him apparently. He's at all your locations. But there isn't any press coverage about him."

"The Indian press is not as bloodthirsty as the Brits or Americans," I said. "I keep Pratham out of the public eye as much as possible– at least with me. He is beginning to get some attention now though."

"He is a budding cricket star."

"Yes, you are well informed." She made no effort to hide her pride. "He may be destined for greatness."

"I hope he gets what he wants," I said. "It is all any of us can ask for."

"You found out he is close to thirteen years old."

"Yes," I said, "which would lead one to believe he arrived some thirty-eight weeks or so after you left your prep school without attending the commencement ceremonies even though you were one of the top graduates."

Now it was her time to nod. "What is it you want, Mrs. Chatwal?"

"You know what I want, Ms. Rai. And it is only fair and fitting." She reached into her purse, handed me a plastic bag containing a hairbrush, and stood. "This is Vikram's. Thank you so much for your time, Ms. Rai," she said. "Whatever the outcome, I am in your corner."

CHAPTER SIXTY

VIK

I HAD PLAYED IN CRITICAL CRICKET matches. Some of the putts I faced against Miguel were for bigger stakes than was prudent. For a while at the beginning, Bombay Baby hovered on the edge of failure. But I'd never felt more tension than what filled the house for several days after my admission to my parents.

Both of them now graced the dinner table. They were polite and hospitable, probably because Lita seemed to have moved in with us. The conversation during the meals was intentionally banal. We discussed nothing of consequence. At one point Lita asked Harlow about going to the movies.

"Last thing I am interested in right now," Harlow said.

Lita scrunched her face in embarrassment.

Amar called every night precisely almost as soon as we finished desert. He knew *Ma's* timing. Once Lita's phone rang, she excused herself and was gone for the next two hours. *Papa* and I resumed our chess matches. He held a 1241-1228 advantage; I was determined to even the tally, but my concentration was shot, so I only fell farther behind. Never fearful to press his advantage,

Pa crushed me with the zeal of an angler pulling in a prize marlin.

"You brought your queen out too early," he said after his first win.

"I know."

"You know better than to leave your king exposed." Second win.

"I know. Again."

"If you are not going to use your rooks, why are we playing?" Third win.

I capitulated for the evening only to return for another drubbing the next night.

One evening before dinner, a FedEx letter arrived. It was addressed to *Ma.* My parents immediately left the table and went upstairs.

"What was that?" Harlow asked.

"I don't know," I said, "but something tells me it's not good. Did you see the look they gave each other?"

"Yep," she said. "You're right. Not good."

We stood at the base of the stairs and strained for any indication of what was happening. Cemeteries at midnight have more noise. We heard nothing for over twenty-five minutes. Then, out of nowhere, my father's voice echoed off every wall.

"I don't care what he wants to do. We have the proof right here. Social propriety be damned. He will marry that woman. It is the right thing to do!"

CHAPTER SIXTY-ONE

VIK

CUTTING AN OVERCOOKED PIECE OF PORK with a plastic picnic knife would have been easier than sawing through the tension in the parlor. My father was wearing the dark blue suit I had seen him put on for funerals. Mother looked a little forlorn in a saree of forest green. Except for her wedding band, she sported no jewelry.

This was serious.

Papa stood in front of the mantle, arms across his chest, and began. Similar to the look of his funeral suit, his voice sounded like someone delivering a eulogy.

"Vikram," he said, "yours has been a life of position and privilege. From childhood to this moment, we now realize you have been indulging and pampered. While I know you are enjoying a modicum of success in your stateside business, the reality is you continue to sidestep your responsibilities as a son of India and the presumptive head of this family. On two different occasions your mother and I have laid out considerable expense to secure a wife for you, an Indian wife—someone with whom you could build a life, have children, and secure the Chatwal legacy. Each time you have found a way to slide out of the commitment we made on your behalf."

My shirt was beginning to stick to the leather upholstery. I changed positions in my chair. *Ma* was sitting with her hands in her lap. She steepled her fingers, a signal for me to remain quiet.

"As the head of this family, your protests and aspirations not withstanding I have come to a decision. The letter we received contained the results of a DNA test. We know for certain the paternity of Amrita's Rai's child. In light of this information, you *will* be married within the next few months. Before we came down, your mother called Isha, who is putting everything in motion. I anticipate you will go to Atlanta for a while to get things in order. Then you will return here for the nuptials."

I looked at Harlow out of the corner of my eyes. Her jaw was clenched. There was no sparkle in her deep eyes. They looked dejected...no...they looked dead. *Papa* shifted positions and addressed her.

"My dear Harlow, you are a lovely, patient, and intelligent woman. I have seen your work with jewelry. You have an eye for beauty and a deft touch. You should be very proud of what you are putting together. I anticipate you will soon become one of the most sought-after jewelry designers anywhere. I have never wanted to cause you pain, so it is with the most profound apologies when we tell you..."

He stopped mid-sentence and looked at *Ma*.

That's strange.

Then, they combined their voices and said, "...that Vikram is going to marry *you!*"

My head throbbed. It took a while for me to realize I had just heard the most beautiful duet ever performed—my parents granting permission for us to marry. Then I noticed something.

Harlow, *Ma,* and *Papa* were standing in front of me, huddled like a three-person rugby scrum, and jumping up and down. They were crying…from laughter. *Papa* kept shouting.

"We got you…we got you…we got you. All hail the conquering heroes. The master prankster Vikram Chatwal has been defeated once and for all time!"

Harlow threw her arms around me. She was sobbing and laughing at the same time.

"I'm so sorry, honey, but they insisted." She looked at my father. "You, sir, are a master thespian."

"Oh no," he said, "your performance was the best. Perched on the edge of your seat, clasping your hands, looking for all the world as if your life were about to end. Brilliant!"

Ma, my own mummyji as I affectionately called her in my youth, continued her giddy dance. "The king is dead! Long live the king—Kavyansh Chatwal!"

Once they tired of their histrionics, Harlow explained everything.

"You're not the father," she said. "The report came via email earlier this afternoon. Your parents told me immediately. Your father decided it was time to pay you back for all the devious things you have done—the practical jokes you have pulled—and maybe jab you a little for some of the heartache you've caused. He and your mother staged the FedEx delivery, then went upstairs for their 'fight.'"

Ma could barely talk. She kept giggling. "Whi…while your fa…father was screaming ab…about (she dropped her voice as low as it would go) … 'It is the right thing to do!'…I had to put a pillow over my face to keep from giving everything away."

I'd never seen my mother so completely out of control. She

collapsed on the couch, wrapped her arms around Harlow and shrieked with delight.

CHAPTER SIXTY-TWO

VIK

WHEN THE COMMOTION FINALLY SUBSIDED, I looked at my father, then my mother, then Harlow.

"That is the single meanest thing anyone has ever done to me," I said. I shrugged. "And, considering everything—including some stuff you don't know about—probably justly deserved."

"What things," *Papa* asked.

"Let's leave that alone for a while," *Ma* said. "This is a joyous time. Besides, you have more news."

"There's more?" I asked.

Papa's face sparkled like the Christmas tree outside Atlanta's Atlantic Station. "Yes," he said. "All the time I was pouting in my room, I had time to think. I am not ancient by any measure, but neither am I a young man. I want to enjoy life while I still can and I don't think I can do so if I continue to worry about stock prices, oil reserves, supply chain issues, and personnel decisions. Consequently, I have decided to sell Chatwal Enterprises. While I do not need your permission since your mother and I are majority stockholders, I will not do so if you disapprove."

My smile threatened to split my face. "I call for a vote of the stockholders," I said. "All in favor say Aye."

Four voices said, "Aye!"

"Harlow, honey, I'm sorry, but I don't think you get a vote," I said.

"I own five percent," she said. "Your parents signed the papers this afternoon. I think it's a bribe to go through with the wedding."

"Well," I said, "third time's a charm."

Before I could hit him, Mrs. Jain, tears streaming from her eyes, came around the corner carrying a tray with four champagne glasses filled to the brims. We toasted the decision and spent the rest of the evening in conversation and laughter.

VIK

Louis XVI probably looked better on his way to the guillotine than Sajin did standing in front of *Pa's* desk.

"In anything other than a family-owned business, you would be fired," *Pa* said. "And very possibly, criminally prosecuted."

"*Chacha*, I—"

"Stop! Please do not insult me or worsen your position with another lie. I know all about your payments to East India Talent. I know they were funneled to Amrita Rai. Do you deny it?"

"No, *Chacha*."

Damn, I almost feel sorry for him.

"There is only one question remaining. Why? What could you possibly have hoped to gain."

Sajin morphed from contrition to scheming before I could blink. "I did it to save Chatwal Enterprises, *Chacha*," he said. "I am dedicated to its future—to its expansion. There are limitless possibilities open to those who want nothing but the best for the corporation. My brother has his own career and, as I understand it, he is busy trying to save his marriage. My cousin, your *son,* who should have spent the last five years learning the ins and outs of international business, continues to play Julia Child in a foreign country. I am the only one who cares enough to move things forward in the decades to come."

"And the checks to Ms. Rai were going to accomplish that exactly how?" *Pa* asked.

Sajin kept looking at me. Perhaps he thought I was going to bail him out. Maybe he figured he could make me mad, start an argument, and escape reality somehow. I remained in a leather chair in the corner, legs crossed, arms folded across my chest, acting for all the world like the disinterested dilettante he assumed I was.

"Vikram fathered a bastard," Sajin said. "I found out quite by accident. I have a friend in the entertainment business. One day we were discussing movies and he mentioned Ms. Rai. I commented that she was pretty."

You made some disgusting comment, and you know it, I thought, but I said nothing. My face remained a mask of detachment.

"My friend asked if I knew she had a child," Sajin said. "After he left, I got curious and did a little digging. I found out she had been in a girls' school down the road from Vikram's. A few conversations later, I learned the two of them had been acquainted. Before too long, I figured it out."

Pa looked disgusted. "Why in the world would any of that matter to you?" he asked.

Sajin's eyes grew wide. He took on the appearance of someone witnessing a five-car pile-up. "Why wouldn't it." The pitch of his voice rose about an octave. "The woman is not of our class. She is *an actress* of all things."

He said "actress" with all the disgust he could muster. I never let my expression change, but I had to pinch my arm to keep from leaping from my seat and pummeling his smug face.

"Under the law, the child has a claim to the corporation. If Vikram were to assume a leadership role, it would be disastrous. He must be stripped of all his stock—compensated a little I imagine, but at a considerable discount as punishment—and banned from taking any part in business activities. He had to know the disaster this could cause." He pounded his fist into his thigh. "He...had...to... know."

His breathing was erratic. He'd almost stopped blinking. I could see the veins in his temples bulging. He kept saying, "He... had...to...know."

Clarity hit me like an Anshul Jubli[1] punch. "You organized the break-in at Xanadu," I said.

He whirled and snarled. "Someone had to get you back here—away from that—"

"Stop!" *Pa* came around his desk and stepped within inches of Sajin's face. "If you say anything—*anything*—about Vikram's fiancée, I will change my mind about your punishment and let the law decide what to do with you."

Sajin was suddenly struck mute. His Adam's apple bobbed and weaved. His nostrils flared. I realized what was happening, stood, and guided him to my chair. I filled a crystal glass with water from a decanter. He chugged it.

"Thank you," he said. He held out the glass. I refilled it. He drained it. "What will be my punishment?"

---

1 "The King of Lions," Anshul Jubli competes as a lightweight in the Ultimate Fighting Championship (UFC). He was the first Indian to win a fight in the organization.

If *Pa* was shaken by the revelation of the break-in's origins, he did not show it. "No one will know of this but those in this room—and my wife…and Harlow," he said. "Your actions are detestable, but I do not wish to destroy your reputation. That would haunt you for the rest of your life—and sully the Chatwal name as well. First, you will return or replace every article that was removed from Xanadu. If, for reasons I cannot imagine, you have sold any article or squandered the money you took, you *will* make restitution. Effective immediately, you are reassigned to the Logistics Department in Kanniyakumari.[2] The foreman there will determine your responsibilities. Once we divest ourselves of our holdings, you will be responsible to the new owners."

"New owners?"

"Yes," *Pa* said. "No one is going to carry your water anymore, my boy. The Chatwal name will be like any other. If you work hard, you will make something of yourself—or not. Either way, you are on your own."

---

2 A smaller city deep in southern India.

CHAPTER SIXTY-THREE

VIK

HARLOW LAY IN MY ARMS IN the king-sized bed of my room. Neither of my parents had given their permission, but we'd given them no possibility of refusal because we had not asked. Still, to observe the proprieties of the household, Harlow was still spending the nights in the room she was sharing with Lita.

"I need to know something," she said.

"My life is an open book," I said.

"It's about Amrita."

"You want to know if I loved her."

"No," she said. "I will never ask. I never want to know—I never want to hear you say it. Understood?"

"Yes. So, what do you want?"

"Will you tell me?'

"Absolutely."

"Promise—no questions asked?"

"I promise—no questions asked."

"Where can I find her?"

HARLOW

The day was unusually beautiful. Though the sun blazed away, a slight breeze from the north kept the temperature from rising to its customary "hinges of Hell" level. White clouds skittered across a cerulean sky. I looked up into the bleachers and saw a familiar face shaded by a multicolored golf umbrella.

"Hello," I said.

"Well, well, if it isn't my favorite *chhataree* companion," the little man said. [1] "It's been a while since I have seen you at a match."

"It is lovely to see you again, Mister…I'm sorry. I don't recall your name."

"That would be because I never gave it to you," he said. "I am Chaitanya—Chaitanya Thongbam."

"I don't think I've ever heard that surname before," I said.

He offered his sterling water cup without comment. I took a sip.

"It is from the northeastern state of Manipur," he said. "Not many people share it."

"What does your first name mean?" I asked. "If I may be so bold."

"An inquisitive mind is never intrusive," he said. "It means 'consciousness' or 'life.'"

"Fitting," I said. I took another sip and returned the cup. "Thank you."

"It is important to stay hydrated," he said. "But an intelligent woman like you already knows that."

---

1 For more on this character, see Chapter 55 in *Karma Under Fire.*

I pointed to the field. "Are you familiar with any of the players?" I asked.

"Only by reputation," he said. "I am here to see the younger boy. I want to see for myself if the stories of his youthful prowess as true. He's wearing number 63."

"Is that significant."

"Currently worn by Suryakumar Yadav, a middle batsman and occasional right-arm break pitcher for the Mumbai Indians. The youngsters in the orange shirts with the green trim are an all-star team from that area."

Makes sense, I thought.

"I used to play many years ago," he said. "I miss it, so I attend as many matches as possible before karma catches up with me."

"You have plenty of time," I said.

"We have only what we have," he said. "And hopefully, more than we deserve." He applauded a good play in the field. There was a break in the action while the team changed sides. "I was sorry to hear about the postponement of your nuptials."

"You never cease to amaze me with what you know about my personal life," I said. "Things have been a little rough, but they are improving,"

"Never fear, my dear," he said. "The stars are in your favor. Everything will work out."

"I believe they will."

Even now, his eyes remained locked on the field. He grunted when a ball skipped past a fielder. "That one was easy," he said. "The coach will not be pleased, but if he is a good instructor, it will be a chance for the young man to learn." He poured water into the cup from a silver bottle and drank some before sharing it again. "Do not doubt. Maintain hope and trust. All lasting relationships are based on hope and trust. I know whereof I speak.

I have been married to Grizelda for seventy-five years."

"Good heavens," I said. "How old *are* you?"

"Now you are just being nosy," he said. His chuckle sounded like a chirping bird. "I don't mind. I am ninety-two. We were married very young."

"Since I have already proved to be a rude American, would you explain your wife's name?"

"Certainly," he said. "It is the last ingredient of a successful union. Her name means 'endless patience.'"

CHAPTER SIXTY-FOUR

HARLOW

THE GAME CONTINUED.

"Your companion is waiting for you," he said after a while.

"What companion?"

"The woman on the back row, one section removed. Ms. Rai is wearing an enormous hat and sunglasses."

"First," I said, "how do you know who it is?"

"In a former life, I might have been in the Intelligence Service although, as the old expression goes, 'I could tell you, but I'd have to kill you.'" The edges of his mouth turned up a little. "If such were the case, I would be more than accustomed to noticing people in disguise, especially one as poorly executed as hers. She might have thought about a wig, you know. Her hair is one of her best features."

I shook my head. "You are a most amazing man. What else."

"As much as I enjoy your company, and you mine I hope, you did not come to this field today hoping to find me."

"A happy accident," I said.

"Indeed," he said. "For another thing, she have been stealing glimpses at you continually throughout the game. Either she was expecting your visit, or she recognizes you."

"How would she do that?" I asked.

"My dear, are you not acquainted with the contemporary social network?" There was the little chirp again.

"Point taken."

"Lastly," he said, "you spotted her before you recognized me. You were on your way to speak to her but veered off when you saw my umbrella. I assume you are up here screwing up your courage."

"Yes," I said.

"Hope and trust," he said. "Now, go and do whatever it is you came here to do."

HARLOW

I don't know how it was possible, but Amrita Rai was more beautiful close up than on the big screen. Even hidden behind sunglasses the size of coasters her face glowed. She wore a simple, flowered sundress that might have been considered immodest except for the pink long-sleeved shirt she had on underneath. Instead of a fabulous designer chapeau, she was sporting a wide-brimmed straw hat a laborer might wear in the sugarcane field.

Like my umbrella companion, she was riveted to the action, but she held out her off hand to grasp mine. "Ms. Kennedy, I presume."

"Good guess," I said. My comment sounded a little snarkier than I intended. I could feel resentment corkscrewing its way into my stomach.

"Not really," she said. "Ever since the paternity test, I figured you would come calling. You're happy Chatwal isn't the father, but you aren't going to rest easy until you know who is."

"To my everlasting shame, you are correct," I said. I took a deep breath, "Listen, Amrita—"

"If we're going to be friends, you have to call me Ahmi," she said.

"I'm sorry," I said. "Can we start over. And please, call me Harlow. Being friends would be nice."

She shifted in her seat and faced me. She glanced left, then right. There were not a lot of people nearby. When she removed her glasses, I could tell she'd been crying.

"I'd like that," she said. "Might not be easy, but I'd like that a lot."

She began at the beginning—how she met Vik. And the longer she talked, the more distinctly I could hear the voices of all the characters involved.

CHAPTER SIXTY-FIVE

VIK

HERE TODAY…GONE TOMORROW.

That was Ahmi—it's what I'd called her almost from the beginning. The final prep school term had ended. Exams were finished. Once again, I anticipated a position near the top of the class—at least high enough to satisfy *Papa* and convince him I was neither as lazy nor as debauched as he suspected.

Ahmi and I had plans for the evening, plans that included activities of which neither of my parents would have approved, but we'd been going out for just over three years. I wasn't anywhere close to considering "forever"—after all, I was only three days short of prep school graduation and still had my university days ahead—but Ahmi and I had talked a little about the days to come. In retrospect, when we spoke of the future, I did more of the talking than she did.

She was an audiophile—not much musical talent, but she knew and loved all genres. She was particularly fond of old, American rock 'n roll and her favorite group was The Beach Boys.

After we'd been seeing one another for a while, she asked me to listen to one of their cuts, a tune called "Wouldn't It Be Nice." When the group got to one line, I saw her wince.

Baby, then there wouldn't be a single thing we couldn't do.

Oh, we could be married…

And then we'd be happy, oh wouldn't it be nice.

She looked at me from the corner of her eye. "Too much?"

"Nope," I said.

"Too soon?"

"Just about right," I said.

"Okay if I say it's our song."

"Sounds good to me," I said.

Our relationship was easy and low stress. She didn't deal in drama and neither of us smothered. The years passed. It was great.

But, before I knew what was happening, prep school was over, and graduation approached—along with my father.

Papa's face bore no expression—pretty standard for our "serious" conversations. His voice was well modulated, almost flat—very matter of fact.

"Vikram," he said, "it's time for us to talk."

"Sounds good," I said. "I enjoy talking to you. What's the subject today? Cricket? World events? Politics?"

"Your future," he said.

In the back of my mind, I heard a voice: *Uh oh. This cannot be good.*

"Vikram, we have been greatly blessed in this life," he said.

"I know," I said. "I don't take anything for granted. I don't think you spoiled me—"

He interrupted. "No, your *Maata* took care of that."

The laugh we shared was a little uneasy.

"Anyway," I said. "I have never wanted for anything."

"You have had the best of everything," *Pa* said. "Not many young men in India have their own polo pony when they are twelve."

"Not many twelve-year-olds can compete in polo with adults," I said. I winced. "I am sorry, *Pa,* that was arrogant."

"One of your less appealing attributes," he said. A pause. "Apology accepted." There was more coming. I waited. After what seemed an elongated interval, he resumed.

"You and I have talked about your aspirations. There was a time when you wanted to be a professional batsman. And before you say anything else—ah—less than humble, let me assure you that I know you were, and are, good enough to compete at the highest levels."

"Thank you," I said.

"It is not bragging if it is true," he said. "If I may be so bold as to break my own rule about self-promotion, your game reminds me a great deal of the way I used to play when I was a young man."

"I have seen some of the old newspaper clippings *Ma* saved. You swung a mean stick."

"Thank you," he said. "But enough about me. First, there was cricket. Then you toyed with the idea of becoming a chess master." He held up a restraining hand before I launched into another round of patting myself on the back. "I know you were a very young junior master, but you did not have the prolonged concentration the game requires."

I nodded in acceptance of his critique. "Not quite enough action," I said.

"Your ma and I talked just before I came here."

Uh oh.

"She tells me you want to pursue a life in the kitchen—like a woman."

I was savvy enough to hold my immediate response. This needed to be measured. "As you know, *Papa,* most of the world-renown chefs are men," I said. "Tom Colicchio, Daniel Boulud, and Chris Cannon in New York. There's Timothy Hollingworth in California." I stopped. "You don't care, do you?"

"If you mean, am I interested in knowing men who have devoted themselves to living in the kitchen…" (he did not say, "like a woman" again, but he held off long enough for me to know he was thinking it) … "then, no—I am not. But my level of interest is not important. I want to know about yours."

"Whether I am interested?"

"No, whether you are *committed.* I know you. You will not want to work for or with anyone. You are a wonderful athlete, but you are *always* the captain. You are a natural leader. You are not going to be satisfied with being…I believe the term is, 'a line chef.'"

He waited. And then waited some more.

"No sir," I said. "I dream of opening my own place." *In for a penny,* I thought. "My own place. I want to introduce authentic, Indian food in a totally new way—in America."

I could see his mind working. He was a lousy card player because his eyes always told everything. The rejection was there. He was trying to figure out how to soften the blow—to determine how best to inform me that I was condemned to a life behind a desk in Chatwal Industries, an endless string of board meetings, personnel issues, corporate engagements. My stomach started to churn.

Then…

"Okay," he said. "I will make the arrangements. But there are three, immutable conditions."

"Yes sir."

"The first is that you graduate from university with a degree in business. If the restaurant concept fails, I will want you prepared for Chatwal Enterprises."

"Absolutely," I said. "I will need the expertise in the food business as well. The second?"

"You go to Harvard Business School and work in the financial industry in America for a while. You will need the foundation for whatever you choose in life."

"Done," I said. "The last?"

I was willing to jump through fiery hoops, wrestle a tiger, wrangle a cobra—anything. Except for what he said next.

"Marriage."

CHAPTER SIXTY-SIX

VIK

PAPA OUTLINED THE PLAN. I LISTENED. I ignored the protests screaming in my head and agreed.

After my father left, I walked down the road to Ahmi's school. She was not there.

She was gone.

It was the worst night of my life.

AMRITA

Vik's door was cracked when I snuck in his dorm. School was done for both of us. Since it was graduation time, I had a special present for him. We'd been very careful in our physical relationship, but once we turned eighteen, we became bolder. Our times together were limited because of strict chaperoning. It was hard to find "alone" time, but, as they say, "Where there's a will…"

Still, we'd never done it in his room. This would be the perfect graduation present. What were they going to do if we were caught? Nothing—no way anyone was going to expel Vikram Chatwal for inappropriate conduct *after* classes were completed. The Chatwal family was as close to royalty as you would find in Mumbai, and I was a girl from the wrong side of everything was lucky enough to get a scholarship to a good school.

That night, I was wearing my raincoat and very little else. My hands were a little clammy. I was not daring by nature. I loved a good time, but for the most part, I played by the rules. Vikram had been my one *massive* exception. I knew I loved him from the moment we danced the first time.

The door was cracked a little. My hand was on the knob when I heard someone else in the room. I was a little surprised. Vik was a senior and enjoyed the privilege of a single. It was well after hours. His friends would have already been in for the night. I moved closer. The voice was obviously an adult. I heard a terrifying word.

"Marriage."

Vik's voice answered almost immediately. "Okay, I agree to your conditions, *Pa*. But my choice, right?"

"By that, you mean the young woman at the school down the road with whom you have been spending so much time," his father said. "Yes, I know all about her and I suspect there is more to the dalliance than you would prefer to discuss."

Vik said nothing. Mr. Chatwal spoke again.

"From everything I have ascertained, she has done laudable work considering her background. Not very many scholarship students can boast her accomplishments."

"She is brilliant and talented," Vik said.

I smiled. *Glad you noticed.*

His father's voice carried an edge. "Stop," he said. "I have no doubt she is a very nice young woman, but you are a *Chatwal*. There are certain standards you are expected to meet, particularly in the matter of your spouse. It is great for you to have friends from all walks of life, but you must marry within a certain scope. Your lady friend is not of our class or background."

I inched the door open a tad, praying all the while it would not squeak. I could see the man's hands folded in his lap. His voice was level, but I detected some strain while he continued. "Vikram, you have agreed to my terms, the last of which is marriage. Your decisions end there. You will wed a woman selected for you by your mother and me. In fact, Isha has already identified a candidate we think is most suitable—a lovely young woman from a good family. Her name is Haiya Tak."

I waited for Vik to say something. After two full minutes, I heard him. "Yes, father."

It was the worst night of my life.

RISHI

It was well past eleven in the evening when I heard a faint tap at my door. I always slept with the lock on—no telling what sort of evil prank Vik and the others might concoct. I rose, flipped on the dim light next to my bed, and rubbed my head on the way across the room.

When I cracked the door, someone shoved it and knocked me back. By the time I recovered, the door was shut and locked. I heard the click.

I blinked several times, not believing the vision in front of my eyes—Ahmi, a raincoat around her ankles, naked to the waist.

"It's now or never," she said.

It was the greatest night of my life.

CHAPTER SIXTY-SEVEN

HARLOW

"Rishi?" I shouted the name so loudly that Ahmi immediately dropped her head and put her shades back on while several of the spectators stared. When they went back to the game, she raised her head.

"Didn't see that one coming, did you?" she said.

"Vik is absolutely certain it was Nitin."

"So would everyone else. Fact of the matter is, it could have been. But when I knocked on his door, he was either out partying or passed out on his bed. Those two competed in everything like two bulls. Every game was blood sport. The coaches finally quit putting them on opposite teams in scrimmages because someone was going to be killed."

I could tell she was embarrassed. "It's okay," I said. "You don't have to tell me if you don't want to."

"No," she said, "it's alright. I need to get this out." Deep breath. "I was angry but mostly I was hurt. I wanted to lash out—to do something that would sting Chatwal. When Nitin didn't answer, I went to the room next door."

"Rishi? I've never met him, but from everything Vik told me, he wasn't your type."

A loud "Ha!" exploded from her mouth. "I was eighteen. I didn't have a type. Since I was with Chatwal, he thought *he* was my type—you know, tall, handsome, rich."

"Like Nitin."

"Nitin comes from money…not Chatwal money…but his father has done every well as a commodities trader."

"To hear Vik tell it, they were closer than two hogs in a tote sack."

"You Americans love your images, don't you?" she said.

"I reckon," I said—just to drive home the point. I kept looking for reasons to dislike the woman—a hint of phony baloney—some sense she was playing a scene instead of being genuine. I could not find one. She was forthright, winsome, genuine, and abso-frickin'-lutely gorgeous. "So, what gives with Nitin's ghost act. He doesn't call or write. He almost never answers texts—skips the reunions."

"You know about the gag we pulled on Chatwal, right?" she asked.

"Classic," I said. "Not very many put on over on him. "Served him right—well done."

"Thank you," she said. "Well, I knew there was no way in the world those chuckleheads could pull it off without at least one rehearsal. Turned out we needed three. After the last one, I stepped into the ladies' room. When I came out, everyone was gone—except for Nitin. He was outside cursing at his car—a brand new BMW. Some sort of electrical problem. I offered him a ride home. Met his wife and three children."

"I don't think Vik knows he's married," I said.

"I didn't either," she said. "Lovely bunch, but that's not the point. On the way home, I asked him about his absences from the Musketeers reunions. I see Rishi regularly—our industries intersect—so I knew when the guys got together. Nitin told me he still loved everyone, still reveled in the memories of prep school, but he never quite got comfortable with how competitive he was around Chatwal. Nitin's not upset or resentful, he's just moved on."

"Moved on?" I asked.

She looked over the top of her sunglasses. "Seriously, Harlow, how many high school chums do you still hang out with?"

"Good point," I said. "Is there more you want to tell me?"

"Yes, if you care to listen."

CHAPTER SIXTY-EIGHT

AMRITA

THE FIRST THING I DID ON the morning after I overheard the conversation between Chatwal and his father was ditch my phone and get a new one. I didn't want to hear Chatwal's voice, not after what I have done with Rishi—and I mostly certainly was not going to meet him face to face.

I didn't think Rishi would be a problem. He was a nice enough guy—remarkably clumsy as a lover, his experience was limited—but like most guys, I assumed he would bask in the glow of his "conquest" for a few days before it ever occurred to him to call me. Of course, he also had to see Chatwal on a regular basis. Not my problem.

Guilt beat on me with the merciless of the Indian summer sun. I imaged people were looking at me strangely. The shame Hester Prynne felt was suddenly all too real. Betrayal was not in my nature. I had reacted without thought—and I had ruined a future about which I regularly dreamed.

I knew I was pregnant within the first few weeks. Don't ask me how. I can't claim "womanly intuition" because I was all of eighteen, but my body felt different. I went to the chemist and got a test. I was right.

Disappearing was the thing to do, and it was pretty easy. My only living relative, my *daadee ma*, had died during my penultimate year at prep school. There was no one to contact.

I was not of a high enough class to chase an arranged marriage, even if I could have afforded a matchmaker. Besides, my purity was long gone—not so much my virginity, but my integrity. How could I have done what I did? Was I really so petty not to have given Chatwal a chance to discuss the issue with me?

More likely, I suspected he would cast me aside. I was a scholarship student at a second-tier girls' school. Some things in my country will probably never change. I understood my culture. The wondrous time with Chatwal and his friends had been most illuminating about the ways and wiles of my nation's upper crust. Though Chatwal was unfailingly polite, gallant, and protective of me, when I was around his friends, I could almost taste their entitlement.

They spoke of fabulous vacations I'd never even imagined. The cost of the casual clothes they wore when they were not in their school uniforms of khaki pants, white shirts, and school blazers could have fed several families in my hometown for weeks. In my more honest moments, I realized I liked being around the "haves"—and I regularly fantasized about what life might be like if I ever became Mrs. Vikram Chatwal.

The lovely illusion was shattered with one word from *Papa* Chatwal's mouth: "Marriage."

I had never seen anything more beautiful than my son's face on the day he was born. I named him Pratham because, for me, he would be "always first." I found a job as a domestic in Bangalore for a friendly family that allowed me to bring my son to work. I told them I was a widow. He was a good boy, never fussy except when he needed to eat. Somehow, he knew he needed to be cooperative if we were to survive.

I worked long hours and saved as much money as I could. My son and I were not going to be without forever—I was very determined. And then it happened.

Film and stage history is full of stories of stars discovered by chance. Vin Diesel was caught breaking into a theater with some friends. Instead of calling the police, the owner cast the boy in his play. Rosario Dawson was watching a commercial being filmed outside her apartment when the director walked over and asked her if she'd ever done any acting. Pamela Anderson's face and figure appeared on a Jumbotron shot at a BC Lions game, then exploded onto the celebrity scene. Norma Jean Mortensen was working in an aircraft factory. An Army photographer snapped her picture, and the legend of Marilyn Monroe was born.

The same thing happened to me. I was sitting on a park bench with my three-year-old. Pratham threw bits of bread to the birds and squealed in delight when they scurried after the morsels. A round little man walked up to me.

"Excuse me," he said. "Are you someone famous?"

It was a public place. The stranger posed no threat. I was not afraid. "I am not," I said.

He handed me a business card. "If you come by my office any time in the next week, you will be."

Two days later, I did. He was right. And I was.

CHAPTER SIXTY-NINE

AMRITA

Pratham's paternity was not an issue for me, so I never bothered to investigate the matter. I did not care. In a fit of anger and despair, I had made a poor decision. Now, karma dictated I would live alone with my son. But Pratham represented a joy, not a punishment. We reveled in each other's company. Every minute we shared afforded the possibility of a new adventure, even if only in the Land of Make Believe.

I was on location one day. Travel presented no problems. After school, I'd changed my name from Ahmi Varma to Amrita Rai—pulled the last name out of the air. Once I was established, "people" took care of my every need, one of which was proper identification. Even the biggest stars require passports and the like.

As in every country, money gave access. The day before my first shoot outside of India, the director handed me an official Indian passport. I didn't ask any questions.

Along the route of my career, I had taken every role I could get. My first appearance was as a waitress in a forgettable rom-com. But the director liked the way I looked on camera, so he insisted I get a few lines—meaningless banter about the menu, but I got extended "face time."

Someone else saw me and I landed another part—this time with a credit. Within three years, I was a named co-star in a movie featuring several of India's leading actors. Against all logic, I received a Film Awards nomination. I always suspected the Academy simply needed another name to read at the ceremony since the winner was a foregone conclusion.

My agent—I had acquired a very good one by this time—kept fielding calls. I insisted that he tell me about all of them, even the ones he thought were dogs. I never took more than a week between gigs. Pratham always accompanied me. I made sure he had excellent tutors. He was a bright child, quick to grasp concepts. There were always a lot of children on the set. No one ever asked about anyone's parentage.

Pratham had a great, imaginative mind. But we discovered his real genius through a happy accident.

As I mentioned, we were involved in a location shoot. After we'd wrapped for the day, several members of the crew were fooling around with a cricket ball and bat—taking turns and wagering on who could launch the ball the farthest.

"May I try, *Mummyji*," Pratham asked.

Overprotective as I was, I hesitated. One of the grips heard the question and came over. He took Pratham by the hand. "I will watch him, Ms. Rai. I promise, no harm will come to him."

Pratham trotted over to the group. Someone produced a smaller bat and showed him how to hold it. "The bowler will bounce the ball," he said.

Pratham bristled a little. "I know how cricket is played," he said. He immediately lowered his head. "I am sorry. That was rude."

"Buck up, old boy," the man said. "We're all chums here."

Pratham watched one pitch go by. It sailed wide of the wicket.

"Throw me a good one," Pratham said. "I won't be swinging at rubbish."

The bowler smiled. He trotted forward and bounced a lazy pitch toward my son. Pratham's bat flashed so fast I wasn't sure I'd seen it. The ball rocketed over several trailers to the great delight of all the players.

"Harder," Pratham said. "My *mummy* could have hit that one."

He smiled at me in his impish way. The bowler rubbed up the ball, then unleashed a savage pitch. Pratham hit is so high, I was surprised it did not bring rain.

And thus, we uncovered his greatest ability. For lack of a better term, my son was a cricket savant.

CHAPTER SEVENTY

AMRITA

I HAD NOT THOUGHT ABOUT THE identity of Pratham's father in years. It could only be either Rishi or Chatwal, and the chances of it being the latter were much higher. I had run into Rishi a few times at industry banquets and the like over the years. The company where he worked routinely set up the parties. Our conversations were always cordial—and brief. Neither of us ever mentioned "that night." He was, after all, at his job and did not have a lot of time for reminiscing—or questions.

Since Pratham never attended such soirees, I imagined Rishi had no idea I even had a child. Surely if he had seen the boy, he might have put two and two together.

According to the grapevine, always alive and well in India, Chatwal was in America. He'd honored his agreement with his father, attended university, and graduated from Harvard School of Business. As far as I knew, he was working for an investment group across the Atlantic.

One afternoon during a brief hiatus from filming—I was now routinely starring in features—I heard an interesting tidbit.

It seemed Chatwal's arranged engagement had steered onto the rocks. Rumor and speculation surrounded the entire affair. Some said infidelity was involved—didn't sound like him. I was the philanderer. Others suggested a problem with alcohol or illicit drugs. Highly unlikely. One account purported that Chatwal was closeted. I laughed out loud.

Time marched on. Late one afternoon about a week after Pratham's eighth birthday, a messenger service delivered an envelope to my door. After I tipped him, I went into the den and opened it. Inside was a check from my agent Rohan. It was for fifteen thousand dollars, U.S. There was a note.

Amrita, Yesterday, I opened a letter to you. I assumed it was from a fan. There was a check made out to our agency—in rupees. The memo bore your name. The note (unsigned) said an equal amount would be mailed every month. I have no idea what the money is for, but the sender very clearly intended for you to have it. The signature was illegible but the name on the check was Chatwal Enterprises. You owe me no explanation (unless you have hired another agent—haha). Your business is your own. Just let me know if there is anything related to this matter—or any other—wherein you require my assistance. Rohan I had no idea how Chatwal knew but given the reach of the empire his father captained, I figured there were ways. It was naïve of me, but I chose to believe the matter was settled. I considered the check, then looked at a picture of Pratham I kept on the table next to the couch.

"Well, my son," I said, "it appears your *Pa* is trying to do the right thing.

CHAPTER SEVENTY-ONE

HARLOW

"Does Rishi know now?" I asked.

"Called him the day I got the results of the DNA test," I said. "If it wasn't Chatwal—had to be him. He was devastated."

"Didn't want to be a father? Too much responsibility?"

"No," she said. "He was crushed because he had missed so much of Pratham's life."

"Where to from here?" I asked.

"Rishi and I have been talking on the phone. His travel schedule is almost as crazy as mine. He's a good guy. We have a lot in common."

"Really?"

"Yes. Like me, he was a scholarship student."

"Seems like he'd have resented Vik."

"Not at all," she said. "Loves the guy. Unlike all the other Richy Riches—"

"Nice reference," I said.

"I'm an actress, remember," she said. "Macauley Culkin, John Larroquette, Christine Ebersole—I've watched more movies than you can count."

"I can relate," I said. "Daddy was a film junkie."

"I knew I liked you," she said. "Don't look so surprised. It's all good. Anyway, for all his money and privilege and despite all the *crap* Chatwal owns—you know about the polo ponies?"

"Yep."

"Well, regardless, in our school days, he acted like a regular guy. He knew he was just as full of shit as everyone else. Seemed like he went off the deep end a little when he cut the apron strings and went to America. I mean he was in *People Magazine's* 'Sexiest People' edition three years in a row. Really?"

"I know," I said. "Sort of ridiculous."

"But predictable," she said. "He spent so much time trying to be a regular guy, only natural he went a little nut for a while. But something tells me you would not be with him if he hadn't gotten his act together."

"We've had our moments," I said.

"And you always will, I suspect," she said. "But what do I know. I swore off men after that one night."

"Seriously?" I asked.

"No kidding," she said. "The studio always asks me to go out with the next hot actor, but to quote Damon Wayans, 'Homey don't play that.'"[1]

"Nobody?" I asked. "You sound like my pre-Vikram life."

"Then you know the truth. Sometimes being happy and alone is better than being with someone and miserable."

"That'll preach," I said.

She stared at me and shook her head. "Like I said, Americans

---

1 Catchphrase of Homey D. Clown, played by Damon Wayans. Homey is Herman Simpson, a hostile, bitter convict condemned to a never-ending sentence of community service.

and their expressions." She lowered her voice as if afraid someone might eavesdrop. I think it was for dramatic effect. The closest person was about thirty feet away and upwind. Our conversation was not going to carry. "Understand this. I loved Chatwal, still do in the nostalgic idealism of my younger days. But it never would have worked—not then at least. I may be a *big star* now, but I grew up on what Americans would call the wrong side of the tracks. His parents would have never—I mean not if the Earth had been hit by an asteroid and I was the only available young woman left on the planet never—have approved of our marriage. You understand, don't you."

"I do."

"If Ma and Pa Chatwal have joined the rest of the twenty-first century and are willing to put their stamp of approval on your union, go for it if you want—and may all the gods, angels, ancestors, and whoever else you need bless you from now until the end of time. I am dead serious." She took a moment. "Oh and tell whatever stalker at Chatwal Enterprises is sending me money to stop. Now, it's creepy."

I don't know why—I hugged her. She hugged back.

It was, indeed, all good.

CHAPTER SEVENTY-TWO

VIK

THE NEXT TWO WEEKS WENT BY in a blur. Every day began with a quick breakfast where *Pa* and I lined out the tasks for the day. We were about our duties long before anyone else arose. *Pa* huddled in his office with a retinue of accountants, attorneys, and executives. They were outlining the transition once a deal was in place. I was tasked with locating and vetting potential buyers.

No one was waiting in line to purchase Chatwal Enterprises— the idea of the conglomerate being on the market was beyond plausible. But everyone took my call and the moment I stated my purpose, I heard nothing but enthusiasm on the other end of the line. After five days, the list of potential buyers was littered with the names of the biggest corporations and investment groups in the world.

"I don't want to sound gauche," Harlow said after dinner one evening, "but…"

"You want to know how much, right?" I asked. "A normal question since *we* are in for twenty percent."

"Twenty-*five*," she said. "Don't forget who you're speaking with."

"Sorry," I said. "Indeed, you hold a considerable stake in this." I stared off in the distance and struck my best "thinking deep thoughts" pose.

"Quit screwing around and tell me," she said.

"Well, I don't have exact numbers because we haven't entered into negotiations. And something like this will take time—considerable time. Even after the deal is struck, nothing will be finalized probably for a year or so."

"*How much?*" She poked me in the ribs.

"Okay, okay…and *ow.*" I raised my hands in full surrender. "Like I said, no exact numbers, but once this is done, you and I could probably buy most of the NFL."

"Holy samolies!" she said. "We'll have more money than Carter has little pills!"

I shook my head. "One of these days, I would appreciate *English,* but I think I understand. Yes, we will be very wealthy. We will be able to do anything we want…buy whatever our hearts desire…go anywhere at any time."

Neither of us spoke while we let the reality set in.

"You really want to live that way?" she asked.

"Not in a million years."

HARLOW

We talked a long time. I was glad we were on the same page. We were both entrepreneurs of a sort. My jewelry business was nowhere near as successful as Bombay Baby, but I was making headway. Some of the nicer stores in Atlanta had placed orders with me. And we both knew the restaurant would be expanding sometime soon—probably within the year.

"What do you think about living off what we make?" I asked.

"Sounds good to me," Vik said.

"So, you going to sell your polo ponies?"

His smile was genuine. "Let's not get crazy," he said. "But, since my folks are going to move to America, trying to ship those lovely animals seems a little cruel. So, yes, I will sell the ponies… and the boats."

"Sounds like a plan," I said. "Any idea where your mother and father will live?"

"Had a few places in mind," he said, "but *Pa* blew them up today."

"Change of heart?"

"Not really," he said. "But they've decided not to move to Atlanta. *Ma* doesn't want to 'cramp our style.'"

"Sounds like code for being afraid she might walk in on us while we're practicing making babies."

"Exactly," Vik said. "Frankly, I think *Pa* is relieved. I imagine he's a little reluctant to spend his retirement as an on-call babysitting service."

"Makes sense to me. Bet he wants something close enough to visit but far enough away that we won't drop the kids off on the way to the airport."

"Caught him researching houses on Sea Island yesterday."

"Great place to visit," I said. I yawned. "I'm beat. Lita and I shopped all day. Getting ready for a wedding is hard work."

Vik was always most gorgeous when he was smiling. "You think that's tough. Wait until you have to live with me full-time."

I kissed him. "Can't wait," I said. I leaned in to kiss him again—with some intent.

"Easy," he said. "Let's not start something we can't finish."

"Good point," I said. "Night, babe."

"Goodnight," he said. "Tell Lita I said hello. Haven't seen much of her with everything that's going on."

I stopped at the door. "Speaking of Lita—we've got to do something about that situation."

CHAPTER SEVENTY-THREE

VIK

I ALWAYS KNEW MY FAMILY HAD money, but the enormity of our prosperity hit me when I saw numbers. I'd joke with Harlow about buying sports teams but, jeez, the amount of cash we would receive boggled my mind. We could not have burned through the money if we tried—and neither of us wanted the lifestyle of the idle rich.

"I've got an idea," I said.

"'Hit me with your best shot,'" Harlow said.

"What movie is that?" I asked.

"OMG." Harlow looked stunned. "I'm fixin' to marry a guy who doesn't know Pat Benatar. Say it ain't so, Joe."

"Well," I said. "If we're going to be married, you are going to have to quit speaking in code. But never mind, like I said, I think I'm on to something."

♨ HARLOW

Vik's concept was stunning.

"It like the School for Kids Who Can't Read Good," I said.

"Exactly," he said. I'd made him watch *Zoolander*. "Only it's about cooking and will be for folks that are slightly older. We'll have at several tracks. Right now, I can see three. One would be for the everyday citizen who wants to learn to cook or do it better—maybe a young woman who's engaged but a little unsure about her skills in the kitchen."

"What about a guy who wants to learn the basics?" she asked.

"Unlikely given social pressures," he said, "but we will give everyone due consideration."

"Not everyone in this country has a kitchen," I said.

"Already thought of that," he said. "We'll offer opportunities for open fire cooking as well as something more modern."

"You said three tracks."

"Second one will be for men and women who are considering working in the food industry. We'll do basic techniques, cover a lot of different styles—I mean, everyone in a commercial kitchen needs to know how to make a decent omelet, right?"

"Right."

"But not everyone needs to know the secrets of preparing sweetbreads."

"Or anyone." I mimed a gag. "I'm not big on eating internal organs."

"One person's internal organs are someone else's pièce de résistance."

"Don't even think about it," I said.

"Duly noted," I said. "But we will concentrate on Indian

cuisine. Our students will be able to find work all over the world."

"Third one?"

"People who are considering opening an Indian restaurant," he said. "And I do not mean those who want to purchase and profit. No, these folks must be chefs. They don't need a piece of paper, but they will have to demonstrate a certain level of skill."

"People can scale up from one track to another, right?" I asked.

"Absolutely," he said. "And here's the great part. There's no charge. We'll start with a small test group in each grade, as it were. We'll move them along while we hammer out the kinks. I am more interested in quality that quantity. I want it to mean something when someone announces they are a graduate of the Kennedy School of Cuisine."

I must have looked strange.

"You don't like the name?" he asked.

"I love it," I said. "Not very Indian though."

He wrapped his arms around me. I was enveloped by his warmth. "Darling," he said, "none of this happens without you— none of it. You deserve some small recognition. So, are you okay with the name?"

"On one condition," I said.

"Name it."

"I never have to give a cooking demonstration."

"Oh, Harlow," he said. "I want to *attract* people to the school—not run them off."

He got out of the room just in time to avoid the pillow I threw. He ducked his head back in. "By the way, I think this will kill two birds with one stone."

I reloaded with another pillow, and he disappeared. I heard him cackling all the way down the hall.

"My god, I love that guy."

CHAPTER SEVENTY-FOUR

LITA

IN MY WILDEST DREAMS AS A child, I never believed I would be summoned to the office of Mr. Kavyansh Chatwal. But he was my *chacha* by marriage. My first knock was so timid there was no answer.

Suck it up. I knocked harder.

"Enter."

Instead of stygian darkness, I found a room with floor-to-ceiling windows.

Wow, did they re-do this place after the break-in.

I guess I was gawking. Mr. Chatwal's resonant voice came from my right. "Do you like the renovation, my dear?" he asked.

"It's stunning," I said. "Very...very..."

"Don't be afraid to say 'contemporary' or 'chic,'" he said. "That's what I was going for. I doubt we will sell Xanadu, but if we are going to have a place to visit, I want it to reflect the newness of our situation."

Harlow had told me all about the plans...selling Chatwal Enterprises...the new school... and, best of all, *the wedding.*

When the family moved back to Xanadu, I'd tagged along. No one objected, so I figured I was okay.

"My dear," he said, "I believe it is time for you to leave."

Ooops, spoke too soon.

I breathed in through my nose to get centered. "I understand, Mr. Chatwal," I said. "You and your wife have been more than gracious to allow me to stay so very long. I apologize for any inconvenience."

"Nonsense," he said. "You are like a daughter to us now. You are welcome to visit whenever you wish—wherever we are living. But, for the time being and to restore balance in the Universe, you must reunite with your husband."

Life over the past however many weeks—I'd lost count—had finally enabled me to settle a little. I'd worked through my rage with Amar's mother, but still have not quite figured out how we were going to pick up the pieces as long as there was so much outside interference.

"Yes, sir," was all I could think to say.

Mr. Chatwal moved to behind his desk. He motioned me to a chair. I sat. "Your life is not my business," he said, "but it is my concern inasmuch as you are dear to Harlow, who is dear to us. If you will allow, I believe I may have an idea to help you."

"I'm all ears," I said.

"Would you like some tea?" he asked.

An odd question, but… "Yes, that would be lovely."

He pushed a button on his desk. Less than thirty awkwardly quiet seconds later, there was a knock. "Enter," Mr. Chatwal said.

A sterling tea set on a sterling tray came through the door—carried by—"Amar!"

I jumped from the chair. My husband barely had time to set down the tray before I threw my arms around him. Propriety be damned, I kissed him full on the mouth. After a while, Mr. Chatwal cleared his throat.

"Excuse me," I said. I released my death grip. I could feel myself blushing. "I just haven't seen him in a while."

"As is readily apparent," Mr. Chatwal said.

He pointed to a chair. Amar sat. Mr. Chatwal poured tea for us, gave us each a cup prepared as we requested, then returned to his seat.

"I have a proposal," he said. "You are free to refuse it. I have no desire to impose my will on you. Are you interested?"

We both said yes. He pushed the button again. Vikram and Harlow entered. Vik was carrying a sizeable cardboard tube. He directed us to swing our chairs around; Amar was to my right. Harlow was across from me. Vik stood at the open spot. He extracted a set of blueprints from the tube and spread them out on a table he had placed in the middle.

"Amar," he said, "you are probably wondering why I asked you to come over."

"I guess you needed a butler," Amar said. He pointed to the tea service and grinned. "Do I get the job?"

"Absolutely not," Mr. Chatwal said from his spot. "You are monumentally overqualified."

"You have a business degree from Wharton," I said. "So, I want to put it to use." He pointed to the heading on the plans. "This is my...I mean, our...new concept."

CHAPTER SEVENTY-FIVE

VIK

AMAR SAID YES. I OFFERED HIM several days to think over whether he wanted to direct the Kennedy School, but he insisted he didn't need any time.

"You don't even know what it's going to pay," I said.

"Vikram," he said, "you are my *bhai*. There is no way you are going to be less than fair." He looked me directly in the eye. "And I would rather die than do anything to disappoint you."

He was well aware of that Sajin had done.

"But why not take some time?" I asked. "It's going to be located in Mumbai."

Lita had not said a word, but she fairly jumped out of her chair. "Precisely!" she said. "It's over fourteen hundred kilometers from—" She stopped.

"My mother," Amar said. He touched his wife's hand. "No worries. She was driving me crazy as well. I just couldn't say much. If it's any consolation, she has been pretty upset about your absence. She knows she was the cause."

"I should apologize," Lita said.

Everyone started a little when Mr. Chatwal spoke. "No, my dear," he said. "That is the old way. We still have many customs worth preserving, but I believe—from everything I have been able to ascertain—that Bhavita has been her usual meddlesome and irascible self. It's time for her to make amends. And, with some encouragement from my beautiful Rachana, I am sure we can make that happen."

"Then, again, I accept," Amar said. "I will need to give notice. When do we start?"

"Nothing will happen with the sale of Chatwal Enterprises for some time," I said, "but I imagine I can find an interested investor who will be willing to front the money for this concept."

I looked across my father's desk.

"I might know someone," he said.

"At no interest," I said.

"Well…" He was the master of the poignant pause. "I still imagine someone can be found."

CHAPTER SEVENTY-SIX

SOPHIA

I ALWAYS WONDERED WHY SOME RELIGIONS emphasized the importance of silence. After several months away from Atlanta, I understood—at least in part. I had not read a paper, watched television, or powered up my phone in all that time. Everyone knew I could take care of myself, and no one had turned out a search and rescue mission.

I enjoyed healing on many levels at the Six Senses Spa nestled in the opulent halls of an ancient women's palace near the heart of Delhi. Nothing like round the clock meditation, clay masks, and massages to reset the balance. Singing bowls and a small brass gong helped chase my demons away one by one. I owned the mistakes of my past. I accepted my part. But I refused to let my past define me.

Life was clearer now. I felt stronger, happier, and healed when I knocked on the door. It opened.

"Hello, Harlow," I said.

HARLOW

My screams were so loud, I was surprised no one called 9-1-1. I bear hugged Mother, then dragged her into the house. Then I stopped dead in my tracks.

"Wait a minute," I said. "Why didn't you just walk in?"

"I felt like I needed permission to reenter your life," she said. "I sort of abandoned you in your hour of need."

"True," I said, "but that's ancient history. I have *a lot* to tell you."

And, for the next six hours, that's exactly what I did.

CHAPTER SEVENTY-SEVEN

HARLOW

Three months later

I HAD DEBATED THE COLOR OF my panetar. Lita had worn red at her wedding, very traditional. I was not wild about copying her, so I decided to read up on Indian weddings before I made up my mind. I discovered I was free to wear any color I please—there were no hard and fast rules. I liked orange and peach...either would look great with my complexion. I had been forced to make up my mind before I left India; ninety days was not a lot of time.

I discovered a few things. Red symbolized power, beauty, and fertility in India. Emperors and queens of that magical land had worn the vibrant color for centuries. When I realized how the color was emblematic of creating something new with a determination to carry forward the values and traditions of the past, I was convinced.

"Red it is," I said.

"Perfect," Sophia had said when I told her about it. "It will be my gift." She shook her head when I began to protest. "I know all about the tradition, but there is no uncle on my side to give it to you and it will mean a lot to me." She took on a sly expression. "But this offer is only good for *one* wedding."

Her laugh was genuine as was mine.

"Trust me, Mother," I said. "I have no intention of doing this again—ever."

"Good," she said. "Vikram is a wonderful young man. I know you will both be very happy."

When the ceremony commenced, I occupied one side of a scarlet and golf antarpat. It was in place like a screen to prevent Vik from seeing me when I entered the room. We were in the massive great hall at Xanadu. Since weddings are affairs with invited guests, therefore a private function, they are never held in a Hindu temple. By tradition, my soul united with Vik's once the antarpat was lowered, the point at which we would begin our spiritual journey together.

When the cloth sank low enough for me to see Vik, I could barely breath. He'd chosen a more contemporary look, a Bandh-gala suit of shimmering white linen, white jutti shoes, and a stunning white turban trimmed in gold to match the edges of my gown. A brilliant peacock feather was attached to the front of the headgear and swept back like a contrail of iridescent blue, green, brown, and yellow.

For a moment I thought the feather might be his idea of a joke and I almost laughed. But I remembered his name meant "bright peacock." This was an homage to his heritage in general and, more specifically, to his parents who sat beaming on the front row.

VIK

Nothing, not sunrise over the Bay of Bengal or a double rainbow after a summer storm—nothing was more radiant than the vision of Harlow when the antarpat dropped. I wondered if I was suffering some sort of respiratory failure because my throat constricted and I had trouble drawing breath, but I realized I had never experienced a more joyful moment in my entire life.

Harlow Kennedy was going to be my bride.

HARLOW

I leaned forward and placed a garland around his neck. I'd selected sunflowers, quintessentially American. They looked amazing against the stark white of his jacket. There was a sound from the congregation. I took a quick, sideways glance. Mother was sobbing into her omnipresent monogramed handkerchief.

VIK

For the *jayamala* ceremony, I had asked for jasmines and lotus flowers for the necklace I dropped over Harlow's gorgeous neck. She was now a daughter of India. *Ma* joined the sniffing chorus of weeping mothers.

Sophia came forward in an understated blue saree and poured water over my hands. It trickled from my palms to Harlow's—a symbol of the continuum of generations. The sacred stream joined our two families in perpetuity.

HARLOW

We lit the sacred fire. At first, I thought my hand was trembling until I realized it was Vik's.

I whispered as softly as I could. "Nervous?"

"No," he said. "I've never been more thrilled.

I wanted to kiss him, but I remained decorous.

VIK

I offered my hand to Harlow while she stepped over a rock next to the sacred flame, an act through which she demonstrated both her inner strength and her willingness to overcome any obstacle. We bowed our heads and asked Agni, the god of fire and divine knowledge, to safeguard our home and to serve as the messenger for our prayers for children, health, and long lives together.

HARLOW

When we mentioned "children," Vik squeezed my arm, and I flashed back for a moment. I didn't think I would make it through the prayer, but my rock was next to me. He would not let me fall or falter. We completed the prayer, then circled the fire four times.

Vik sprinkled red kumkum powder into the part between my braids. I understood the powder was a symbol of my place in society as a married woman, it was an essential part of the ceremony.

VIK

I was careful with the powder. Her hair was stunning. I did not want to ruin what obviously represented hours of work. But the powder was important to *Ma*, who had been Harlow's champion.

We walked seven steps together. With every stride, we repeated traditional prayers for children...character...prosperity... involvement in the world...

HARLOW

...involvement in the world...an industrious life...the seasons of life...and friendship.

When we completed the steps, the crowd erupted and assailed us with a shower of flowers. Orchids, blossoms of lotus and jasmine, marigolds, and roses rained on us and covered our shoes while we embraced and kissed.

"I love you, Mr. Chatwal," I said.

VIK

Her face beamed at me through a torrent of fragrant flowers. "I love you, Harlow," I said.

CHAPTER SEVENTY-EIGHT

HARLOW

MANY OF MY FAVORITE MEMORIES OF my father involved watching old movies together. He especially liked westerns. One scene played out in almost every story—no, not the gunfight in the street—the one in the bar. The doors swung open, boots echoed on the wooden floor, the piano stopped jangling, the saloon ladies gasped, the gamblers lowered their cards, and everyone stared at the new arrival.

With considerable modification of the scene, that was how Sophia walked into the reception in the ballroom of the Imperial Club. Even though the band kept playing, there was a discernible hitch in the song tempo. Waiters momentarily forgot where they were supposed to go …bartenders quit shaking martinis…and every single person—male and female alike—locked eyes on the vision entering the room.

Sophia had changed clothes. She'd worn a modest, attractive outfit to the wedding, a muted blue saree in which she looked wonderful. Hair up, no jewelry, simple and elegant. But this was a party—and Sophia knew how to get down with the best.

Her gown was brilliant yellow. It hugged her toned contours like a Formula One driver maneuvering through a hairpin turn. A daring slit up the left side exposed her stunning leg from the straps of her Louboutins to the middle of her shapely thigh. A diamond and emerald choker encircled her long neck. Her makeup screamed, "Perfection!"

She glided across the dance floor. Her walk was sensual but not trashy, provocative but nor lurid. Every step was a renewed announcement of confidence. Her hair fell in cascading cornrows below her shoulders.

"My God," I said. "She makes Jenny Hanley[1] look like a mud fence."

Vik, who'd never seen *10*, was lost.

"I'll explain later," I said.

The crowd parted in front of her—Moses walking across the Red Sea. When she got within arm's length, I proffered my cheek for her customary *mwah*. Didn't happen.

She embraced me with an intensity I could never remember feeling from her. She clung to me. She was fighting for self-control. I whispered in her ear. "Don't cry again. You'll ruin your makeup."

"I don't care," she said. "I am so damn proud of you." She would not release me. I decided to go with it.

"I didn't do anything," I said.

"You are your own woman, Harlow," she said. "You are confident, self-reliant, intelligent, and creative." She pushed back a little a locked me in her gaze. I...am...so...proud. And I love you."

I blinked two...three...four times but the tears would not be denied. "I love you too, Mother."

---

1 Played by the incomparably beautiful Bo Derek in the Blake Edwards' movie, *10*.

SOPHIA

I danced with almost every man at the party. Some were old enough to be…well, they were considerably older. Some could not have been very far north of twenty. But I never sat, and I had a marvelous time.

I knew who she was when she approached. I held out my hand. "You must be Isha," I said. "I've heard so very much about you."

"Nothing bad, I hope," she said.

"Not at all. From what I can ascertain, you are responsible for quite a number of the marriages in this place tonight."

"My best guess is about seventy-five percent, though I can't take any credit for tonight's happy couple—except perhaps tangentially." She pointed to Harlow and Vik who were slow dancing in the middle of the floor while the band played an up-tempo tune. "They have no idea what the band is doing. They are truly in love."

"I believe they are," I said. "And I could not be happier."

There was an odd twinkle in her eye. "I hesitate to say anything because we do not know one another, and I do not want to offend you," she said.

"I do not offend as easily as I used to," I said, "but if you're going to criticize this dress, I might get crankier than a drunk raccoon in a corn maze."

I seldom spoke in colloquial idioms, but I was having a hell of a good time. Isha looked at me. Her face was blank.

"Never mind," I said. "What do you want to tell me."

"Let me begin," she said, "by assuring you that your ensemble is stunning. Next to your daughter, you are the most beautiful woman in attendance." She swept her arm across the room. "No small feat as you can tell."

"You are too kind," I said. "But I sense you have something more on your mind than compliments."

"You are most astute, Mrs..."

"Just call me Sophia," I said.

"Fine," she said. "Sophia, as odd as it may sound to you, over the course of the evening I have collected at least four marriage inquiries for you to consider. All are from men who claim to be of considerable financial and social standing. They are close to your age except for the one over there." She tilted her head to the side. "He says he is thirty-five."

I looked across the room and saw a fine looking, younger man—but thirty-five was considerably in his rearview mirror. He was zeroed in on my conversation with Isha.

"He's not by chance standing by the bar and staring holes through me, is he?"

Isha looked. "He is indeed. His name is Samir Gupta."

Thank goodness the band had cranked up the volume. Otherwise, everyone in the room would have heard my guffaw.

"Oh no, no, no, no," I said. "He's the same one who draped himself all over my daughter like ugly on a bulldog."

Isha's face twitched a little. "I do not completely understand your reference, but you are correct. He had an interest in your daughter. She did not return his advances." She leaned in close. "And I would have warned you away from him, but I am honor bound to make a presentation on behalf of a client, however much they resemble a...what did you say?"

"Bulldog," I said. "No way he was invited. How the hell did he get in here?"

"Mr. Gupta is what I believe you Americans call 'a wedding crasher,'" Isha said. "He shows up at a great many events always with the excuse that his invitation has been lost in the mail or something equally lame. High class people like Mr. and Mrs. Chatwal would rather suffer the fool gladly than make a scene—and he knows it. You probably know Mr. Gupta has a rather unsavory reputation. Rumor reports he has taken financial advantage of innumerable unsuspecting women in the States. While it is unlikely the U.S. will pursue extradition, I do not think he will be leaving the country anytime soon. Eventually, he will become persona non grata and drift into oblivion, unless he can cajole someone into marital bliss. Interested?"

"Hard pass," I said.

"Agreed," Isha said. "Now, let's talk about the legitimate suitors."

I took a moment to compose myself. "Ms. Isha—"

She stopped me with a raised palm. "Not to be rude, but before you reject the offers out of hand, you should know, the other three are very serious and very wealthy. You will want for nothing. And they will make a generous contribution towards your future security should you wish to accept."

Curiosity prodded me a little. "How generous?" I asked.

"The gentleman in the corner sitting alone," she said.

"The one in the awful vermilion dinner jacket?" I asked.

"The very same," she said. "What he lacks in fashion sense, he more than makes up for in generosity. His is the highest offer—four billion."

"Dollars?" My voice squeaked a little. Three people turned to see if I'd been frightened by a rodent or something. I lowered my volume. "Four billion dollars?"

"I am afraid not, my dear," she said. "Rupees. But the amount in U.S. dollars would exceed four million."

"Let me get this straight," I said. "That lump of a man in the loud tux with the atrocious hairpiece—a man who's never so much as spoken to me—he wants me to marry him. And he's willing to give me *four million* with no strings attached?"

Isha nodded. "Well," she said, "except for the…ah…anticipated marital duties."

Bile rose in my throat. I'd always heard about someone's life flashing in front of their eyes when they were facing death. I was not close to the Pearly Gates, but I had a moment. Vivid pictures played in my mind, a slide show of everything I had endured…

…a philandering husband…

…banishment from my home and daughter…

…living on the streets…

…working for Mama Jasmine…

…degrading myself in a series of loveless, but financially profitable marriages.

What's one more? I thought. *I could leave a nice chunk to Harlow and Vik and any children they might have.*

Isha touched my arm. "Sophia?"

I put out my hand again and took Isha's. "Thanks for the offers, but I don't need to hear any more," I said. "Please tell the gentlemen I am flattered by their interest. But, I'm very happy in my current unattached state."

Isha nodded politely and went off to convey my message. I looked out on the dancefloor at my daughter and her husband, still swaying to a tune only they could hear.

I am, I thought. *I'm on my own and I'm really, really happy.*

CHAPTER SEVENTY-NINE

VIK

I HAD NEVER UNDERSTOOD THE LINE from the old musical until that very moment, but in truth, I could have danced *all night* with Harlow. The party revealed everything anyone needed to know about *Ma*. She was the hostess extraordinaire. Everything was perfect. Banquet tables overflowed with food. The bar was so expansive I would not have been surprised to learn it was stocked with mead. Three different bands played throughout the evening—music for every person's taste.

Harlow sang quietly in my ear while we swayed. "Embrace me, my sweet embraceable you."

"How do you know this song?" I asked. "It must be fifty years old," I said.

"Closer to a hundred," she said. "Music and lyrics by the Gershwin brothers. Part of an unpublished operetta entitled *East Is West*. In addition to classic movies, Daddy loved music. I know 'em all."

"And I can't wait for you to educate me," I said.

She nestled into my shoulder. The music swirled around us. It was bliss. Someone tapped my shoulder.

"May I cut in?"

I stopped moving. Harlow looked over my shoulder.

"Hello, Haiya," she said.

VIK

Harlow said something about powdering her nose. Before I could protest, she was gone. I did not move.

"Well," Haiya said, "are you going to make me stand here looking foolish or are we going to dance?"

It was a slow tune. I extended my left hand in the proper ballroom position. Haiya took it in her right. With the caution I would have exercised while petting a tiger, I put my right hand on her waist and braced for a pelvic thrust. It never came. Haiya maintained a proper distance and we began to dance.

"I'm not going to bite, Vikram," she said, "but if they switch to a tango, I'll have to be closer than a foot."

"Or we could sit down," I said.

We moved around the floor for a very uncomfortable, very elongated two minutes or so. Haiya leaned close to my ear.

"Let's go outside. We need to talk."

She dropped her hands and headed for the terrace. On the way out, I prepared a short speech. Focusing on what I was going to say helped me avoid staring at the magnificent view of Haiya's backside. I *was* married but I *was not* dead.

The evening air was warm and pleasant. A crescent moon

hung over the treetops. *Mendhak*[1] croaked and *tiddywon*[2] chirped in a harmonious nocturnal duet.

When I opened my mouth, Haiya put a finger on my lips. "Vikram, you have every right to be angry with me," she said, "but I would appreciate the chance to go first. Okay?"

"Fine."

"I owe you an apology. To begin, I was a fool to break our engagement. Your career is the stuff of legend here. I should have believed in you and supported you in your dream. I was arrogant and obsessed with status. I thought moving to America was a terrible idea; I imagined your dream of becoming a chef was worse. I was a fool." She stopped and looked at the moon. "Beautiful, isn't it?"

I tilted my head skyward but kept my eyes on her. She turned her head a tad and swiped at a tear on her cheek. I pretended not to notice.

"Yes," I said. "Stunning."

"When you came back to India for what turned out to be Amar and Lita's wedding, I acted abysmally. I was angry with myself. I had too much to drink at the party. I am told I acted like a shrew. I said and later did some horrible things. [3] For everything, I am truly and profoundly sorry. I hope you can forgive me."

She stood on her toes, kissed me quite properly on the cheek, then walked toward the ballroom door.

"Thank you," I said.

I saw her shoulders heave. "Congratulations on your marriage, dear Vikram. She is lovely. I wish you nothing but the best," She did not turn around.

---

1 Frogs.

2 Locusts/Cicadas.

3 Chapter 25, *Karma Under Fire*.

CHAPTER EIGHTY

AMRITA

It took everything in my power to get out of the car and walk to the entrance. The doorman stared at me the entire time. I stopped and waited. He seemed frozen in place.

"Are you okay?" I asked.

"Ms. Rai," he said. It seemed like he wanted to say something else, but when his mouth moved, there was no sound. Finally, instinct kicked in. He snapped to attention, bowed deeply at the waist as if I were royalty of some sort, and opened the door. "Please excuse me. I never thought I would have the honor. My wife will be so jealous. Welcome to the Imperial."

Two steps inside, I stopped.

"Is something wrong?" he asked.

"No," I said. "Everything is fine. I just wish I had something for your wife." I thought for a second and opened my sequined clutch. "Would you be so kind as to give her this?" I handed him a silver lip gloss case.

"Th…tha…thank you," he said. "This is so very kind. She will never believe it."

"It has my initials on it," she said. "That should help."

He beamed with the intensity of a premiere spotlight and let the door close. I walked across the lobby. Just outside the grand ballroom I exhaled deeply.

Here goes nothing.

VIK

I saw Ahmi the moment she entered. She came through the door and immediately slipped to the side where she could not have stayed closer to the wall if she'd been suctioned to it. Her saree was elegant but not showy. Her jewelry was minimal and understated. She had no intention of being the star of this show.

Harlow tapped me on the shoulder. "Beautiful, isn't she?"

Everything in my head screamed, *Trick question,* but I answered truthfully. "Always has been." A thought occurred to me. "Why is she here? Did you…"

"Yes," she said. "I made absolutely sure she was invited. Had to talk her into coming."

"You *talked* to her?"

"Vikram," she said, "Ahmi and I have conversed several times. Everything is fine with us. Now it's your turn."

There was a gentle nudge. I locked my legs like a dog unwilling to go outside in the rain. The nudge became a shove. "Go on," she said. "If you don't, you will regret it."

CHAPTER EIGHTY-ONE

VIK

WE STROLLED THE GROUNDS OUTSIDE. IT was fully lit. There would be no scandalous gossip, but we needed to be away from the party. I didn't want to shout to be heard over the crowd and the band. Once we raced through the pleasantries, I dove in.

"I didn't know," I said.

"That was pretty obvious at the cricket match," she said. "All the color drained out of your face."

"I wish I had," I said.

"What would you have done?" she asked. There was no rancor in her voice. She was simply the matter-of-fact woman I had known so long ago. "You and I both know marriage was never on the table. And, to be honest if we had married, I might never have found my calling. I love what I do."

"You're very good," I said. "I've watched everything."

"Oh?" She raised her brows above her sparkling dark brown eyes. "Movie night with the fiancée?"

"Once a smart ass," I said.

She punched me lightly on the shoulder. "I learned from the master."

"Harlow tells me that Rishi knows."

"Yes," she said. "We've gone out a few times. He's met Pratham but we haven't told him yet. We're taking it slow."

"Will you marry?"

"I don't know. But Rishi is determined to be a father and I am convinced it will be good for Pratham to have a dad, in whatever form it takes. But—maybe for the first time in a long while—I am absolutely sure everything is going to be alright."

"I'm sorry," I said.

When she shook her head, her dangling earrings tinkled like the whispers of angels. "No," she said. "I am the one who is sorry. I did a terrible thing out of immaturity and spite. I betrayed your trust—and I am ashamed."

"Ahmi," I said, "please look at me." There were wispy tears at the corners of her eyes. "I cannot be angry about something I didn't even know about from a dozen years ago and life is too short for bitterness. All of this is in the past. As the poet says, 'The moving finger writes and having writ, moves on—'"

She interrupted to complete the recitation from *The Rubaiyat* of Omar Khayyám. "Nor all thy Piety nor Wit shall lure it back to cancel half a line."

"You still remember Master Banerjee's Lit Class," I said.

"How could I forget?" she asked. "The shared, co-ed class on your campus was one of the few times I got to see you during the week."

"I always wondered why your school never offered a reciprocal arrangement. We could have come down the road," I said.

"And let a leash of foxes loose amongst the hens? I don't think so."

Her famous laugh replaced the tears.

"I will always hold the memories of you and our time together in my heart," I said. "And if you ever need me, all you have to do is call." I reached for her hand. "Be well."

"Shemamailru,"[1] she said.

There was nothing else to say. We gave each other a "Three Bears" hug—not too long… not too short…just right. She kissed me on the cheek. We looked at each other.

"Goodbye, Amrita," I said.

"Goodbye…Vikram."

---

1 Blessing: "May you lead a happy, peaceful, and prosperous life forever."

CHAPTER EIGHTY-TWO

HARLOW

THE LAST BAND PACKED UP. THE catering van drove away. All the guests departed. Rachana and Kavyansh, my new in-laws, said goodnight, kissed their son and their "new daughter" and rode away in their limo. Mother was on her way to the airport. She'd told me she wasn't going to run anymore.

Vik and I were alone, still slow dancing to the music we could both hear in our heads.

"I love you, Mrs. Chatwal," he said.

"I love you back, Mr. Chatwal-Kennedy," I said.

His soft laugh vibrated through my body. "Wouldn't that be Kennedy-Chatwal?"

"It's whatever *we* decide," I said.

"I can live with that," he said.

We finally stopped dancing, got in the Mercedes, and snuggled while Hussein drove us to the hotel. *Ma* and *Pa* had offered their guest house, but neither of us wanted to endure what would have undoubtedly been an awkward "morning after" breakfast. *Pa* would have made suggestive eye movements and *Ma* may well have offered me a pregnancy test kit.

I must have fallen asleep because the drive was much quicker than I imagined and before I knew it, Vik was helping me from the backseat. Our luggage had already been delivered to the Honeymoon Suite of the Lodhi. The room was amazing, but I was only interested in one of the furnishings—my new husband.

Vik kissed me. I returned the favor with more passion than I knew I possessed. For reasons I did not need to understand, I was shaking with anticipation. I began clawing at his shirt buttons.

"Whoa…whoa…slow down," Vik said. "We've got all the time in the world."

I took a breath. "Sorry," I said. "I'm just so very happy."

"I am too," he said. "I want to take it slow—and make it last."

We did.

I have a surprise for you," he said.

I was draped across his naked body like a Roman toga, our legs intertwined, our bodies virtually inseparable.

"I fell for that trick an hour ago," I said. "But I'm game—if you're *up* to it."

He popped my fanny with his palm. "You are naughty," he said.

"And you love it," I said.

"I do, I do," he said. "This is something different, I promise."

I grunted. "Well, that's a little disappointing." My smile felt like it might break my face. "But go ahead."

A warm glow surrounded Vik's eyes. I might have seen a little glisten. He looked genuinely moved by whatever he was about to reveal.

"You know how Amar is going to oversee everything at the Institute," he said.

"Yes. It's a great idea."

"Well, I want to do the same VIP dinner thing there that we do in Atlanta."

"Baby, that's a wonderful idea," I said. "You'll need someone to run the program."

"I know," he said. "Someone with experience with the concept—someone who can understand what it means and what it can do."

"Got someone in mind?" I asked.

"I do," he said. He leaned in close and whispered the name in my ear.

"Vik, that is amazing. Do you think you can make it work?"

"I sure hope so. It would be a win-win."

"Do you think you can handle round four."

"I think it's round five," he said.

"Pride goeth before a fall," I said, "and a haughty spirit before destruction."

His eyes grew dark and intense. "I love it when you talk dirty."

EPILOGUE

HARLOW

Several weeks later

DAKOTA'S EYES SPARKLED WITH INTELLIGENCE AND wonder. [1]

"This is where you cook?" she asked.

Vik put his hand on her shoulder. "Well, I *can* cook here," he said, "but I am leaving Amar in charge of everything. He has a whole staff of great chefs. I have to go back to Atlanta to run my restaurant."

Dakota scowled for a moment. "Let me get this straight," she said. "You brought Mama and me over here to run this place and now you're abandoning me? This is *India* you know."

Vik laughed. "I am aware," he said. "But your mother and I had a long talk—several, in fact. And let's be clear. *She* is going to supervise the program—one single program, the VIP dinners. She doesn't have any responsibility for the Institute."

Dakota leaned in and tried to whisper. People in Chennai [2]

---

1 For Dakota's backstory, please see Chapter 7, *Karma Under Fire,*
2 Largest city in southern India, over 2000 km from Delhi.

could have heard her. "Good thing," she said. "She's a terrible cook."

This time, everyone laughed—even Dakota's mother. "I haven't poisoned you yet," Eunice said.

"Not for lack of trying," Dakota said. She giggled when Eunice fanned a sweeping right palm in her general direction.

"Child, you know I make the best cornbread and collard greens in Atlanta. Don't go storying to people. You might hurt my feelings."

Dakota was instantly solemn. "I'm sorry, Mama," she said. "I'm just playin.' Everyone knows you're the best cook in Georgia—probably anywhere."

Now it was Vik's turn. "Hey, I live in Georgia," he said.

"I stand by my statement," she said.

"Turned into a little smarty pants since you finished the fourth grade."

"She reads on a twelfth-grade level," Eunice Duncan said. She made a face. "Sorry, maternal pride."

"And completely justified," I said. I knelt down and put my hands on Dakota's shoulders. "If you don't want to be here, it's okay. No one is going to make you stay."

Dakota's smile lit up the room. "Mama says this is going to be an adventure. I like adventures."

"She's going to oversee the VIP Night," Vik said. "It'll be just like the one in Atlanta—once a week—"

Dakota interrupted. "Half dozen elementary kids, their brothers, sisters, and parents or other adults. Dial the spices back a little until they get used to the pop—but I guess you won't have to do that here, will you?"

"No," Vik said.

"Maybe you should serve American food," she said. "You

know, fries, shakes, hambur…" She trailed off, then covered her face with her hands as if in shame. She looked up. "Well, that was stupid—Hindus and all." She cut her eyes at me.

"Nice catch," I said.

"Okay," she said. "You going to offer to-go…I mean 'take away'…service once a week like back home?"

"Three courses," Vik said. "Each meal enough for eight for everyone who's ever been invited. The list will grow every week."

Dakota narrowed her eyes in thought and put a finger to her lips. "Okay," she said. "We'll take it. Let's talk about the cash."

"Dakota Duncan!" Eunice was scowling.

Vik's laugh bounced off the walls. "It's okay, Ms. Duncan," he said. He knelt alongside me and looked into Dakota's mischievous eyes. "Your mother and I have already ironed out all the details. Salary, housing, a driver, the whole deal."

"Is there an allowance for a rising fifth grader who seriously needs to update her wardrobe?" Dakota asked.

Before Eunice could protest again, I said, "Absolutely. But it will be controlled by her mother subject to behavior and grades."

Dakota looked like she'd stuck her finger in an electrical socket. "Grades? I still have to go to school."

"Of course," I said. "How else are you going to become the boss of this whole thing."

"Good point," she said. When the laughter died, Dakota looked at Vik. "Mr. Chatwal, there's one more thing. It's kind of private."

"I can take a hint," Eunice said. "I'll go talk to the chef."

After she was out of earshot, Dakota stared into Vik's eyes with the intensity of a priest taking confession. "Mr. Chatwal, do you think you could help my mom?"

"I hope we already have," he said. "She is certainly helping me."

"I mean with the other things," Dakota said.

"What other—" He stopped and remembered Dakota's father, a soldier who'd died in service to his country. "You mean…"

"With one of those arranged marriage things," Dakota said. "She needs something more than work and I won't be around forever."

Vik's shoulders sagged with the weight of his helplessness. He was waaaay out of his league. I took over.

"Dakota," I said. "I hope your mom will be very happy here. She'll make a lot of friends. And I am certain, when the time is right, she will meet someone special. She doesn't need an arranged marriage."

"You really think she'll find someone without help?" she asked.

I studied her deep, dark, wise eyes then twitched my head towards my husband.

"Worked just fine for us," I said.

AUTHOR'S NOTE

HAVE YOU EVER HAD A PLACE grab hold of your heart after just one short visit? That's what Mumbai did to me over a decade ago. What started as a brief stop on the way to the beach in Goa turned into a lifelong fascination with this incredible city and its evolution from Bombay to the Mumbai we know today.

My love affair with film began during my screenwriting fellowship at Columbia University, but Bollywood truly captured my imagination. I binge-watched everything from intense dramas that left me in tears to gloriously over-the-top musicals that had me dancing in my living room. Each month, I'd eagerly dive into the latest issue of Vogue India, soaking up the fashion, culture, and the magnetic pull of India's entertainment powerhouse.

Here's what I find magical about Bollywood: beneath the sequins and choreographed dance numbers, these films tell stories that touch the soul. They speak of love, family, and tradition in ways that cross cultural boundaries while remaining authentically Indian. This beautiful contradiction drew me in, and I wouldn't let go.

Remember the characters you met in Karma Under Fire? Well, they're back, but this time, we're diving deeper into their past.

Bombay Baby peels back the layers of decisions made decades ago that still echo through their lives today. Think of this book as your personal invitation to the ultimate dinner-and-a-movie experience—except we're crossing continents, exploring how ambition, secrets, friendship, and food weave together in the shadow of Asia's largest film industry.

This isn't your typical tourist's Mumbai. This is the Mumbai of my imagination—where every street corner whispers secrets, where dreams take flight among the skyscrapers, and where magic feels not just possible but inevitable.

Love Hudson-Maggio

RECIPES

Bollywood Popcorn

Popcorn is essential to any movie night. This spicy version, seasoned with masala, will please your taste buds with each bite.

Makes two batches (total servings 4 to 6)

Ingredients
2 teaspoons of salt
2 teaspoons ground coriander
2 teaspoons ground cumin
2 teaspoons paprika
1 teaspoon garlic powder
½ teaspoon Indian red chili powder (or cayenne)
2/3 cup popcorn kernels divided
1 teaspoon canola oil divided
4 tablespoons (1/2 stick) butter, divided
1 teaspoon freshly squeezed lemon juice, divided

Instructions

Create the Bollywood masala (or spice blend) by mixing the salt, coriander cumin, paprika, garlic powder, and red chili powder in a small bowl.

Measure 1/3 cup of the popcorn kernels into a small bowl and pour over ½ teaspoon of the oil. Stir to coat.

Melt two tablespoons of the butter with ½ teaspoon of the lemon juice in the microwave for around 30 seconds.

Pour the kernels into a paper bag and fold over twice. Place the bag on top of a paper towel or plate (to absorb excess oil) and microwave on high for 3 to 4 minutes until the popping slows to every 3 seconds.

Open the bag carefully and pour the popcorn into a large bowl. Drizzle with the melted butter and toss to coat. Then sprinkle with one teaspoon of the masala and toss well. Adjust the salt to taste.

Repeat for a second batch.

Vada Pav (potato fritter sandwich)

Vada Pav is the most popular snack in Mumbai, India. It can be found at any street vendor. Vada Pav is a thick bun (pav) cut open and loaded with a fried potato patty (vada). You can season it with chili chutney, spicy green chile chutney, coconut, or garlic. This vegetarian delight is usually paired with a steaming cup of chai.

Vada

3 russet potatoes

2 tablespoons vegetable oil, plus more deep-frying

1 teaspoon brown mustard seeds

1 teaspoon cumin seeds

½ teaspoon hing (asafetida)

4 fresh curry leaves

1 teaspoon ground turmeric

½ teaspoon Kashmiri or other red chile powder

1-inch piece of fresh ginger peeled with a spoon and finely chopped

2 garlic cloves, minced

Kosher salt

½ cup lightly packed, finely chopped fresh cilantro leaves

2 teaspoons chaat masala

Fresh lime juice

1 cup chickpea flour

1 teaspoon ground coriander

Chaat
1 tablespoon of unsalted butter
4 flaky white buns, such as potato or brioche buns
Chutney (store-bought is fine)
Pan-fried serrano chiles (optional)

Instructions

Make the vada: In a saucepan, combine the potato and enough water to cover the potatoes by 3 inches. Bring to a boil over high heat, reduce the heat to medium, and simmer until tender, about 15 minutes. Drain, and once the potatoes are cool enough to handle, peel them using your hands (the skin should slip right off). Place the potatoes in a bow and mash them with a fork until they are mashed but still slightly chunky.

In a sauté pan, heat two tablespoons of oil over medium-high heat until the oil glistens. Add the mustard and cumin, and sauté until they hiss for about 2 minutes. Add the hing, curry leaves, turmeric, chile powder, ginger and garlic. Sauté, stirring often, until the garlic is tender, about 4 minutes. Remove the pan from the heat. Season with salt and then transfer to a large bowl.

Add the potatoes, cilantro, and chaat masala to the spice mixture in the bowl. Stir with a wooden spoon until everything is incorporated, season with lime juice and salt to taste. Form the mixture into four 2-inch balls and arrange them on a plate in a single layer. Cover with a damp cloth and set aside at room temperature.

In a large bowl, whisk the chickpea flour and enough water (begin with ¼ cup) to form a paste resembling a thick cake batter. It should not be rummy. Stir in the coriander and season with salt.

Line a plate with paper towels. Pour 5 inches of oil into a

deep, heavy-bottomed pot and heat to 350 F on an instant-read thermometer. Dredge the potato balls in the chickpea batter until they are well coated. Shake to remove any excess. Using a slotted spoon, gently lower a vada into the oil and fry until golden brown on all sides, 4 to 6 minutes. Turn with the spoon as it fries to ensure even cooking and browning. Transfer to the paper towels to drain and season with salt. Repeat with the remaining vada.

Assemble the chaat: Melt the butter over medium heat in a sauté pan. Spit the buns and place them in the pan, interior-side down: fry until lightly golden brown, about 1 minute. Place one bun, open and interior sides facing up, on each of four plates. Slather both sides of the bun with your preferred topping. Serve with additional chutneys on the side.

DISCUSSION QUESTIONS

1. Bombay Baby is a title that has a lot of different meanings. Discuss the title and different meanings throughout the book.
2. Vik and Harlow are a couple from different cultures. How do their cultural differences cause their love to grow and divide them?
3. Relationships with family play a significant role in this novel: father-son, mother-son, mother-daughter. How do the inner dynamics of these relationships shape Harlow and Vik's decisions in their lives and throughout their relationship?
4. The novel's themes are forgiveness (external, internal), guilt, and a sense of obligation. How do each character's guilt and sense of obligation shape their decisions, and how does the need for forgiveness ultimately affect the penultimate choices of the characters?
5. Vik and Harlow face their pasts in this novel. How does the past ultimately affect their futures, and how do you think the things they have reconciled from their pasts will affect their future?
6. India and its culture inform a lot of this novel and the behavior of its characters. If you were to partake in "matching season,"

what qualities would you hope you would be matched with? How surprised were you to learn what goes into Matchmaking and arranged marriages?

7. Gossip and outside validation play a role in this novel regarding Harlow and Vik's relationship. Societal and family pressure, past relationships, secrets, and worries put a lot of obstacles in their way. How do you think they overcame these differences? Have you ever been in a relationship society viewed as "not a good match"? Would you have made the decisions that the characters did?

8. Film, food, music, and pop culture are throughout this novel. Did this novel make you want to learn more about the Indian culture or the Bollywood movie industry?

9. If there were to be another story based on these characters, which character would you like to read more about? Why?

10. Discuss the cover. Talk about the colors and the cultural significance of the photos; why do you think the author chose this design? What would you think it would be like if you were to judge this book solely on the cover?

11. Discuss the friendships throughout this novel. How do these friendships affect the dynamic between Vik and Harlow?

12. The Bombay Baby story takes us to Bombay/Mumbai. What is significant about this location for Vik, Harlow, and their families?

ABOUT THE AUTHOR

LOVE HUDSON-MAGGIO'S journey as a storyteller began at age five, and she hasn't stopped writing. Her passion for weaving narratives has seamlessly blended with her professional career as a marketer, where she helps brands transform their product messages into compelling stories that resonate with customers.

Love's mantra, "Do the thing you love, love the things you do," reflects her belief that passion should infuse every aspect of life. This philosophy has guided her through diverse experiences, including earning an Executive MBA from Georgia State University and a screenwriting fellowship from Columbia University.

As the founder of Mar Dat, a boutique marketing technology consultancy with offices in Atlanta and New York City, Love continues to bridge the gap between technology and storytelling.

Her innovative spirit led her to create Martonomy, where she serves as the technology founder and CEO, further pushing the boundaries of marketing technology.

When she's not crafting narratives or revolutionizing marketing strategies, Love cherishes moments with her husband, two sons, and their cuddly dog. Her sequel, *Bombay Baby*, promises to captivate readers with the same heartfelt storytelling that made *Karma Under Fire* a beloved read.

Connect with Love at lovehudsonmaggio.com
Instagram: @love.hudsonmaggio
Facebook: @love.hudsonmaggio
BookBub: @lovelhudson
LinkedIn: @lovehudsonmaggio